TUMBLED GRAVES

Stonechild and Rouleau Mysteries
Cold Mourning
Butterfly Kills
Tumbled Graves
Shallow End
Bleeding Darkness
Turning Secrets
Closing Time

A STONECHILD AND ROULEAU MYSTERY

TUMBLED
GRAVES

BRENDA CHAPMAN

DUNDURN
PRESS

Editor: Jennifer McKnight
Cover designer: Laura Boyle | Interior designer: Jansom
Cover image: © grybaz/istockphoto.com

Library and Archives Canada Cataloguing in Publication

Chapman, Brenda, 1955-, author

    Tumbled graves / Brenda Chapman.
    (A Stonechild and Rouleau mystery)

Issued in print and electronic format
ISBN 978-1-4597-3096-0 (pbk.).--ISBN 978-1-4597-3097-7
(pdf).--ISBN 978-1-4597-3098-4 (epub)

    I. Title. II. Series: Chapman, Brenda, 1955- . A
Stonechild and Rouleau mystery

PS8605.H36T84 2016   C813'.6   C2015-902893-0   C2015-902894-9

  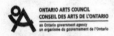

We acknowledge the support of the Canada Council for the Arts and the Ontario Arts Council for our publishing program. We also acknowledge the financial support of the Government of Canada through the Book Publishing Industry Development Program and The Association for the Export of Canadian Books, and the Government of Ontario through the Ontario Book Publishers Tax Credit program and the Ontario Media Development Corporation.

Care has been taken to trace the ownership of copyright material used in this book. The author and the publisher welcome any information enabling them to rectify any references or credits in subsequent editions.
    — *J. Kirk Howard, President*

The publisher is not responsible for websites or their content unless they are owned by the publisher.

Printed and bound in Canada.

Dundurn Press
Toronto, Ontario, Canada
dundurn.com, @dundurnpress 🐦 f 📷

For Ted

In the faint moonlight, the grass is singing
Over the tumbled graves, about the chapel.
— "The Waste Land," T.S. Eliot

Stars will blossom in the darkness,
Violets bloom beneath the snow.
— Julia C.R. Dorr

CHAPTER ONE

At first, Catherine Lockhart wasn't worried. Perplexed, possibly even annoyed if she was honest, but definitely not worried. It wasn't until she and Sammy stood on the country road in front of Adele Delaney's house that a sense of foreboding rolled slowly upwards like a bad meal from the bottom of her gut. Her shoulders wriggled as a shiver travelled up her back, even as her face was warmed by the late-April sun. *Something doesn't feel right*, she thought. She'd remember that exact moment of trepidation for days afterward.

Sammy tugged at her arm until she looked down into his freckled face. "They're home," he said, pointing a chubby finger toward the rusty Fiat halfway up the long driveway. His blue eyes brightened and his voice rose joyously. "Can I play with Violet?"

She'd meant just to walk by, to assure herself that Adele had been ignoring her phone messages because she'd been called away suddenly. The sight of Adele's car standing unashamedly in the drive felt like a betrayal — as if she were thirteen again and her best friend had just ditched her for the cooler crowd. The bit that didn't feel right, though, was the front door. Wide open, it swung gently back and forth on its hinges in the gusty spring breeze.

Catherine and Sam had moved into the small white house with the blue shutters a kilometre down the road a year and a half ago. She'd wanted Sam to grow up surrounded by trees and space, not in a scuzzy high-rise in the east end of Toronto. Luckily, her freelance writing job meant she could work anywhere. This stretch of land just east of Kingston and north of Highway 2 was close enough to civilization but far enough out of town to feel like they were living in the countryside. They'd met Adele and Violet at a mom-and-me fitness class and their kids had hit it off. Naturally, they'd started meeting up for coffee and playtime during the weekdays when Adele's husband, Ivo, was at work.

Catherine ruffled Sammy's ginger hair, soft and fluffy from his morning bath. The strands felt like warm silk in her fingers. "I'm not sure Violet and her mommy are up for company just now." She checked her wristwatch. "Maybe Violet's having a nap."

"Violet doesn't nap," Sam said, scowling. "She said that napping's for babies."

Before Catherine could stop him, Sam had sprinted across the gravel shoulder of the road and was halfway up the long drive. He stopped long enough to check that she was following before turning and running toward the front steps. A premonition made her call out to him.

"Wait, Sam! Wait for me."

She stepped around the puddles left over from the morning rain. Sam had barrelled through the mud and water in his black rubber boots, not caring about the muck splashing up onto his pants and jacket, but what four-year-old ever cared? She was panting when she reached him. The cigarettes were going to have to go or she would be on a ventilator before she hit forty. For the second time that day, she made a solemn promise to herself to quit. The same promise she made every time she exerted herself beyond a brisk walk. Sam had found a stick and was poking it into an ant hole. She spit onto her fingers and rubbed a smear of mud from his cheek.

"Why's the door open?" Sam looked up at her, his brow creased as he tried to work out what an open door could mean. She glanced up the steps into the shadowy hallway.

"No idea, kiddo, but we shouldn't just rush in. I'll knock and you wait here until Violet's mom tells us to enter."

Sam shrugged and moved over to a mud puddle where he began digging in the muck with his stick. Catherine slowly climbed the steps and grabbed onto the swinging door when she reached the top. She knocked and called down the hallway. The lights were off and gloom thickened towards the kitchen. "Adele! We've just come by to see if everything is okay. Are you home? Adele?"

Catherine kept one hand on the door and listened. The house smelled of cinnamon and apples.

Adele must have been baking pies with apples she'd bought during an outing they'd all gone on that Tuesday. She looked back at Sam. He'd made it to the bottom step and looked up at her. "Can we go in?"

She hesitated.

No noise except the normal house sounds — the furnace kicking in, a clock ticking, the shudder of the fridge cycling on. She suddenly felt ridiculous, standing on her friend's steps, imagining the worst inside.

"I'm just going to make sure everything's okay since the door was left open," she said to Sam. "Come wait here in the hall while I have a look."

"I want to come too," Sam said, stubbornly climbing the steps until he was next to her.

She took his hand and led him into the living room. All looked in order. The furniture was frayed and second hand, but cozy. Sunlight filtered through the white lace curtains. Sam dropped down next to the basket of Lego and started pulling pieces onto the floor. A moment later and he was laying on his stomach, fitting pieces together, their search for Violet forgotten.

She backed out of the room and walked quickly down the hallway into the back of the house, leaving Sam engrossed in building a spaceship. She stood at the entrance to the kitchen and glanced around the large space. The smell of cinnamon and spices was stronger but other smells competed. A container of open milk had been left on the counter, a half-filled glass beside it. A carton of eggs and a block of cheese were next to the stove. Plates of uneaten scrambled eggs and toast sat patiently on the table as if waiting for Violet and Adele to sit down and tuck in. Catherine stepped farther into the room until she was standing beside the kitchen table. A greyish crust had formed on the eggs, which looked the consistency of rubber. She reached a hand out and touched the toast with her fingertips. It was stone cold, unbuttered. She looked around the kitchen, her eyes searching the attached family room for any sign of them. She didn't know whether to be relieved or worried that they weren't anywhere to be seen.

She returned to the doorway to the living room. Sam was still busy with the Lego, so she had time to finish her search. She crossed to the stairs and climbed toward the light coming in from the window halfway up. The carpet was red and frayed but it muffled the sound of her footsteps. The landing was empty except for a laundry hamper at the far end. Catherine took a deep breath and darted the length of the corridor, checking each room as she went. Satisfied that nobody was lying dead on the floor in any of them, she took her time returning with a good look inside the three bedrooms and bathroom. *Nothing. Jesus.* Her overactive imagination was going to kill her before the cigarettes. She laughed out loud at herself before taking the stairs two at a time back to find Sam.

"Let's go, honey bun," she said to him.

He looked up. "Where's Violet?"

"They must have gone out." *In a big hurry.*

"Then why's their car in the driveway?"

Catherine stopped and looked at his scrunched up features, serious eyes so like the father he would never meet. She had no answer to his question or to the others that crowded in alongside. Why had the front door been left unlocked and swinging in the breeze? Why hadn't Adele answered her phone all afternoon? The anxious feeling returned. She reached into her pocket and pulled out her cellphone. She checked if Adele had responded to one of her calls, but no voice mail or text messages. What to do? She didn't feel right just leaving. Ivo worked in a bank downtown on Princess. She knew his direct line because she'd returned his call the summer before when he was organizing a surprise birthday dinner for Adele. She found his number and tapped the screen. He answered on the second ring.

"Catherine," he said as a way of greeting. His voice quavered as it always did when he spoke to her. He'd been a big awkward boy who'd grown into a man without quite recovering from his shyness. "What a pleasant surprise to see your name pop up. Everything okay?"

Now why had he asked that? "I'm not sure. Adele and Violet missed our appointment so I came by to see if they were feeling well. We were supposed to meet at playgroup in the church basement after lunch. The car's in the drive but the front door was open. Nobody's here."

A pause, then, "Are you sure?"

"Yes. Sam and I came in to check on them since the door was open. Their breakfasts are on the table uneaten. Could they have gone out with someone spur of the moment? Maybe in a friend's car?"

"I wouldn't know who. Adele doesn't have any other friends that I know of. I'm going to come home. Can you wait until I get there?"

"Of course." She wanted to say no, but his voice had picked up the worry she'd been trying to ignore for the past half hour.

She was sitting on the couch with Sam in her lap, reading a book about trucks, when Ivo clumped into the front hall. She heard the sound of his keys hitting the bowl on the entrance table and something heavier dropping onto the hardwood floor. A moment later and his six-foot-three hulk entered the living room. His shoulders were stooped from trying to hide inside himself and from sitting at a desk all day. His wavy brown hair needed a cut and his glasses were small and round and could use an update. The mystery was why Adele had found him attractive enough to marry. Catherine studied him for hidden depths of character whenever Adele invited her and Sam for supper. They had to be there but so far she hadn't detected anything spectacular. She'd always thought that Adele treated him as an afterthought.

"Any word?" he asked, voice hopeful.

"I'm afraid not," Catherine said.

"Well, I have no idea where they could have gotten to. When I got up this morning, Adele said that she was going to let Violet sleep in and they were going out in the afternoon. What time is it now?"

"Going on four."

"You checked the kitchen?"

Are you thick? "Yeah, and upstairs. Their breakfast is still on the table … uneaten."

She and Sam trailed behind him into the kitchen. He stood looking at the food, then spun around to face her.

"Did you try the basement?"

"No. I couldn't imagine what they'd be doing down there." Even as she said the words, a kind of hysteria began bubbling somewhere around her ribcage. Wild horses couldn't get her to go down there now.

"Well, I'll just run and check. You wait here."

"If you like." She leaned against the kitchen counter and listened to his footsteps clumping down the stairs, fainter as he descended. Sam came over and tugged on her arm.

"I want to go home," he said.

"In a minute. Let's just wait to say goodbye to Ivo." She kept an ear open as he made his way around the basement. What if Violet and Adele were down there? What would that mean? She pulled out her cellphone again and hit Adele's number. Tapping the fingers of her free hand on the counter, she listened to it ring once, twice, three times and then Adele's voice telling her to leave a message. Catherine didn't hide her worry as she had in her last messages, or her growing impatience. "Where are you, Adele? We're worried sick. Call me or Ivo as soon as you can."

She shut her phone and listened for Ivo. Just as she was thinking about calling down to him to make sure he was okay, he reappeared at the top of the stairs, holding Violet's pink knapsack with rabbit ears sticking out the open pouch. Puzzled lines creased the width of his forehead.

"That's odd. Violet never goes anywhere without her rabbit. It looks like she was watching a movie this morning while Adele was making breakfast. The television is still on but the movie is over."

"I wonder if we should call the police."

The words had popped out. They held both of them motionless for a moment. Their meaning had opened a box of fear that neither of them had wanted to acknowledge before now. Ivo looked across to the table where the full plates of food sat untouched. His eyes circled the family room and the mess on the kitchen counter before sweeping back to meet her own.

"You might be right," he said, "because I have absolutely no idea what is going on here. There has to be a logical explanation, but for the life of me, I can't think what it could be."

CHAPTER TWO

The desk sergeant, Fred Taylor, took the call at exactly 4:23 p.m., and after a moment's reflection punched it through to Staff Sergeant Jacques Rouleau. Taylor knew his decision to send the call to Major Crimes might be an overreaction, given that the mother and child were only missing a few hours, but the details put their disappearance into the higher risk category. And hadn't he been warned to pay more attention when a child was involved? In any case, his conscience would be clear. Rouleau could decide.

Rouleau was in his office with Paul Gundersund when the phone rang. He held up a finger and smiled at Gundersund. "Hold that thought. I really want to know why you keep giving the Leafs your blind devotion when they finished in the basement again this year. It might be time to cut your losses and join the Habs' fan club."

Gundersund shook his head and watched Rouleau as he listened to whoever was at the other end of the call. His own stomach tightened when

Rouleau's features changed from relaxed to attentive, his mouth settling into a stern line. He reached for a pen and pad of paper and jotted down an address. Gundersund's first thought was that something had happened to Rouleau's ex-wife, Frances. The talk around the station was that she was in a hospice in Ottawa. Nobody knew where the rumour started, but it hadn't come from Rouleau. Gundersund hadn't known how to broach the subject with his boss.

Rouleau ended the call. He was still for a moment, deep in thought. His green eyes met Gundersund's. "I think we should send someone to have a look at this one."

Gundersund reached across the desk and took the paper from Rouleau. "What have you got?"

"A woman named Adele Delaney and her young daughter, Violet, didn't turn up at an appointment after lunch. Her friend Catherine Lockhart went to check on them and found the front door open, breakfast still on the table. She called the husband, Ivo Delaney, and he beat it home. He says that he has no idea where they could be. That's the address. Apparently in a rural area just outside of Kingston, but still within city limits." Rouleau looked out his open office door and spotted Kala Stonechild at her desk. He checked his watch. "See if Stonechild can manage the call with you. I'll be in a budget meeting with Heath but check in and let me know what's going on."

Gundersund unfolded his large frame from the chair. "I'm on it."

"Let's hope it's nothing."

"I won't go looking for trouble."

Gundersund left Rouleau's office and walked over to Kala Stonechild's desk. "Got time for a run just outside the city? A woman and her kid have gone missing. Rouleau thinks it's worth checking."

She looked up at him, black eyes expressionless. "Yeah, just let me make a quick call."

"I'll meet you outside."

This had become their way of operating. Clipped sentences. All business. Gundersund couldn't figure out why Stonechild had decided to freeze him out, but she was doing a hell of a job. He walked down the hall and into the fresh air. The station was out of the downtown on Division Street. A modern building low to the ground with a large outdoor parking lot on the south side. He kept going until he reached his vintage Mustang. He leaned on the front hood and waited. Puddles dotted the ground, left over from the early morning rain, but the sun was out and felt good on his face. It had been a wet, bone-chilling winter. He needed something warm to chase away the bleak lethargy that was keeping him in front of the television night after night like an old man in his undershirt.

A few minutes later Stonechild sauntered toward him, wearing a black leather jacket and sunglasses, looking more like a biker than a cop. She pointed toward her truck. "I'll follow you. I have to get home right after this."

He wanted to tell her how ridiculous it was to take two vehicles when they lived so close to each other. He could drive her home and pick her up in the morning, and her truck would be safe in the police parking lot overnight. Instead, he nodded and asked, "Do you know where we're going in case we get separated?"

"It's not like we're driving through New York City. Don't worry, I won't lose you."

He shrugged and got into his car. He waited until Stonechild had started her engine before easing out of his parking spot. When he reached the Princess Street intersection, she was still right behind him. They headed down the one-way through the downtown toward the harbour. He waited at the lights and turned left, straight past the armed forces base and across the bridge out of town. The water level was up with spring runoff. It sparkled in the sunshine, giving an unexpected jolt of pleasure. Highway 2 followed Lake Ontario and ten minutes out he turned north on a side road. The houses were spread out on large wooded lots. He slowed, checking house numbers until a few minutes later he spotted the Delaneys', a two-storey house with grey siding. Two cars were lined up in the drive but there was room for a couple more. He pulled in and Stonechild swung in behind him. They walked up the drive together.

"How's Dawn doing?" Gundersund asked. He looked sideways at her. She kept her eyes straight ahead, the angular lines of her face looking as if they'd been chiselled into a block of granite. Her long black hair lifted back from her face in a sudden gust of wind.

"Not great. Having your parents in prison and living with a stranger can be hard on a thirteen-year-old." She finally turned to look at him. Her cheek muscle twitched. "Sometimes I wonder if I'm up for this. Then I remember that I'm all she has."

"You'll be fine. Just give it some time."

"Well, we've got nothing but. Her parents aren't going anywhere for a good number of years anyway."

Gundersund leaped up the steps and rang the bell. A plump woman in her thirties with a pleasant face answered the door. Her eyes flashed relief when they said they were from the Kingston police. "I'm Adele's friend, Catherine Lockhart," she said. "Ivo, Adele's husband, is in the living room. He seems … at a loss." She held the door open until they were inside, then turned and started down the hall.

Gundersund shot Stonechild a worried look that she returned. They both knew this could turn odd very quickly. They followed Catherine into the living room. Ivo Delaney sat hunched into himself on the couch. Gundersund took a second to realize that he was reading something on his phone. A boy who looked to be four or five was building something out of Lego on the floor. He had the same reddish hair and freckled pug face as Catherine. The child who had been reported missing was a girl, so this had to be Catherine's son — if the resemblance hadn't already confirmed it.

"Ivo," she said louder than she need to. "The police are here."

"I gathered that." Ivo set the phone down beside him and pushed himself to his feet. Gundersund could see that Ivo Delaney was a man ill at ease in his own body. Being a big man himself, he knew the feeling of always being on display with nowhere to hide. He instinctively reached out and shook Ivo's hand. It was soft and sweaty, no pressure returned.

"I can't imagine where Adele and Violet have gotten to," Ivo said, releasing his hand and sinking back onto the couch. He leaned forward and ran his fingers through his hair, scratching both sides of his head before letting his hands fall between his knees. Catherine seemed unsure what to do. She glanced worriedly between them before walking over to sit on the edge of the couch next to Ivo.

Gundersund and Stonechild pulled the only two chairs in the room closer and angled them in front of Ivo. Gundersund nodded at Stonechild to take the lead.

"Mr. Delaney, when did you last have contact with your wife?" Stonechild asked. She kept her eyes focused on his face until he finally looked at her.

"She was in bed when I left for work at the bank. It's the CIBC on Princess. That would have been around six-thirty. I'm an accountant and this is a very busy time of year. I hadn't had a chance to call her all day, but tried before four o'clock, after Catherine phoned me to say that my wife had missed an appointment. I rushed right home."

"Has your wife ever done this before? Left for the day without telling you?"

"No. At least, not that I know of. She's always home when I get back or she tells me where she is."

"Your daughter ..."

"Violet, yes, she's missing along with Adele. My daughter is three years old. She'll be starting kindergarten in the fall."

"Was Adele upset about anything?"

"How do you mean?"

"Oh, I don't know. Had you been fighting about anything? Was something bothering her about living out in the country?"

Ivo's cheeks reddened. "No, nothing unusual. She talked yesterday about us going on a trip to celebrate our wedding anniversary. She liked living in the country."

"Have you checked with your friends and family to see if they've heard from Adele?"

Ivo raised his head and hope crossed his features. "I hadn't thought of that! She has a sister. They're not close, but maybe that's where she's gone." He grabbed his phone and flipped through a couple of screens until he pressed her number.

"What's the sister's name?" Gundersund asked while they waited.

"Leanne Scott. She lives in Gananoque."

Stonechild sent Gundersund a questioning look. "About half an hour from here," he said. She nodded. He could tell by her eyes that she also thought Ivo was a man grasping at straws.

Ivo spoke a few words into the phone before he dropped it back onto the couch. His shoulders rolled in further. "She hasn't heard from Adele today."

Gundersund almost felt sorry for the guy. Sorry until he reminded himself that the husband was always the first suspect when a wife went missing. "I'll take her phone number and address and your wife's cellphone number." He jotted them down in his notepad before asking, "Do you mind if we have a quick look around? I understand she left food out in the kitchen."

Catherine jumped up. "I could take them, Ivo."

"It's okay. You stay here with Sam." He stood and led Stonechild and Gundersund into the hall. He stopped and turned to look at them when they entered the kitchen. The ruddy colour was back in his cheeks. The hand he lifted to his forehead had a slight tremor. "I've already checked the basement. I found Violet's knapsack and stuffed rabbit on the floor and the television left on. She never goes anywhere without her rabbit. Puts up a big fuss if we forget to pack it. I didn't want to say this in front of Catherine and the boy, but I have a very bad feeling about this, officers. A very bad feeling."

CHAPTER THREE

Kala Stonechild looked at the food on the kitchen counter and the meals left uneaten on the table. Adele and her daughter had been interrupted while they were getting ready to sit down to their meal, no question. They'd left on an emergency or somebody had forced them out of the house. As the afternoon slid into evening, the second option was becoming a dangerously real possibility. If it had been an emergency, Adele would certainly have called her husband by now. She wouldn't have turned off her phone. But who would take them, and why?

"Do you want to see the basement?"

She looked into Ivo's eyes — a nondescript pale shade of blue, small dark centres. He seemed so unsure of himself, a man who cared too much, perhaps. She wondered what type of woman would have joined her life to his. One equally as unassuming? "Yes, thank you," she answered.

She followed him down the steps while Gundersund called into the station. The room was large, carpeted, and wood-panelled. A flat screen perched on one wall with a couch facing it. A colouring book and crayons lay scattered on the floor. Violet had been colouring a duck in galoshes holding a bright yellow umbrella. Kala walked past the picture to check the laundry room and small bathroom. The furnace room was also empty. No sign of Adele or Violet, but she hadn't expected there to be. Ivo was waiting for her at the bottom of the stairs.

"How did you the two of you meet?" she asked.

He seemed startled by her question before a smile lifted the corners of his lips. He looked younger, not handsome but passable, when the worry lines in his face relaxed. "Adele came into the bank and I was asked to help her with a problem. For some reason, we got along. She asked if I had time for coffee. Before I knew it we were seeing each other every day. I owned this house in the country and she asked if she could stay with me."

"Were you married by then?"

"No, we'd only known each other two weeks, but she just moved right into my bedroom. We decided to get married and went to city hall the following week."

"Two weeks. That was quick."

"Yeah, I could barely believe it myself. A woman like Adele falling for me. You only get a chance like that once in a lifetime, if ever. I wasn't going to let it go by hesitating."

The conversation felt intimate, as if the real Ivo was letting himself out. Kala was sorry when

Gundersund pounded down the stairs and broke the moment.

"Do you have a couple of recent photos of your wife and daughter, Ivo? We can get started on circulating them."

"Of course. They're on my computer."

They all filed back up the stairs. Catherine and Sam met them in the kitchen. "We need to get on home. Sam is hungry and it will soon be his bedtime. Will you be okay, Ivo?" Catherine asked.

"I'll be fine. I'll call you as soon as I hear anything from Adele."

"I want to play with Violet," Sam said. He pulled on his mother's arm until she restrained him with her free hand.

"We'll be back another time when Violet is home," Catherine said. "Say goodbye to Ivo."

"No."

Catherine smiled an apology. "Make sure you call me as soon as you hear anything. We'll let ourselves out." She took a firm grip on Sam's arm and frog marched him toward the kitchen door that led into the front hall.

"I'll just jot down your phone number and address," Gundersund said, following her. "We might have more questions if Adele isn't home by morning."

"I'll be by the phone, waiting to hear from somebody," Catherine tossed over her shoulder before disappearing from view with Gundersund right behind her.

"I'll get you those photos, shall I?" Ivo asked Kala when they were alone.

She nodded. He led her through a second door down a short hallway into a small study. She took a moment to breathe in this sanctuary, tucked into a corner of the building. On first entry, she'd liked the feel of this house. High beamed ceilings, double paned windows with stained-glass transoms, hardwood floors and comfortable, well-worn furniture. Ivo's office was more of the same, dominated by an antique oak desk and swivel chair. It faced a window with a view of the woods, darkening now in the purple and indigo shadows of evening.

Ivo sat down at his desk and clicked on the keys. A series of images appeared on the screen. He clicked again and a woman and child filled the space. Kala leaned in, surprised. Adele Delaney was a looker: long brown hair with honey highlights, direct blue eyes, full lips, and pointed chin. Strength emanated from her eyes, the set of her jaw. Kala had no doubt this was a woman who would not put up with bullshit. The child was tiny and blond. Eyes like a doe and delicate features in a heart-shaped face. She was going to break some hearts in the school yard. Adele had her arm wrapped around Violet's shoulder, holding her close. Kala would never have placed either one of them with Ivo.

"This will do," Kala said. "Do you have separate head shots of them?"

Ivo nodded and brought up two more pictures for her approval. He transferred them to her mobile and she sent them on to Rouleau. Seeing the two missing people made this more real and urgent than before.

"Do you know of anyone who would want to harm your wife or child?" she asked the back of his head.

Ivo's shoulders drooped. "We lead a quiet life, Detective. Adele wanted it that way. I have no idea who would force them out of our house." He turned and fixed eyes glistening with anguish upon her. "I just want everything to go back the way it was this morning when I left them safe and sleeping. I want you to bring them home."

"I know. I need to ask though: if Adele was depressed, would she take Violet into the woods? Have you checked the grounds around the house?"

"My wife wasn't suicidal. I checked the yard before we called and they aren't there. They rarely go into the woods."

"They never disappear with the front door open either. We have to look everywhere."

He bowed his head. "This makes no sense. Adele isn't flighty or unpredictable. She wouldn't do anything to put Violet in harm's way. I know that as surely as I'm standing here."

"We don't need to jump to any conclusions either, but we need to eliminate possibilities, no matter how remote. My partner and I will walk around the grounds before we leave."

"I understand, but I must insist that wherever they are, Adele wouldn't just leave me unless she was being forced. She's my wife, Detective. I know her better than anyone. Something is very wrong."

Descending darkness and mist made the search difficult and less than thorough. Kala walked the east perimeter of the half-acre yard, venturing several feet into the woods when the foliage allowed. Gundersund was mirroring her search on the western edge. The temperature had dropped along with the disappearing sun and Kala shivered in her short-sleeved shirt, having left her jacket in the truck. Her shoes were soaked through from wet grass and pooled rain that had fallen earlier in the day. Her hair was damp from the moisture in the air. She cursed quietly when a branch slapped back and struck her cheek. Maybe they shouldn't be stumbling around back here in the semi-dark. If something untoward had happened, they might be trampling on evidence that would be more apparent in daylight. Something told her that Violet and Adele were not going to be found this close to home. She pushed back a low-hanging branch and stepped back onto the lawn. Gundersund's tall, dark shape was moving toward her across the last stretch of property. He stopped a few feet away, closer than felt comfortable.

"Find anything?" he asked.

"Nothing. Unless we have a better idea of where they are, this could be a fool's mission."

"Yeah. They might be halfway to Europe by now. I phoned Rouleau a few minutes ago. He said to give it a night and see if Adele makes contact. He agrees the whole situation is suspicious, but we can't be sure a crime has been committed. She might have run off with a boyfriend for all we know."

They started walking toward the lights of the house. They should have led to a safe, warm harbour. Now, they seemed eerie in the foggy night air. "What do you make of this?" she asked.

"Not sure. He's an odd one though. I wonder if he would have reported this if the neighbour hadn't entered the house. Maybe he did something to chase them off … or worse."

Kala stopped. "You think he killed them and then planned to come back after work and tidy up the kitchen and carry on as if nothing happened? He'd never get away with it."

"I'm just running around possibilities. We both know that a husband is suspect number one when a wife goes missing."

"I just don't get that vibe off the guy. Why kill his child?"

"No idea, Stonechild, but people do crazy stuff all the time."

"So, we just leave him here tonight?"

"Nothing more we can do. I'll check in with Rouleau and we can be on our way."

"I suppose we don't have any other choice. Let's hope they turn up by morning and Ivo's dire prediction that something is wrong proves unfounded."

CHAPTER FOUR

Kala pulled into her driveway just past eight thirty. She was relieved to see the lights on. The feeling of having someone inside waiting for her return was still strange. Of course, Taiku awaited her return, but this was different. Dawn was somebody she had to interact with and learn how to mother. Kala wasn't sure the responsibility suited her. She had no role model to draw from. Sometimes, in the middle of the night when she couldn't sleep, having a thirteen-year-old girl in the house felt like a noose around her neck.

She opened the truck door and jumped onto the ground. The night air was even foggier here, so close to Lake Ontario. The stars and moon were hidden from view and the darkness was absolute this far from town. She started up the driveway and heard the back door slam as loud as a pistol shot in the evening's stillness. A soft thudding of paws and then Taiku was upon her, jumping up and licking her arm and face. She laughed and pushed him down, then bent and rubbed his head all over while his tail thumped against the pavement.

"That's my good boy," she said and looked up as Dawn ran around the corner of the house. The girl stopped a few feet away and stood silently watching Kala with Taiku. She was tall for her age, long straight hair braided, black staring eyes. Her body language was unsure, neck bent, arms wrapped around her stomach. Kala wanted to reach out and hug her slender frame but resisted. The last time she'd tried, Dawn had stood frozen with her arms stiff at her sides. The counsellor had said to give her time and space. The past year's events had made her fragile, untrusting.

Kala settled on a neutral greeting. "How was your day?"

"Fine."

They started walking toward the back deck, Taiku between them. "Sorry I'm so late. The case was at a house the other side of Kingston. How was school? Bus on time?" She stole a sideways glance. Dawn's eyes were fixed on the ground as she walked.

"Yes."

Inside the brightly lit kitchen, Kala glanced over to the table. It was filled with Dawn's school books. A pencil lay on a half-filled lined sheet in an open binder. "How's the homework going? All done?" She mentally kicked herself. Dawn's one word responses were turning her into an inquisitor.

"I just have to finish my story."

"Well you do that and I'll get supper heated up. Stew okay?"

"Yes."

Another question. She'd done it again. *Shit*.

The stew was soon bubbling away in a pot on the stovetop. Kala cut thick slices of multi-grain bread and poured Dawn a glass of milk. She poured herself a glass of iced tea and set bowls of the thick beef stew on the table. Taiku stretched out at Kala's feet.

"I'll pick you up tomorrow," Kala said when they were nearly done eating. "You have an appointment with Dr. Lyman that'll run until five. I'll be waiting in the parking lot."

Dawn nodded, head down.

Kala resisted reaching out to brush back Dawn's bangs from where they fell into her eyes. "If you want to go watch TV before bed, I can clean up," she said instead.

Long after Dawn had disappeared into her bedroom and shut the door, Kala sat outside watching the band of lake from her spot on the deck. She'd wrapped herself up in a wool blanket and tucked her feet under herself. Taiku was off chasing shadows in the woods. She'd received a call that morning that Gil Valiquette, Dawn's mother's boyfriend, had been sentenced to ten years in Millhaven Pen. Her mother, Rose, would be doing five years in Joliette prison outside Montreal. Armed robbery and a police chase through Manitoba with Dawn in the car. When Kala had taken custody, Dawn was nothing like the girl she'd met twice in Ottawa. The light in her eyes had died and been replaced by something flat and lonely.

She hadn't even asked when she'd see her mother again. Compounding the misery, her father, Paul, was already in prison and not due out for four years. He'd been friends with Valiquette and while they'd been partners in crime Valiquette had managed to stay out of jail … until now. Kala found out that Paul had been moved to Millhaven when Kingston Pen closed. She wondered if the two men would team up inside. Her main concern at the moment was deciding the right time to tell Dawn this latest news. Perhaps the best thing to do would be to give Dr. Lyman a call in the morning to seek her advice. Even better if she could convince the counsellor to break the news to Dawn herself.

Kala stood and called for Taiku to come. A cold wind blew back her hair and made her shiver inside the blanket. She could hear the distant roar of waves slapping the shore at the far end of the property. This guardian role that she'd agreed to take on was filled with landmines. One wrong word, gesture, look could topple the delicate relationship she'd managed to keep going the past few months since the night she'd picked up Dawn from the police station. In some ways, that night felt like a lifetime ago; in other ways, the sight of Dawn's bruised face and terrified eyes could have happened yesterday.

"There you are, Taiku," she said as his nails clattered up the cedar steps. "Let's get some sleep before the night gets away. We have another busy one tomorrow."

Sergeant Jacques Rouleau hefted his father's battered leather suitcase into the trunk of his car and hurried around to the driver's side. His father, Henri, was already inside, belted into the passenger seat.

"All set," Rouleau said. "Got your train ticket?"

"I do." His father patted his breast pocket. His thick white hair was newly trimmed and he was wearing his good black coat. He'd tucked a silk cravat the colour of a robin's egg around his neck. "And it's not too late for me to order a cab. You need to get into the office." He squinted through the front windshield. "Nice to see some spring sun for a change."

"Work can wait half an hour, Dad." Rouleau put on his sunglasses before pulling out of the condo parking lot. He turned right onto Ontario Street then left onto Brock, a one-way that would merge onto Division. Division was a main road that led past the police station to the train depot closer to Highway 401. The trip would take under half an hour this time of the morning. He put the heater on low to take the chill out of the car. By mid-morning the temperature would climb and he'd have the windows open.

"Will I be seeing you on the weekend?"

Rouleau felt that he should nod, but knew he had no way of knowing. "We got a report yesterday about a woman and her daughter gone missing. It could be nothing or it could turn into a major case. I might not be able to get away this weekend."

"Well, I've taken a suite at the Delta on Lyon in case you can make it."

Rouleau felt the weight of his father's sharp blue gaze without turning his head. "You really need to spend the next few weeks rooting around in Library and Archives, Dad? I worry that this might be too much so soon after your surgery."

"I do, and you shouldn't worry because I don't. The doctor says I'm fine to resume my normal routine." He paused. "Since I'll be in Ottawa anyway, I'll probably go visit Frances. Anything you want me to pass along?"

"No."

His father's voice got softer. "You can't keep pretending this isn't happening, Jacques. She'll want to see you."

Rouleau felt the tightening in his chest that would soon have him sucking in air like a fish. He worked to control his breathing. He checked the rear-view and glanced toward his father. Henri was now staring straight ahead, his elbow resting on the armrest, bearing his weight. The pain in Rouleau's chest eased. "I'll try to make it, Dad. I just can't guarantee anything with the woman missing."

"Well, I'll be there a couple of weeks. Offer stands."

"I'll come to Ottawa if I have time."

"Can I count on that, Son?"

"All I can do is promise you that I will try."

CHAPTER FIVE

The team was waiting for Rouleau in the small meeting room when he arrived fifteen minutes late. Someone had brought in doughnuts and everyone had a mug of coffee. He selected a Boston cream from the nearly empty box and sat in the chair at the head of the table they'd left vacant for him.

"Caught in traffic?" Gundersund asked, smile tugging at his lips. Even on the worst days, Kingston roads were not an issue this time of the morning.

"I see you've managed to fill in the time without me," Rouleau said before biting into the doughnut. He chewed and then asked, "Any word on the missing woman and child?"

"Nothing," Gundersund said. "Stonechild called this morning and spoke with the husband, Ivo Delaney."

Rouleau saw Stonechild fix her eyes on Gundersund. He knew what she was thinking. Gundersund would be wise to let her speak for herself. "Delaney didn't hear from his wife overnight?" Rouleau deliberately turned to face Stonechild.

She stared back. "Nothing. He was up all night."

Zack Woodhouse was sitting across from Stonechild, leaning back in his chair, arms crossed over his potbelly. "Or at least that's what he told you. He probably has a better idea where she is than he's letting on."

"We haven't ruled that out yet."

Rouleau picked up the file and read through Gundersund's report of their visit to the Delaney house. The others silently drank their coffee and waited. Rouleau looked across at Gundersund. "No sign of a struggle and her car still in the driveway. Breakfast on the table uneaten and the front door open as if they left in haste." He was speaking aloud, sorting the facts and wondering at their significance. "You checked the woods?"

"Just the perimeter. It was getting dark when we finished inside the house."

"Although unlikely, we need to make sure they aren't wandering around lost. Stonechild, take Bennett and Woodhouse and have another look around the property. See if Mr. Delaney sticks to his story. Talk to the neighbour again and see if she can provide more information about the Delaney marriage. I'll pull in someone to check out the airport and the train and bus stations." He looked back at the notes. "She has a sister named Leanne Scott who lives in Gananoque. Can you follow up with her, Gundersund? It's a short drive. Might be good to talk to her in person."

"Right."

"I could get the Amber Alert in motion, but if the child is with her mother, and we have no reason to believe otherwise, an alert appears premature. So far this is baffling and worrisome, but not criminal. It's quiet right now so we may as well move on this one until somebody hears from Adele Delaney. I'll be in court this morning testifying on the Mendelson case but keep me informed by text."

Four heads tipped in unison.

Rouleau watched them file out. Nobody had bought into a crime yet, but they were definitely intrigued. Even Woodhouse moved more quickly than usual. He was infamous for dogging it but Rouleau had hopes that Woodhouse would turn around now that his partner Ed Chalmers was retired. Andrew Bennett had replaced him, a bright young cop from the Ottawa force who wouldn't be satisfied skirting over investigations and taking shortcuts. Already Bennett had asked to be partnered with Stonechild. They'd worked a case together in Ottawa and he liked her investigative skills, could learn from them, at least that was the reason he gave for wanting to work with her again. Rouleau doubted that was the only reason. If Stonechild knew that Bennett found her attractive, she'd given no sign.

Bounded on the southern end of town by the St. Lawrence River, Gananoque is known as the Gateway to the Thousand Islands. Gundersund had taken Fiona on the Thousand Island cruise one August day several years back. They'd caught the ship, along with another hundred tourists in the harbour, outside the Gananoque Hotel. The day had been overcast and cool, but he and Fiona had huddled together on deck, his arm around her, not wanting to miss the beauty of the islands slipping past or the feel of her body pressed against his. She'd been captivated at the sight of Boldt Castle, a magnificent six-storey masonry masterpiece built in the early 1900s on Heart Island. They'd docked and spent a happy afternoon traipsing around the island, exploring the restored structures, and posing for pictures. She'd agreed to marry him standing under the stained-glass window in the central hall. Once back in Gananoque, they'd walked up Stone Street to downtown with the requisite charming small-town shops, restaurants, and bars kept alive by the summer tourist trade. A leisurely supper with two bottles of wine to celebrate and then lucky to get a room in the hotel. One of the few idyllic memories he had left from their time together. Until now, he'd had no reason to return.

Leanne Scott lived on Elm Street on the west side of town in a bungalow: white siding, green trim, and detached garage on a small lot. The windows and front door had been recently upgraded and a small verandah added to the front. A modest house well maintained on a quiet street.

Unlike his last day in Gananoque, the spring sun and clear sky gave the day a promising feel. He spotted tulips pushing up in the small garden that lined the walkway. The smell of earth and damp rotting leaves rose up to greet him as he passed by. Purple and white crocuses had pushed through and would soon be in bloom. Leanne Scott was waiting for him and opened the door at the top of the steps before he rang the bell. She'd already brewed a fresh pot of coffee and served him a cup in the living room, snugly fit with a plaid couch, coffee table, rocking chair, and recliner.

He took a moment to study her as she settled into the rocker. She was an older, faded version of her sister, from what Gundersund had seen in Adele's photo. Leanne's eyes had the same blue directness, but the brown in her hair was overtaken by grey. She was a tall woman but her body had thickened in the middle, fat dimpling her arms and what he could see of her legs. She was wearing a striped v-necked T-shirt, pink Bermuda shorts, Birkenstocks over socks, pushing summer and fashion sense just a bit, Gundersund thought.

"Have you spoken with Adele this week?" he asked. He took a sip of coffee and waited. It was strong and sugary, flavoured with hazelnuts and chocolate. The unexpected sweetness made him wince. He raised the back of his hand to his lips to hide his involuntary response. He preferred his coffee bitter and unadulterated.

"I'm fifteen years older than my sister. We keep in touch, but not daily, or even weekly for that matter. I guess the last time I spoke with her was just after New Year's."

"I guess not even monthly then."

She returned his smile. "No. I guess not even that." She paused, "Although, we did exchange emails this week."

He should have been less specific with his question. "Can you share what she wrote?"

"Of course. She was asking how Randy and I are doing and mentioned that she and Violet were due for a visit. I emailed her back and said next weekend would be great. She said that she was hoping for this weekend but could hold off until then. I still have the exchange if you'd like to read it."

"I'll give you my email address and you can forward the emails. Did she use the words 'hold off'?"

"Yes."

"Did these words strike you as odd?"

"A little, since I hadn't heard from her in so long. They made me think that she had something to tell me. Naturally, I wondered about her marriage since she didn't mention Ivo."

"How would you describe your sister's marriage?"

"Okay. It had been okay." Leanne shifted, groaning softly. Sweat glistened on her forehead and cheeks. A flush travelled upward. Even her hair shone damp in the lamp light.

Gundersund had felt a chill from the moment he entered the house. "Are you feeling alright?" he asked.

Leanne waved a hand back and forth in front of her face. "Hot flash. Getting damned inconvenient. Randy's sleeping in the spare bedroom, I sweat that much at night. Nobody's ever died of them though. Where were we?"

"Your sister and her marriage."

"Oh yeah. Ivo seems like a nice enough man. A little bland maybe, but Adele was looking to settle down. She seemed happy with him."

"I hear some hesitation in your voice."

"Adele and I weren't exactly close growing up, being so far apart in age, so it's hard for me to pass judgment. I just, well, I wondered if Ivo was enough for her."

"Was she happy being a mother and living in the country?"

"I guess. It's not where I thought she'd end up by a long stretch." Leanne laughed. "She was a wild one back in the day."

"How so?"

"We grew up in Gananoque but she moved to Montreal after high school. Couldn't wait to leave. Had to see the big city. She ended up working in a bar in the east end the last six years she lived there. We lost touch for several years until she moved back to the area. From the little bits she let drop, I gathered she was running with a wilder crowd in Montreal."

"Do you know the name of the bar where she worked?"

"Let me think. It was a man's name. The … Henri? No, that's not right." She snapped her fingers. "The Louis. She worked at the Chez Louis. She told me that it wasn't a place that Randy and I would like. A bit rough."

Gundersund jotted both names down in his notebook. "What was your surname before marriage?"

"Dufour. My father owned a hardware store on the main drag. Randy works at the Home Hardware on Stone Street. Life can be one big circle."

He had her spell the name and wrote it down too. "Is your husband at home?"

"Randy?" She hesitated as her cheeks flushed bright red for the second time. A fresh coating of sweat covered her nose and cheeks. "No, he's gone to town. I don't expect him back anytime soon."

"I'll give you my card with my email, cell number, and the central police number. I'd appreciate if you would call if you hear from Adele."

"Of course. I imagine she just took Violet on a vacation somewhere for a few days. Maybe someone from her past life showed up and surprised her and she jumped at the opportunity to have a change from her routine. I wouldn't be surprised."

"You're not worried then."

"Not overly. I know Ivo is though. He probably has no idea what my sister can get up to when she gets it into her head to kick up her heels." Leanne held his gaze. "Just one thing, Detective. I'd appreciate if you keep our names out of the press. We value our privacy and I don't want any media at our door asking us about Adele. My sister and I weren't close and I don't want to have to explain that to anybody."

"Of course. We'll keep your names out of it."

"You can do that?"

"Yes, we certainly can at every stage of the case."

"Thank you. I'll hold you to that."

He was surprised by the relief on her face because the world had turned into a reality TV show with everyone trying to become famous. He found it refreshing to know that she and her husband had no desire to make themselves into media stars. He'd respect their request for privacy and make sure that they weren't bothered by journalists looking for a family connection for their stories.

CHAPTER SIX

Kala was shocked at the paleness of Ivo Delaney's skin and the tortured look in his eyes when he opened the front door at ten past nine. His tall body was more stooped than she remembered; his expression defeated. Had something happened between the time she'd left him the evening before and now? She followed him inside the hallway and touched his shoulder. "Tell me what's going on."

"Nothing. I'm just losing faith with every passing minute." He turned to face her. "I didn't sleep at all last night."

"Understandable, but we have no reason yet to think anything bad has happened. I checked the newswire before coming here and there's nothing of concern. No need to fear the worst." *Unless you know something.* She could sympathize with his distress, but whether it came from worry or guilt, she had no way of knowing. She pointed through the open door toward the driveway. Bennett and Woodhouse stood talking on the lawn next to their car. They'd convinced her to take one vehicle, although she didn't like to be without her own truck.

Another police car pulled in behind them. Rouleau had rustled up two more officers for the search. Bennett looked toward her and smiled. He was smiling at her way too much, as if trying to get on her good side. She frowned and looked back at Ivo. "We're going to check deeper into the woods, just to be sure that Adele and Violet aren't roaming around lost. I wanted you to know before you spotted us trooping around."

"Go ahead. I know they aren't there."

"Oh? How would you know that?"

He closed his eyes. "Violet hates the woods. She thinks it's full of monsters. Adele wouldn't want to frighten her."

"We'll check just to make absolutely certain and then I'll come back to see if we've forgotten to ask you anything from yesterday." She started to leave the house but stopped in the doorway. "Is there anybody you could call to come stay with you? Waiting can be more difficult alone."

"No, I'll be fine. We liked … like our privacy."

"Right. I'll be back soon."

She left him and walked over to Bennett, Woodhouse, and the two uniformed officers. The day was warming up and she unzipped her leather jacket before she reached them. Woodhouse had taken charge. He'd brought up a map of the area on his iPad and was pointing to different sections of the property. The others took turns looking at the screen. Kala leaned in past Bennett.

"Is that a creek?" She traced her finger along a ribbon of dark terrain.

Woodhouse enlarged the image. "You're right. It is a creek of some sort."

"It'll be larger with the spring thaw," Kala said. The snowfall had been nearly record-breaking in February and March. She pointed along a route through the bush. "I'll hike that way to the water to have a look around."

"I'll come with you," Bennett said. "Two sets of eyes are better than one."

Woodhouse nodded. "We'll do a sweep and if you're not back we'll check the houses along this road. Maybe someone noticed the two of them leaving with somebody else. Stay in touch by text if you find anything."

Kala would have liked to head out on her own. She knew Bennett would put up an argument so she decided not to fight his offer. "Let's get going," she said to him. "I saw a path over there somewhere. It was dusk when I looked last time, but it shouldn't be hard to find.

They crossed the lawn and separated to search. It wasn't long before she found the opening in the underbrush and a path heading north. "This looks like the route," she called to Bennett, who was several metres away. He jogged over and she started into the woods.

"The path is a bit overgrown but not hard to navigate," she said. "I've been through thicker bush up north."

"Lead on then. I'll try not to hold you up."

She kept a keen eye on the ground and bushes, searching for signs of recent activity. She remembered that it had rained the day that Adele and Violet went missing. A steady rain near lunchtime that turned to drizzle mid-afternoon. Even now the path was boggy in the lower lying places. Sumac, raspberry, and honeysuckle bushes lined the path with scrubby cedar leading into pine and birch trees. Tree roots crisscrossed the dirt trail and she heard Bennett stumble and curse more than once.

Five minutes into the woods her eyes spotted a patch of pink on a low-hanging bush. She stopped and parted the branches carefully. She reached for her camera to record what she'd found. If the piece of clothing wasn't related to the missing woman and her daughter, all the better, but it was best to make a record just in case.

"What have you got?" Bennett asked. He was so close that she felt his breath on her cheek when she turned her head.

"Looks like a mitten. A child's mitten."

He pulled back the branches while she took photos. Then he took the mitten from the bush with a gloved hand. They inspected it carefully.

"It's not been here long," Kala said. "It's too clean to have been subjected to the elements over winter."

"No, I'd say it was left here recently. It's still damp, likely from yesterday's rain." He pulled out a plastic bag and inserted the mitten. "It could belong to a three-year-old. It's the right size."

"The thing is, Ivo Delaney said his daughter never comes into the woods because she's scared of them. If this is her mitten, how did it get here?"

The smile disappeared from Bennett's face. "This is turning damned weird." He thought for a second. "Do you think he might have told you that to keep us from coming into the woods? Maybe he has something to hide."

"Let's look around some more. Be careful not to disturb anything that you find." She didn't have to elaborate on what that might be. They were both thinking the same thing.

Ten minutes later, they met on the path. "Nothing," Kala said.

"Me neither."

"Well, that's a relief. Let's keep going."

The path widened and walking was easier for the last five minutes leading to the river bank. With all of the melted snow over the past month, the creek was deeper and wider than it had looked on the map, just as Kala had predicted. She could see a current pulling the blackish water in a southerly direction toward Lake Ontario. Trees hung over the water, tangles of roots and brush making the terrain along the sloped bank difficult to negotiate.

Bennett stepped closer to the water's edge and looked upstream. "I think we should split up to save time."

"I'll head downstream. We can meet back here in half an hour."

They separated and Kala followed the line of the river as best she could. It was slow going. She looked out over the water every few feet, checking for clothing or dark shapes bobbing in the water. She was crouched down, poking a stick under tree roots in the water to release what turned out to be a plastic bag when Bennett yelled. His voice startled her and one of her feet slid into the water before she caught her balance. She climbed back up the bank and pushed her way through the scrub and bushes to their starting point. Bennett was nowhere in sight.

"Where are you?" she called.

"Just over here." His voice was closer, sounding like it came from around a short curve in the bank.

She jumped over a fallen log and continued on through scraggly cedars until she saw his head above some bushes, further down the bank. She scrambled down the ridge to where he was kneeling. He reached a hand to steady her, then half turned and pointed to a clump of tree trunks standing in the water. Her breath stopped. "No."

The hood of a child's pink raincoat was caught on a branch, bobbing up and down between two cedars. The bad feeling she'd had at the sight of the mitten in the bush was suddenly full blown. Kala looked at Bennett and pulled out her phone.

"Rouleau will have to send out the dive team. Lots of daylight left."

Bennett stood and looked out over the water while she made the call. When Kala finished speaking with Rouleau, he said, "If the child is in the river, the mother must be too. You figure a murder-suicide?"

"Maybe. Rouleau's going to meet me back at the house to lead them here. You okay to keep watch?"

"No problem."

"I'll try to be quick."

"I won't be going anywhere."

CHAPTER SEVEN

Kala pulled into the only empty parking spot in front of Dr. Lyman's office, a limestone building at the edge of the university campus. She threw the truck into park and quickly got out. Guilt pounded through her as she ran toward the front door. She'd let time get away from her as she stood watching divers plunge into the river searching for the bodies of Violet and possibly Adele Delaney. The search had stretched on without success and now she was a good forty minutes late picking up Dawn. She'd tried calling Dawn's cell twice before leaving the Delaney property, but maddeningly the calls had gone to voice mail.

The reception area was empty; the woman who answered the phones was not at her desk. Kala scanned the lounge, normally so inviting with pink and purple chairs and pale yellow walls lined with French impressionist prints. Now the vacant space felt like a rebuke. Had Dawn gotten tired of waiting and decided to walk home in the dark? No, it was much too far. Kala forced herself to take a deep breath and calm down. Nothing would be gained by imagining the worst. She had to think about this logically. She had to think like an upset thirteen-year-old girl.

Dr. Lyman's door was closed and Kala suddenly realized that in all probability Dawn was still inside with the counsellor. Dr. Lyman must have taken advantage of Kala's tardiness to get in some more time with Dawn. Kala crossed the hall to stand in front of Dr. Lyman's door with her hand raised. She hesitated. What if Dr. Lyman was in with another patient? What if Dawn was long gone? She squared her shoulders. There was only one way to find out. She rapped lightly on the door.

The sound of a woman's voice and the thump of footsteps carried through the door. It swung open in a sudden motion and Dr. Lyman was standing in front of her, a questioning look in her eyes. "Kala," she said, a smile lighting up her face as she recognized Dawn's aunt. She must have seen something in Kala's face because she immediately asked, "Is everything okay? Stella and I were just going over some accounting since it's that time of year." She looked past Kala into the reception area. "Is Dawn waiting outside?"

"I just got here. I haven't seen her."

Dr. Lyman looked toward the woman sitting at the desk. "Did Dawn say anything to you about leaving, Stella?"

"No. She said that her aunt was picking her up. I left her alone to come work on these books."

Dr. Lyman turned back to face Kala. "Oh dear. But she can't have gotten far. We spent an extra ten minutes in session."

That meant Dawn had a half hour head start at the most. "Did she seem okay? I'd meant to call you this morning about her mom but the day got away from me."

"She was a little quiet today, more so than usual. What's happened with her mother?"

"Sentencing was yesterday. Her boyfriend got ten years and she got five. I was going to tell Dawn this morning at breakfast but we were running late. In fact, I've been running late the whole day."

Dr. Lyman's eyes searched Kala's face. She was a kindly woman, early sixties, tall but plump, with soft white hair. Kala had liked her instinctively. Hoped that she would be the lifeline for Dawn, but so far Dawn was just treading water. Dr. Lyman had suggested giving her space, but three months had passed without a breakthrough. Every day that went by made Kala doubt her ability to look after such a troubled child entering the teen years. Dawn was dealing with demons not unlike those she had faced herself not that long ago. Her own past should have given her insight. All it did was make her scared.

"Dawn might have gone to catch a city bus. She's quite self-sufficient, as we both know."

Kala started backing away toward the main entrance. "I'll have to go see if I can track her down. Thanks for everything." She could barely stop herself from running full tilt out the door.

"Phone me later and we can chat. Perhaps it's time to have you and Dawn in a session together."

"I'll call when I have some time." *Whenever that might be.*

Kala hurried outside and scanned the street as she raced toward her truck. No sign of her. The bus stop was a few blocks over. Dawn knew the route because she'd taken it once when Kala had been stuck in a meeting. She hoped Dawn had decided to take the bus again. Surely, she wouldn't have tried hitchhiking. Images of Ivo Delaney and his missing family were weighing on Kala's mind. This had to be unrelated. Did Dawn even have bus money?

Why hadn't she answered her phone?

The shadows were lengthening as the sun began its incremental descent. There was still a lot of light left, but it was paler and had lost the day's warmth. Kala drove slowly down the streets as she made her way to the bus stop. A woman with a baby stroller was standing next to the route sign. Dawn was nowhere in sight. Kala drove past and continued to scan the sidewalks. Her phone buzzed on the seat next to her and she glanced down, hopeful. Gundersund's name and number held on the screen as the call went to voice mail. She had no time to talk to him about the case. He'd want to compare notes. She ignored the call and backtracked, taking side streets on the chance that Dawn had taken a different route. Twenty minutes later she pulled over and tried calling Dawn again. After three rings, Dawn's recorded voice told her to leave a message.

"I sure hope you caught that bus," Kala muttered, tossing her phone onto the seat. She pulled away from the curb and followed the bus route out of the city toward home, checking for signs of Dawn along the way, but she knew that it was futile the farther she travelled. If Dawn was walking, she wouldn't have made it this distance in so short a time.

What was she going to do if Dawn wasn't home?

She turned right onto King Street West, which became Front Road once out of the downtown. Front Road in turn fed into Old Front Road some twenty minutes on. Old Front Road wound along the shoreline of Lake Ontario, both sides lined in houses set back in the trees on large lots. She was lucky to have landed in a house with prime property backing onto the lake. Her lawyer friend Marjory owned the land but was away for at least the year working in the North on a land claims case.

Kala followed Old Front Road past Gundersund's property. His car was in the driveway but there was no sign of him. Nor was there any sign of Dawn walking along the road. She rounded the corner and took an immediate turn into Marjory's driveway. She slowed and eased past the birch trees, parking between two old growth pines. She craned her neck to look out through the windshield for any sign of life. The lights were off in the front of the house and her heart dropped. She stepped out of the truck.

It was nearly dark now. The wind had come up and she could hear waves striking the shore. Taiku would be desperate to get outside after being stuck in the house all day. She'd let him out and then start making some calls. The problem was that she had no idea who Dawn knew in Kingston. Perhaps Gundersund and Rouleau would help with her search. She started walking toward the back of the house but slowed as she neared the back verandah. A man's laugh warned her that she was not alone. A girl's voice answered and Kala exhaled relief, but she was immediately on guard again. Dawn had made it home, but who was she with?

Kala skirted silently around the side of the house until she had a view of the deck. Looking up, she saw the two figures sitting in the deck chairs close together, out of the wind. The light was on in the kitchen, backlighting them from behind. It took her a few seconds to recognize Gundersund. Dawn was talking and Kala stopped to listen, surprised to hear the girl speaking in more than monosyllables. The sudden relief that Kala felt knowing everything was okay was followed by anger. Her partner and Dawn were settled in having a nice chat while she'd been worried out of her mind.

"I liked living in Ottawa. My mother was a waitress until she got sick but she wouldn't let me stop going to school. She wanted me to go to art college when I get older. She used to like my drawings and always made me tape them up on the wall in the kitchen."

Gundersund's voice carried toward her on the evening breeze. "You still can go to art school, you know. Have you been doing any drawings since you came to live with Kala?"

"No. I don't feel like painting. I just don't want to anymore."

Gundersund nodded. "Sometimes that happens. I remember when my brother died, I didn't play baseball for an entire summer. We used to be on the same team and it made me sad to go to the ball diamond without him."

"How old were you?"

"Fourteen. Charley was a year younger than me. A drunk driver hit the car and Charley was sitting in the front passenger seat. It was his turn, so I was in the back."

"You must have felt bad, but it wasn't your fault."

"I know that now. It took me a while to believe it."

A rush of motion came from the back of the property. Taiku was bounding toward Kala with Gundersund's dog, Minny, at his heels. Kala stepped out of the shadows and waved up at Dawn and Gundersund before Taiku reached her. "There you are, Dawn," she said, knowing she'd been caught eavesdropping. Embarrassment made her voice sharp. "I went to pick you up at Dr. Lyman's and couldn't find you. Why didn't you answer your phone? You must have known I'd be worried. Did you just not care?"

Gundersund was quiet for a moment. Then, he spoke with the same reassuring voice that he'd just used with Dawn. "I met Dawn walking home at the start of Old Front Road so offered to drive her the rest of the way. She was upset because her phone was dead and she hadn't been able to reach you. I left you a message on your cell to let you know where she was, but I guess you didn't get it. Anyhow, we stopped to get Minny and then decided to walk her from my place to let Taiku out."

Kala climbed the steps. She should have answered Gundersund's call. "I was driving when you called." She looked at Dawn, not quite ready to let her anger go. "I'm sorry I was late picking you up, but you shouldn't have left without telling Dr. Lyman or Stella. You knew that I was coming for you."

Dawn's head dropped. "Sorry," she mumbled from under her veil of black hair.

Kala felt herself deflate like a pricked balloon as she looked at her niece's bowed head. After all, she was mainly to blame for having left Dawn waiting so long without sending word that she was late. Gundersund's eyes were studying her and she stared back at him.

"I guess I'll go in and heat up that leftover stew," she said. She walked past the two of them and turned with her hand on the door handle. "You're welcome to stay, Gundersund."

Dawn lifted her head.

"I'd enjoy that," Gundersund said. "All that's waiting for me at home is a frozen dinner and two weeks' worth of dirty laundry."

Dawn finished eating and disappeared into her bedroom to do homework. Kala watched her leave, regretting her earlier harsh words. Dawn had become even more withdrawn during the meal and she knew that it was her fault.

"Well I better be pushing off," Gundersund said. "Busy day tomorrow."

They both stood at the same time and Kala followed him toward the back door. "Any theories on what happened to Violet Delaney?" he asked as they stepped outside onto the deck. Stars glittered above in an ink black sky. The spring wind was still up, but the cold edge was gone.

"I'm leaning toward murder-suicide, but not yet convinced of anything," Kala said. "Ivo Delaney seemed genuinely in shock when he identified her raincoat and mitten."

"Maybe. Hell of a shame when a mother takes that way out. Better to just end her own life and leave the kid."

"She must have been in awful pain."

"It's hard to understand." Gundersund hesitated. "Say, I wonder if I could take Dawn to an art show a friend of mine is having on Wednesday night. I know it's a school night, but I'd get her back early. You could come too, if you like."

"I don't know. Let me think about it."

"Sure, but it would be a chance for her to maybe get inspired again."

"I'll think about it. I promise."

"Great. Well, see you tomorrow."

"Yeah. Bright and early."

He climbed down the steps and whistled for Minny and then disappeared into the darkness. She waited a few moments before calling for Taiku. She'd just decided that she'd have to go in search of him when he appeared at the bottom of the steps, tail wagging.

"Time to call it a night, boy," she said. "Get in the house and let's get to bed." She waited while Taiku had one last sniff around the lawn below the deck before he climbed the steps and padded past her into the house.

A half hour later, lying in bed staring out the open window, Gundersund's words replayed in her head. Losing a brother so young would leave a pain that time would ease, but never completely erase. Sharing his story with Dawn had been an act of empathy. This challenged the opinion she'd built up of him over the past few months. Some of distancing herself from Gundersund had been an act of self-preservation. The rest had been to keep her life simple. Even if he said that he and his wife were separated, Fiona was still very much involved with him at work and not going anywhere. Gundersund's life was a mess and she didn't want to be pulled any further into his world.

Kala rolled onto her back. On the other hand, what harm could it do to go with him to the art exhibit? Maybe Gundersund was right about reaching Dawn through art. God knows, nothing else had worked. She and Dawn were as far apart as the day she'd picked her up at the station. Hobnobbing with artists for an evening might be worth the pain, especially since she couldn't get past the feeling that she and Dawn were running out of time. She'd raise the idea of an outing with Gundersund to Dawn in the morning.

CHAPTER EIGHT

Walter Knight reached for the can of Red Bull and took a long swallow. He glanced over at Jed, his head bobbing up and down to whatever new wave, crazy rap music it was the kid listened to through ear buds hooked up to his iPad. Jed. His oldest and only son: skater boy with frizzy blond hair and skinny as a whip — seventeen with nothing deeper on his mind than what he wanted to eat for supper.

When he'd agreed to take Jed along for the Maritime run, he'd hoped they'd get a father-son bond going. He'd imagined forging one often enough, especially those times when the loneliness of his job got to him. He spent many nights a thousand miles from Windsor, and his family became the star he pinned his dreams on. Never mind that after a few weeks at home he couldn't wait to get back out on the road. So far on this trip, the longest conversation he'd managed to have with Jed had been about whether to order the apple or the lemon meringue pie. Not exactly the deep connection he'd envisioned.

He checked his watch before looking back at the road. Kingston was another twenty minutes on the 401. They'd made decent time and should hit Montreal just after five a.m., usually the best time of day to cut through that city. After making it to the other side, he'd keep going and pull into Rivière-du-Loup to catch a few hours sleep. Not that Jed would care. The kid was pretty much sleeping his way across Ontario as it was.

Walter checked his side mirror. Some asshole in a dark-coloured truck had been riding his ass since Trenton. The number of idiot drivers was on the rise. Time was, he might have had some fun with the driver on his tail, but now he just wanted to get through his run without a hassle. He slowed down to let the guy pass. The Ford pickup pulled alongside when the driver put his foot into it and sped off. Walter had just had time to glimpse a good old boy wearing a ball cap behind the wheel. No accounting for the games drivers played to ease the boredom. He'd seen the gambit from annoying to downright dangerous.

The rain started the other side of Napanee; a hard slanting rain that drummed down on the roof of the cab like going through a car wash. The noise was loud enough to wake Jed from a sound sleep. He pulled the ear buds out and yawned.

"When did the rain start, Dad?"

"A few minutes ago."

"Sounds like bullets on the roof."

"It's one nasty storm. Looks to be coming off the lake."

"Where are we, anyway?" Jed leaned forward and squinted through the front windshield. The wipers were on high, snapping across the glass like they were on steroids.

"We'll be in Kingston in about fifteen minutes. That would be Lake Ontario off to our right. If this keeps up, I'll find a place to pull over so we can get a coffee and have a break."

"I could eat something."

Walter drained the last of the Red Bull and turned his full concentration on the road. The 401 was a four-lane highway — two lanes in each direction — and straight for the most part. He was glad that he wasn't on one of the smaller highways with visibility down to almost nothing. The load of produce in the trailer was heavy enough to keep the wind from battering the truck around too much. The darkness combined with the rain was unnerving. Every so often, red brake lights flashed ahead of him, giving him an idea of curves in the road.

Even Jed appeared to sense that this was a dangerous situation. He put away his iPad and kept his eyes on the road. A bell sounded in his pocket and he reached for his phone.

"Mom just sent a text. She's asking if we're caught in the storm." Jed grinned at his dad. "She watches the weather channel when she can't sleep."

"I know. It's not the first time she's called me in the middle of the night."

"What should I tell her?"

"That we're fine and pulling into the next rest stop to wait this out."

Thunder rumbled overhead as Jed's thumbs worked away on the screen. A jagged streak of lightning cracked the sky. A few seconds after Jed finished typing, the bell rang again. Jed looked down and then up. "She says to let her know when we get there."

"Tell her ten-four."

They passed the first of the off ramps into Kingston. Walter was reluctant to get off the highway. He wanted to be through Montreal before morning and any long delay would be a problem. He passed the second exit.

Walter chanced a quick glance at his son. Jed's face was pale and worried in the glow from the dashboard.

"Dad, this is really bad. Where are we going to stop?"

"Nothing's open this time of night except the rest stops on the highway. I was thinking we could make the one at Mallorytown. I'll even treat you to a hamburger and fries."

"How far?"

"An hour, maybe."

"You're okay to drive that far in this storm?"

"It's letting up."

A crack of thunder made a liar of him. The last exit into Kingston slid past on their right. Now they were committed to keep going until at least Gananoque, another thirty minutes with the storm. He could pull off the road there if the rain was still coming down in torrents. The Mallorytown rest stop was going to be more than an hour the speed they were forced to travel.

"Mom's not going to like this."

"She'll never know. I just don't want to stop in the middle of nowhere. We have to make Montreal before daybreak." He took Jed's silence for agreement, knowing it wasn't. "Send her a text and tell her we're hunkering down."

"But that's a lie."

"Not really. We will hunker down. Just not yet. No need to have her worry."

Jed's thumbs got busy again. After he sent the message, he crossed his arms and slumped deeper into the seat. He turned sideways and looked out the passenger window.

Walter didn't have the energy or time to deal with his son's disapproval. He'd smooth things over when they took the break in Mallorytown. The lights of two vehicles were ahead of him, both in the left lane. He could barely make out their tail lights through the darkness and rain. Still, it was comforting to know they weren't the only fools on the road. Thunder split the sound barrier directly overhead and seconds later fork lightning lit up the sky like fireworks.

"Dad!" Jed's voice came out a high pitched shriek, nearly making Walter swerve into the other lane. "Dad! Pull over! Somebody's lying on the road." Jared lifted an arm and punched his finger on the glass. "On the side of the road." He turned horrified eyes toward his father. "They're just laying there, Dad. They could be dead."

"Are you sure?"

"I know what I saw. You have to pull over now, Dad."

"Maybe it was just some garbage or road kill."

"It was a person!" Jed's voice had risen to frantic.

Walter had been doing forty so it didn't take much to gear down, especially since they were on an incline. He eased the rig onto the shoulder as far over as he could get. He set the air brakes and turned to face his son.

"You're sure about this, Jed?"

"I know what I saw."

He put on the four ways. "Okay, but you stay here. There's no use in two of us getting drenched."

"I want to come with you."

"Stay here. Have your phone ready to call 911."

Walter reached around behind him until he found his raincoat. He put it on, pulling the hood over his head.

"Give me the flashlight in the dash."

Jed opened the glove compartment and reached around inside. He handed over the flashlight, his face grim in the dashboard light.

Walter turned it on, keeping the beam pointed at the ground. He double checked for oncoming headlights before opening his door and jumping out of the cab. His face and jeans were soaked before he hit the ground.

He checked again that no traffic was coming before racing to the back of the trailer and moving as far onto the shoulder as he could. The rain and wind pummelled against him but he had a wrestler's body and was a match for even these elements. He plowed forward, head bowed and chin tucked, keeping his balance as he ran down the incline toward the place where Jed had yelled for him to stop. Even at that, he nearly stumbled over the woman. The feel of his boot jamming into her made him curse and jump back. He stood for a second, breathing heavily, arcing the flashlight along the road and over the grassy slope as far as it would cut into the blackness of the woods. Anybody could be out there.

He pointed the beam to his feet and crouched down beside her, careful to keep one eye watching down the road for approaching headlights, straining to hear over the wind. She was wearing a black shirt and blue jeans, rolled on her side, one arm straight out, the fingers spread wide. Her feet were bare, her legs twisted at unnatural angles. He pushed back her long tangled hair to find the back of her neck. Her hair was a soggy mass and cool to his touch. He couldn't find a pulse. When he pulled his hand away the flashlight beam lit up crimson blood on his fingers.

He squatted on his haunches for a moment more, the rain pouring down his face, trying to make sense of it. Then he took out the oil rag that he kept in his pocket and wiped his hand before slowly pushing himself to his feet. He backed away, careful not to disturb the scene any more than he already had. Shock was setting in and made him feel outside his body. He'd like nothing more than to get back in his truck and tell Jed that it was just a deer on the road. Carry on to the Mallorytown rest stop and have burgers and maybe get Jed to talk about where he planned to go to school in the fall. The talk was long overdue. The woman was dead. She wouldn't know the difference.

He started back up the road, the wind pushing him along this time toward the flashing lights of his transport. The door to the cab fought him as a strong gust of wind blew it wide open. He climbed into the cab and wrestled the door shut behind him. Then he sat for a moment, collecting himself, hands on the steering wheel.

"Dad?"

"Yeah."

"Was it anything?"

He turned his head sideways and looked at his son's face, so young and untested in all the things that could beat a man down. Now was the time to put the truck into gear and get back on the road. Walter inhaled a long draught of warm air from the truck cab into his lungs. He let it out slowly and nodded in Jed's direction.

"Hit 911, Son, then hand me your phone."

Jed's eyes widened before he looked down at his phone. Walter swallowed the lump in his throat at the sight of his boy's bowed head, blond hair sticking up like duck down above the nape of his neck. He'd missed the better part of his kids' lives, telling himself that he was making a good living for his family by being on the road. Telling himself they were better off with him gone most of the time. Sometimes he'd even convinced himself. Jed and his sister had gotten used to his comings and goings, never questioning why he wouldn't find a job in town. His wife had covered for him. She'd kept him tied to them with some invisible, endless string even during those long stretches when he'd taken extra runs, trying to ease something in himself that wouldn't be eased. Lying to Jed now would cross some dangerous line that Walter knew he'd never be able to uncross. It would break the string that held him fast. The kid had seen what he'd seen. The body on the side of the road would haunt his dreams even if Walter made him believe for this moment that he'd been mistaken.

He took the phone from Jed and spoke to an officer on the desk. They'd have to wait around and talk to police when they arrived. He'd have to fight his way through the rain and wind again and light some flares.

So much for making Montreal before sunrise.

Walter reached over and rested his hand on the back of his son's neck. "Text your mother and tell her we'll be spending the night at a motel in Kingston. I got a feeling we're going to be a while."

CHAPTER NINE

Rouleau stood from his crouched position near the dead woman. They'd closed off the highway and erected a tent and hooked up lanterns with enough light for photos and a thorough first inspection. Rain pattered on the plastic material like a kind of hypnotizing background music. He signalled to Fiona Gundersund to take over and ducked outside the protective awning, stepping around a puddle and over to where Paul Gundersund stood talking on his cellphone. After a few seconds, Gundersund tucked the phone into his pocket and pulled his hood down over his forehead.

Gundersund spoke first. "The driver who called it in doesn't know anything. It's definitely Adele Delaney on the side of the highway. The question is how she ended up here."

"Fiona says that she was killed somewhere else. Are you okay breaking it to the husband?"

"I wouldn't mind waiting for Stonechild. She seemed to get along with him better than the rest of us. I found him a bit odd, to tell you the truth."

"You can't wait for her to get here. As it is, she's not going to be thrilled that I didn't call her, but no point three of us standing in the rain." Rouleau squinted through the slanting downpour at a woman walking toward them. The darkness had thinned somewhat as dawn neared. If only the rain would let up. Rouleau recognized the woman as she got closer. He'd seen her from a distance at a news conference in city hall the week before. He turned so she wouldn't see what he was saying. "A reporter's here already. You've got to tell Delaney before this gets out."

Gundersund stared over Rouleau's shoulder. "That's Marci Stokes from the *Whig*. Word is she was a foreign correspondent in the Middle East for an American news outlet until a month ago."

"Kingston isn't exactly a hotbed of excitement. I wonder why she took a job at the paper."

"To make our lives miserable?"

"She can join the line. Take one of the uniforms with you to Delaney's. What time are they resuming the search for their daughter?"

"At first light, so in about an hour, I'd say."

"Check in."

Gundersund nodded at Marci Stokes before he headed over to the parked police cars lining the highway. She stopped just outside the crime scene in front of Rouleau and extended her hand. Her fingers were cool and damp from the rain. He noticed her grey eyes looking him over before she tilted her head to look past his shoulder toward the tent. Her view of the body was blocked for the most part. Again, he wondered what she was doing in Kingston.

"I'm Marci Stokes from the *Whig-Standard*," she said. "Do you have an ID on the body?"

"No. Her next of kin would have to be notified first at any rate. But I'm sure you knew that."

Marci's mouth curved in the smallest of smiles as she pulled a notepad out of her pocket. "So, it's a woman. How old?"

"Hard to judge."

"Because she's in such bad shape?"

"Not necessarily. How did you hear about this anyway? It's the middle of the night."

Marci smiled wider this time. Deep lines crinkled at the corners of her eyes and around her mouth before the smile disappeared. "Was she murdered or hit trying to cross the highway?"

"Too early to say."

She lifted her eyes and studied his face. "How about this? I won't print anything until you give the okay. I know these deaths can be … delicate." She pushed back a strand of wet hair that had fallen into her eyes with the back of her hand. "It could be mutually beneficial if we work together on these cases. I'm good at cooperating with investigators as long as I get the story in the end."

"You're pretty much the only game in town yet you talk as if the competition is beating down my door to get the story. You must have figured out by now that Kingston news doesn't normally make the national stage."

"All small cities have their stories. It's a matter of digging them out."

"That sounds a lot like digging dirt. Has the *Whig* changed its focus from real news to the sensational?"

"On the contrary." She pointed toward the tented area. "Is this incident related to the woman and her daughter who went missing yesterday? Adele and Violet Delaney?" She waited, grey eyes unblinking.

Rouleau managed a poker face while he ran the implications of what she'd said through his head. No doubt now that someone was feeding her information. Heath was not going to be happy. He'd have to be brought in to handle the leak. Rouleau kept his tone guarded. "Then you know that we haven't anything to release yet about them at this point."

"Listen, Detective Rouleau. We both know that the Kingston Police Force is remiss when it comes to sharing information with the public. I'm here to change that. I want to work with you, but it's a two-way street." She reached into her pocket and pulled out a business card. "Here's my cellphone number. Call me day or night if you decide that you have something to share. I won't wait forever though, before I go with what I have."

Rouleau reached inside the white jumpsuit and tucked the card into his shirt pocket while he watched her stride back toward her photographer. He was leaning on the hood of their vehicle parked on the shoulder just past the police barrier. Stokes lifted an arm and pointed toward the tent. Her partner started snapping pictures in quick succession using a telephoto lens.

Fiona Gundersund appeared at Rouleau's elbow. "We're ready to transport the body back to my office. I'll get the autopsy underway right after I have some breakfast. I see you're getting to know our new crime reporter."

"Not by choice. I'll get Stonechild in to watch you work." He checked his watch. "Should we aim for eight?"

"Works for me." Fiona tilted her head toward Marci Stokes. "I hear she's doing penance here in the backwoods until a political story she broke blows over. She offended some mighty powerful American politicians. She could be cooling her heels here a while."

"Just what we need. Someone trying to find a story where there isn't one."

Fiona smiled. "We all have to make a living somehow, Jacques. Personally, I'd rather cut up dead bodies than write about the terrible acts performed by the living."

The forensics team was still hard at work scouring the area around the highway when Rouleau got into his car. He turned the heater to high trying to shake the chill that had seeped into his bones. The rain had slowed to a drizzle but it promised to be a miserable morning — especially for the team searching for Violet Delaney's tiny body in the river.

Some days he didn't like his job much. This was turning out to be one of them.

*　*　*　*

Officer Halliwell jumped into the front seat next to Gundersund and slammed the door. Rain dripped from his coat and his face was slick with water under his police cap. He looked from the radio to Gundersund. "So, should I call it in?"

Gundersund ran his tongue around the inside of his mouth and over his teeth while he thought over what significance to attach to the fact that Delaney's car was gone from his driveway at almost six a.m. The outside light and a lamp in the living room window were both shining brightly, but Delaney wasn't answering the door. He let his eyes wander across the yard to the dark line of trees at the back of the property. The shapes looked like hovering giants in the morning shadows. The child, Violet, had been forced through the woods to the river and thrown into the fast-flowing water, and not by her mother ... or that was how things looked now. Adele Delaney had been taken somewhere else and held for a time before being murdered. The scenario was incomprehensible. Horrific.

The sound of a vehicle slowing on the main road caught his attention and brought him back from his reverie. A set of headlights swung their beams up the driveway as a car turned in.

"Don't call the station just yet." Gundersund pulled up the zipper on his coat and pulled the hood up over his head. "Will this damn rain never end?" He swung the door open and squinted at the car through the sheet of rain as it pulled in next to them. Ivo Delaney was at the wheel. Gundersund turned back toward Halliwell. "Let's find out where Delaney's been before I tell him about his wife. Then we can decide whether or not to bring him into the station.

"Hold up a minute, Delaney!" Gundersund called as he stepped out of the car. Delaney had already jumped out of his and was sprinting for the front door. He wasn't wearing a jacket and rain plastered his hair to his head and soaked his shirt so that it was nearly transparent. He pointed toward the house without slowing and Gundersund gave chase. Halliwell's door slammed and he joined in the run for the front door. They crowded into the front entranceway, dripping water onto the hardwood floor from their coats. Delaney backed up so that he was leaning against the staircase. He wrapped his arms around his chest and shook from the chill he'd gotten in the cool morning rain. Gundersund had never seen skin so pale, the man's cheeks hollowed out in a face becoming more cadaver-like with every passing day. His eyes were wild and bright in the harsh light from the overhead lamp. There was no doubt that Delaney was a man in torment. The question now was whether or not it came from killing his family.

"It's early to be out and about. Where were you?" Gundersund stepped closer to Delaney so that he could catch every bit of emotion crossing his face.

"Couldn't sleep. I thought driving around searching for my family was better than lying in bed going out of my mind." Delaney's teeth chattered behind blue lips. "I can't believe they're in the creek.

I keep hoping to find them wandering ..."

"Can you tell us where you drove exactly?"

"Why?" Delaney's eyes flashed the first hint of defiance. They held Gundersund's for one brief moment before his shoulders slumped and the fight appeared to fizzle as quickly as it had come. "I drove into Kingston and took Highway 2 to Highway 33 into Bath. I drove back through Kingston and took Highway 2 home. I didn't stop anywhere if you're looking for witnesses."

His story was going to be hard to disprove unless a witness could put him elsewhere. Gundersund would leave his travel tale unchallenged for now. He motioned toward the living room. "You might want to sit down and wrap yourself in a blanket. I have some news that is going to be difficult." He hated this part of the job. Delaney might have killed his wife and daughter, but if not he was going to be devastated by Gundersund's next words.

Delaney shut his eyes and his body swayed as if he was going to fall down. Gundersund reached out an arm to steady him.

"Tell me now." Delaney's voice was low and wretched. "Just tell me."

"The body of a woman was found a few hours ago on the side of the 401 just outside Kingston on the way to Gananoque. We believe it to be Adele."

Delaney's body jolted as if a fire had been lit under him. His eyes widened, a crazed expression making his features grotesque. "My wife? Dead on the 401? How can that be? You told me that she'd drowned Violet and then herself. Now you tell me that she was killed on the highway? I could have been out looking for her all this time instead of answering your damn questions? *You* could have been out there doing your job." Delaney pushed himself away from the staircase and began pacing, his arms rising and falling like a bird trying to take flight. A guttural growl came from deep in his throat.

Gundersund and Halliwell stepped forward in unison and somehow got their arms around him. He fought them for a moment before slumping against Gundersund. Between them they walked him into the living room and angled him onto the couch, his body limp, all resistance gone. Gundersund reached for the blanket lying across the back of the couch and wrapped it around Delaney's shoulders while Halliwell kept a firm grip. Gundersund spoke to Halliwell as they worked Delaney into a reclining position. "We'd better get the paramedics out here. Call them and then see if there's some brandy in one of the cupboards. He's going into shock."

"I'm on it." Halliwell let go after Delaney sunk into the cushions and closed his eyes. He crossed the floor to the hallway already speaking into his cellphone.

Not for the first time since they stepped through the front door, Gundersund wished for Kala Stonechild's silent presence next to him. He knew for a fact that she would have handled his botched interaction with Delaney with greater skill and compassion. Delaney had instinctively trusted her on their first visit. He wasn't the first person in trouble who'd reacted to something they saw in her eyes. Black eyes as layered and mysterious as the Canadian Shield. For all her prickly toughness, a humanity could be seen shining from their depths. Gundersund knew this as a certainty because for a short time he'd been allowed into her world. Now he was left on the outside looking in with the feeling that he'd utterly failed her. The problem was, he had no idea why.

CHAPTER TEN

Kala finished her Tim Hortons coffee and tossed the cup into the garbage can on her way to the morgue. She wasn't looking forward to spending the next couple of hours with Fiona Gundersund, her partner's on-again, off-again wife. The way Fiona watched her when nobody else was looking made Kala uncomfortable. Behind the direct stare was a barely hidden dislike and Kala had a good idea why. Fiona saw any woman connected to her husband as a threat. She was territorial. An emotional leech. A wife who wasn't going to let go of him even if she was getting it on with other men. Kala had heard the rumours. She thought Gundersund might be a fool for his devotion but she wasn't going to get involved in his pitiful personal life. She'd done the relationship thing with a separated married man once before and never again. Especially not with her work partner.

Even if she found the kindness in the man attractive.

She pushed open the door to Fiona's work-shop and crossed over to the slab where Fiona was preparing to cut into Adele Delaney's corpse. Classical music provided a soothing background to the whirring sound of a saw. The air was chilly and the smells disturbing but Kala normally took autopsies in stride. She'd shot and dressed deer in a past life. Only the violence of what had been done to Adele made this a difficult viewing. Even in death, Adele's face was strong-boned in perfect symmetry, light reflecting off the golden highlights in her long brown hair. She'd been a good-looking woman and Ivo Delaney was far from a catch. Kala tried to reconcile the idea of the two of them together, but failed.

Fiona turned off the saw and looked at Kala through her protective glasses. Her long blond hair was tucked under a plastic cap. "Nice of you to join me, Detective. Your timing's perfect. Ivo Delaney identified her this morning so everything is in order. The man could barely stand, he was so distraught. I think they took him directly to the hospital. I'm about to start cutting open her chest."

Kala nodded. "You're not wasting any time on this one."

"Rouleau's lucky it's been a slow month. I have nothing else pressing at the moment."

"Do you know what killed her?"

"You weren't at the crime scene this morning with Paul?"

"No."

Kala watched the expressions flit across Fiona's face as she assessed this information before she spoke. "It was likely the knife wounds in her stomach. She bled out but not where her body was found. Her abdomen is a mess." She whipped the sheet away from Adele's body to show the jagged gashes that crisscrossed Adele's stomach. It looked as if an operation had been performed without the final suturing to close the openings. "It would have taken a lot of stitches to close these wounds, as you can see. Not that any surgeon would have made a mess like this."

Kala frowned. Why had the killer carved up Adele's stomach? Was there a message in choosing to brutalize this part of her body? To disfigure a woman so terribly seemed personal. Angry. The door behind Kala opened and she turned. Bennett nodded hello and came over to stand next to her. He took one look before averting his gaze from the table.

"Rouleau sent me to observe."

"Your first time?"

"Yeah. Does it always smell so bad?"

Kala exchanged a glance with Fiona. Fiona's lips curved up and she turned on the saw. The whirring noise cut off conversation. She lowered her head and began cutting into Adele's ribs.

Kala nudged Bennett with her elbow. She leaned in and spoke loudly into his ear. "If you need to get some air, just step outside. I can fill you in later. The first time is always the hardest."

"I can handle it." A muscle twitched in his square jaw.

"Of course."

Fiona was skillful and methodical, Kala would give her that. She spoke into a microphone and recorded her findings as she went. By the time she'd removed and weighed Adele's heart, Bennett was the colour of a pierogi.

Kala took pity. "Ready to make a coffee run?"

"Sure."

He didn't need to be asked twice. Kala figured he wouldn't be in any rush to get back. Twenty minutes later she got a text from Bennett that he'd been corralled by Rouleau. He was on his way to the Delaney house to help with the search for Violet. He was sorry about the coffee. Kala smiled to herself before turning her attention back to Fiona and the work at hand.

"I've never seen anything like this before. Someone removed several of her internal organs, including her uterus, appendix, and spleen. I've heard of killers cutting off fingers so the victim can't be identified, but never this. It's ... bizarre." Fiona jumped up to unplug the whistling kettle. The autopsy had finished late in the afternoon. She turned her back on Kala and filled the teapot with water, then placed the pot and two cups on the desk between them. "I have sugar but no milk."

"Black is fine."

Fiona mashed the teabags with the back of a spoon before pouring. She handed Kala a mug with the words "Made in Canada" stamped on the side. Kala wondered if the double entendre was intentional. Fiona took a sip and sat back in her leather chair. "Heaven. My arms are aching." She looked over at Kala and continued their conversation about the autopsy as if no break had occurred. "So what do you make of it?"

"Not sure yet."

"She died somewhere else but not long before she was dumped on the highway. The marks on her face were from being tossed onto the pavement from a moving vehicle."

"So time of death?"

"I'd say between seven and eleven that evening. She had bruising on her wrists and ankles from being tied up. I found sores on her mouth from been gagged. How was her marriage?"

"Her husband said all was going great."

"Do you believe him?"

"We're looking into their relationship, but it's tough since they were reclusive for the most part." Kala wasn't keen to speculate at this point in the investigation. Fiona seemed in tune with her thoughts because she shifted subjects after another sip of tea.

"I guess you've heard that Paul and I aren't together at the moment."

Kala held up both hands. "None of my business."

"I know you say that, but the station is a small family. Anyhow, I just want you to know that Paul and I've weathered a lot. I'd like to get back with him but he's tentative, even though we've gotten, well, intimate again. I hope ... well I hope that you'll respect that we're trying to make our marriage right." She opened her blue eyes wider as if she was opening herself to Kala.

Kala's cellphone beeped. *Saved by the bell*, she thought. She lifted the phone from the desk where she'd set it and clicked on Paul Gundersund's text. Meeting at the Merchant in ten. She thumbed in an okay before standing and looking down at Fiona.

"I have a debrief to get to. Sorry to run. I wish you well getting your marriage back on track. Believe me that you have nothing to worry about on my account. I meant it when I said your relationship with your husband is none of my business." *And you don't need to know that I'm off to meet him now.* "Thanks for the tea."

Ten minutes later, Kala was in her truck heading down Division Street to Princess. The Merchant Tap House was at the bottom of Princess, not far from the Holiday Inn that looked out over Lake Ontario. She and Gundersund liked to meet at the Merchant when they had notes to compare. She found a parking spot a street over and was only fifteen minutes late when she walked in the front door. She checked out the main room first before crossing the hall to the smaller room to the right of the main entrance. Gundersund looked up from his beer and smiled at her. Rouleau was with him. She slid into the empty seat between them. A waitress arrived immediately afterward with a cranberry soda and lime.

"I took the liberty of ordering for you." Gundersund grinned. "On me."

She took a swallow and set the glass down. "Thanks. I think my drinking habits are getting predictable."

"Not at all."

She looked at Rouleau. "Any word on the child?"

"Nothing yet. Bennett and Woodhouse are still at the Delaneys. I expect they'll be closing down for the night. Her body could be anywhere with the currents. She might have gotten lodged somewhere but so far, no sign."

"Has Ivo Delaney confessed to anything?"

"He's in the hospital. He insisted on seeing Adele's body against everyone's advice, so the ambulance made a stop at the morgue before taking him to the General. The psychiatrist he's been seeing has been called in to check him out."

"He's been having mental problems? Can't say that I'm surprised."

"I haven't been able to reach the doctor to get any details, but we understand that Ivo has an underlying condition. We'll need to follow up and hopefully get some information that isn't doctor-patient protected. We're in the process of getting a search warrant to go through his house and car. A judge should be signing off within the hour."

Kala grimaced. "What a mess. From the autopsy, whoever killed Adele Delaney appears to have been either a sadist or mentally ill." She repeated the results of Fiona's observations. "So what time do you want me to meet you at the Delaney house tonight?" She caught the briefest of eye contact between Rouleau and Gundersund. She fixed her eyes on Rouleau.

"You don't need to come out tonight. Gundersund and I will be there, as will Woodhouse and Bennett."

"But ..."

Rouleau held up a hand. "It's overkill to have all of us there. You're better off spending time with Dawn this evening and getting a good night's sleep."

"I don't want special treatment because of my personal life. You could have called me in to the crime scene this morning."

"We're a team and there'll be times when you have to carry more of the load when another member of our squad needs time to deal with their commitments."

"I didn't ask for any favours."

"I know, and none are being given. We're just doing some of the grunt work so you can get Dawn settled into your life. That's what well-functioning teams do."

Gundersund ran his fingers across the scar on his cheek. He'd watched their exchange without comment. Kala was grateful when he broke the silence that descended by turning focus back to the case. It gave her a chance to hide her frustration.

"What would spark Delaney to drown his daughter and then mutilate his wife? What did we miss when we searched his property?"

Rouleau looked away from Kala and clicked on his cellphone. "You sent a message that Delaney was out in his car this morning when you arrived. Did he say where?"

"On a drive to clear his head in Bath, and home on Highways 33 and 2, although it could as easily have been the 401. I wonder if he would have been as forthcoming if we hadn't caught him returning home at six a.m."

"The man just keeps looking more and more suspicious. If I had to guess, I'd say that he had her in the woods tied up and decided to get rid of her before the police stumbled across her body. We just didn't look in the right spot. How can we prove he didn't dump her on the 401 without a witness?"

The waitress returned with menus. Gundersund and Rouleau accepted but Kala declined. "It's getting late and I have to get home to my commitment." She smiled at Rouleau to soften her words. "Thanks."

"No thanks needed."

"Do we have a plan of attack for tomorrow?"

Rouleau looked up at the waitress. "We need a few minutes. I'll motion you over when we're ready." When she'd gone, he answered. "We'll give the search for Violet another day and will expand the search to take in more of the woods around the Delaney property. If we're lucky, we'll find where she was being held. I'd like you both to interview Ivo when we get the go ahead from the doctor. It might not be tomorrow though. I'd like you both to return and interview Adele's sister in Gananoque."

Kala had forgotten about her. "Has she been informed?"

"Yeah. She decided not to view the body today. She wants to remember Adele alive. She's expecting you tomorrow around nine."

Gundersund looked at Kala. "I'll pick you up at eight."

Kala thought about turning him down but that made no sense. She was crazy to even think about how it would look to Fiona. "I'll be ready." She stood. "Well, I'll leave you to it. If you find anything tonight, give me a call. I'm up until midnight."

"You got it," Rouleau said. "If you don't hear from me before then, Gundersund will fill you in tomorrow when he picks you up."

CHAPTER ELEVEN

Taiku met her at the door and led her into the living room where Dawn was huddled under a Hudson's Bay blanket on the couch. She lowered the novel she'd been reading to her lap when Kala sat down next to her.

Kala tried to get a bead on Dawn's mood but failed. "Sorry I'm so late again."

"The missing woman and her daughter?"

"Yes. It's turned into a murder investigation."

"That's horrible."

"It is." She paused. "I hate leaving you alone so much. How about I find someone to be here to meet you after school?"

"You mean like a babysitter?"

"More like a housekeeper. They could get supper going and clean up. They'd be company until I get home."

Dawn frowned. "Taiku's all the company I need. I could get supper going if you tell me what you want to eat. I can tidy up too."

Kala patted her leg through the blanket. "Have I told you what a great kid you are?" She paused. "I know how hard this has been for you and I'm sorry. I've never … I'm not used to looking after anyone but myself and you'll have to be patient with me."

"It's okay."

"I want you to know that I'm happy to have you with me for however long. You're family. I also need to talk to you about your mom and Gil."

"I know about their sentences."

Kala tried to keep the surprise from her face. "Did somebody contact you?"

Dawn shook her head. "I searched their names in the news on Google. I've known for a few days. Are you sure that you want me to stay so long? They won't be getting out for a long time. Neither will my real dad."

Nothing about wanting to contact her mom. Kala wondered at the toughness of this child. The wounds must lie deep. She chose her words with care. "I want you here as long as you need me. We can help each other."

Dawn looked at Kala. "Then we won't be alone."

"No, because we'll have each other."

Dawn was silent for several seconds. The flash of vulnerability disappeared from her face replaced by an empty stare. "Okay." She picked up the book from her lap. "I want to finish this chapter before supper." She lowered her head, effectively ending the conversation. Kala watched her for a moment. The timing never was going to be right. She asked, "Do you want to visit your parents? I can make arrangements."

Dawn kept her head down. "No."

"Well, if you ever change your mind, promise you'll let me know."

"I won't change my mind."

"Well, if you ever do."

Kala went into the kitchen and checked the cupboards. Grilled cheese sandwiches seemed like the right comfort food. She'd heat up some frozen chicken and rice soup to go with them. She was thankful for those marathon weekends of cooking she'd done the month before. The fully stocked freezer had turned into a godsend.

While the soup thawed in a pot on the stove, Kala leaned against the counter and looked through the window over the sink at the night sky. Until now, Dawn hadn't responded to any overtures to discuss the situation with her parents. It must mean something if she'd been searching out information on the Internet. She hadn't shut off her feelings altogether. Dr. Lyman would tell her not to read too much into this, to be patient and let Dawn reach out in her own time. Easier said.

Kala took the block of cheddar from the fridge. Ivo Delaney's face passed through her mind as she straightened and walked over to the counter. Had she been fooled by his mental illness? Her gut instinct had told her that he wasn't a killer. Now

... well now the evidence was all pointing at him. Something had to account for the way he'd butchered his wife's stomach. Everything a killer did was driven by a reason, no matter how bizarre or twisted. Delaney would be no different. The work was to figure out the logic behind his behaviour. Hopefully, tomorrow Adele's sister, Leanne Scott, would give them the key.

Kala thought about Adele Delaney as she stirred the soup, a familiar uneasiness keeping her from closing off the case in her mind. What were they missing? Why had she married a man with mental issues? She'd walked into the bank and picked him out of all the men in the world. An attractive, self-possessed woman had chosen to live with a mouse of a man in the middle of nowhere. He'd hacked up her stomach and thrown their daughter into the river. If she were looking at this from Delaney's point of view, he was venting his rage on the part of her body that he hated most and the child they'd created. But why? Kala stood silently, holding the wooden spoon motionless in the air while she tried to make sense of the facts.

As if controlled by ESP, her cellphone buzzed from her handbag tossed onto the counter. She turned the heat down on the soup and grabbed the phone from the side pocket.

"Hello?"

"Kala, it's Fiona Gundersund. Sorry to bother you so late."

"I wasn't doing anything much. How can I help you?"

"I think I'm the one who can help you. I was replaying the tape with my observations and something struck me as odd. I went back and had another look at Adele Delaney's body and think you might be very interested in what I found."

Kala listened closely and stood for a long time looking out the window after Fiona signed off from the call, running over the facts of the case through her mind. This new piece of the puzzle didn't square with what they knew about the Delaney family. What they'd been led to believe about the marriage and the child.

They hadn't been asking the right questions.

As usual, Gundersund was right on time picking her up the following morning. The rain had stopped, although the clouds hung low and grey. Kala grabbed her windbreaker from the hook behind the back door and left Taiku with a promise to be home early. She jumped off the back deck and made her way to his Mustang idling in the driveway. She slid into the passenger seat and grunted a hello. Gundersund grunted one back. They didn't speak again until Gundersund pulled into the Tim Hortons drive-through on their way out of Kingston and yelled their order into the two-way speaker. Two coffees with cream, no sugar. Kala nodded at his questioning look and he added a couple of multigrain bagels with cream cheese. *We're becoming an old married couple*, Kala thought.

They ate in the parking lot with the radio tuned to a rock station. The sun was trying to break out from a bank of clouds but it was a tossup as to whether it would succeed. Gundersund took a look at the sky through the front windshield. "Calling for more showers after lunch. At least the search team will catch a break for a few hours at the Delaneys." He crumpled up the wrapper from his bagel and tossed it over his shoulder before putting the car into drive. He looked over at Kala. "I guess we'll take the 401."

"No point taking the scenic route."

They hadn't gone far before they reached the place where Adele's body had lain on the side of the highway. All lanes were now open, the murder scene cleared away. Kala took a drink of coffee and scanned the road on both sides.

"It's a long, straight stretch of road before it starts climbing up the hill." Gundersund glanced over at her. "Whoever did this would have waited until nobody was behind them and pulled over to push her out. They would have watched for approaching headlights, which would have been visible only for a short distance in the rainstorm."

"So this exact location was likely opportunistic."

"That would be my guess."

"There should be traces of her blood in Ivo's car."

"Unless he had her wrapped in plastic."

"That strikes me as something he would do. Being an accountant, he'll have the anal gene." She was quiet while she drank her coffee. A few kilometres farther on she said, "I read the report from your first interview with Leanne Scott. She said that she and Adele weren't all that close."

"Yeah. According to Leanne, Adele moved to Montreal as soon as she could and lived a rougher life. There's a fifteen-year age difference." Gundersund glanced over at her. "You appear to be pondering something."

"I have a few questions for the sister."

"Want to go over a strategy?"

"No, that's okay."

They didn't speak again until they reached Gananoque. Kala had been past the town on the highway but never driven into it. She liked how the road wound along the lakeshore. "Pretty spot. Have you taken the boat tour of the Thousand Islands, Gundersund?" She watched a pained expression cross his face.

"Yeah. It's worth an afternoon if you have one to spare."

Kala thought about taking Dawn one summer afternoon. A day trip might get her mind off the tragedies that were her parents. She might even open up about the robbery and the cross-country run with her mom and Gil Valiquette. The police believed Dawn had been in the car for all of it. So far, she wasn't talking.

Gundersund followed a few of the residential streets until he reached Elm. He drove halfway down and pointed to the black Ford truck in the middle of a driveway. "Must be the husband's. Name's Randy and he works at the Home Hardware on the highway. He wasn't home last time I was here."

They parked on the street in front of the house and Gundersund led the way up the driveway to the front door. They stood silently while they waited for someone to answer the chiming doorbell. The door was yanked open by a bear of a man with a full grey beard, wearing a red checked hunting jacket and ball cap pushed back on his head. The rim of the cap was bent in the middle and reminded Kala of a duck's beak. He held out a hand. "Randy Scott. Good of you to come to us. The wife isn't up to leaving the house."

Kala and Gundersund each shook his hand as they stepped inside. Kala immediately felt the chill in the hallway but it turned out to be warm compared to the living room where Leanne Scott, dressed in a pink nylon housecoat and bare feet, sat in a rocking chair, her fingers rhythmically clicking away on knitting needles. She was making what looked to be a pint-sized yellow sweater. As soon as she saw them in the doorway, she set aside the balls of wool and stood to also shake their hands. Her eyes were red from crying but her handshake was dry and firm. They took seats, forming a circle around the coffee table.

Leanne looked at her husband. "Offer the folks some coffee, why don't you, Randy."

Kala opened her mouth to refuse but Gundersund beat her to a reply. "That would be great, thank you. We both take it with milk, no sugar."

Randy exited and they heard the sound of his footsteps recede down the hallway. Leanne rubbed her hands up and down her thighs. "Won't take Randy long. I had him make a pot not ten minutes ago. I'd prefer to wait for him before we start discussing my sister."

"Of course." Gundersund leaned back as if they had all the time in the world.

Kala studied the needlepoint artwork of kittens and puppies on the wall next to the woodstove, which was unfortunately not in use. She shivered under her light jacket. Leanne met her eyes.

"Sorry about the lack of heat. I can't seem to take it much warmer than frigid anymore. Menopause is not all it's cracked up to be."

"No problem."

Randy clumped into the room and set a tray down on the coffee table. He handed out cups of coffee and sat back down in his leather chair. His eyes were pale blue and bulged like marbles from under a heavy forehead. "What can you tell us about Adele's death? Leanne and I are just starting to get our heads around the fact she was murdered."

Leanne looked straight ahead. Her bottom lip trembled but she didn't cry.

Gundersund took the lead. "All we know is that somebody killed her in a different location and moved her body to the side of the 401 just this side of Kingston. A truck driver found her and called us. We're very sorry for your loss."

Leanne's hands tapped up and down in her lap. "Did she … did she suffer?"

"No. We believe she died instantly."

"Well, at least there's that."

Kala knew this wasn't true but she didn't blame Gundersund for sparing them. She would have done the same.

Randy looked at Leanne then back at Kala and Gundersund. "And what about our niece? Is there any word on Violet?"

"Some of her clothes were found on a trail in the woods leading to the river. We've been searching for her, but nothing yet. However, I must tell you that the river is high with spring runoff and we might not find her body for a long time if she's in the river. Sometimes drowning victims are never found."

Randy nodded slowly. "You're saying that some-body threw her in the river." Leanne glanced over at him. They exchanged grim nods before Leanne looked down at her hands.

"It appears that way." Gundersund waited a few beats. "Is there anything more you can tell me about who might want to hurt Adele and Violet?"

"No. I have no idea. We barely kept in touch, I have to say. Leanne must have told you that she and Adele took different paths in life. Leanne works at the family healthcare clinic in town part-time. She never left Gan but Adele went off to live in Montreal first chance she got."

"You never had any kids?"

"No. Not for lack of trying." Randy smiled, man to man.

Gundersund nodded as if in commiseration. "Did Adele ever speak about those years in Montreal?"

"Not really. Just said she was glad to settle down with Ivo in the country. She told us her wild days were over."

Kala broke into the conversation. "How long have Ivo and Adele been married?"

"Not sure. Do you know, Leanne?" Randy turned toward her.

"Nearly three years, I guess."

Kala also looked at Leanne. "So Violet is not Ivo's child?"

Leanne's jaw tightened. "We think of her as his child. Violet was just a few months old when they married, so he's the only father she's known."

"I don't question his connection with her. Do you know who Violet's biological father is?" Kala felt Gundersund's stillness. Out of the corner of her eye, she could see him straighten up on the coach. She bet the wheels were turning inside his head. He'd be going over the facts, figuring out what they'd neglected to ask.

Leanne raised her eyes to the ceiling. "She never said."

Kala waited. She asked softly, "And did she tell

you that she wasn't the mother?"

Randy's face twisted into a sneer. "Bullshit, officer. Of course Adele was Violet's mother."

Kala continued speaking directly to Leanne. "From the forensic evidence, we have reason to believe that your sister never gave birth. Did you see her pregnant or did she arrive with the baby?"

Leanne's eyes fluttered and a sob escaped her open mouth. A bright red flushed her face underneath beads of sweat. Her words came out like a cry. "I don't know what you're talking about." Her whole body began to shake.

Randy pushed himself to his feet. "If what you say is true, we have no knowledge of it. In fact, we challenge your insane accusation. Adele always said that Violet was her daughter. We'd better end the interview now so my wife has time to grieve. She's not holding up so well. I'm going to have to ask you both to leave."

"I just have a few more …"

Gundersund cut her off as Randy moved between them and his wife. He spoke quickly. "We'll leave it here until you've had some time." He stood. "Thanks again for your hospitality and we're very sorry for your loss. We'll see ourselves out." He made a sharp motion with his right hand for Kala to lead the way out of the room.

She wanted to press on while she had the element of surprise, but she knew that Gundersund was right. They'd get nothing more out of the Scotts for the time being. She stood up and passed in front of him on her way to the door. She stole one last look at Leanne, trying to understand her extreme reaction.

Outside, Gundersund turned and looked down at her.

"Well, that was awkward," she said, trying to head him off. He ignored her levity.

"Did your bombshell come from the autopsy?"

"Yes."

"You might have thought to mention it when we met at the Merchant. Rouleau needed to know."

"Fiona called me last night. I left Rouleau a voice mail with the information."

"And yet you kept it to yourself all the way from Kingston to Gananoque. You should have told me what you were going to ask. At the very least we could have worked up a better way of approaching her."

"It wouldn't have mattered. Either they don't know that Violet was somebody else's child or they're covering up."

He rubbed the scar on his cheek, something Kala knew he did when he was agitated. "Maybe the biological parents of the kid aren't relevant."

"Maybe, but I think it's an avenue worth pursuing. Why did nobody mention that Violet was adopted? We should check out Adele's life in Montreal."

"When people raise an adopted child from birth, they forget somebody else actually gave birth."

"Yeah, except if the kid is kidnapped or murdered.

Then they'd want to consider everyone who might have had a motive."

"The Scotts have had a lot to take in and Violet's parentage is the last thing on their minds. Like most people, they wouldn't be linking Violet's biological parents to her disappearance. The most obvious path would be to focus on Ivo Delaney, but I have a feeling you aren't going to go for the obvious." He started walking toward his car. A sigh made his shoulders rise and fall. He spoke with his back to her. "Let's head back to the station and get started on some research. It'll be something to do while we wait to interview Ivo."

"Okay." She followed slowly behind. Gundersund's logic had holes but he was being obtuse and argumentative for some reason. If Violet was adopted, why wouldn't Adele have told her sister? If Adele had told her, why the denial? And why hadn't Ivo mentioned that Violet wasn't his child? She knew she was onto something even if Ivo turned out to be the one who killed his own wife and kid.

The return trip to Kingston was as quiet as the ride down. Kala tucked herself against the passenger door and kept her face turned to look out the side window. In her blurry reflection, she saw a blond little girl's haunted eyes staring back at her. As the kilometres stretched by, the child's eyes became her own, aged ten, brimming with guilt and loneliness. She let the miles slip past as memories crowded back like unwelcome guests, rarely allowed to see the light of day. This case was getting to her. The violence was opening wounds long put away.

She knew with certainty that Gundersund was wrong about one thing. Nobody forgot that a child wasn't their own, no matter how much they let them into their family. She'd lived in enough foster homes to know the truth of that. Nobody ever forgot where you came from.

Ever.

CHAPTER TWELVE

Rouleau sat next to Malcolm T. Heath while he reassured the public that the killer was not going to strike again and that all was under control. Even Rouleau found himself soothed by the Colombo-like calm of his boss, this man-cherub in police uniform. You'd never know that Heath was feeding smoke and mirrors to the media crowded into the meeting room at city hall. He was subtly leading the reporters to conclude that Adele and Violet's deaths were the result of a domestic incident. The absence of evidence didn't seem to concern him.

Marci Stokes sat squarely in the centre of the first row, madly scribbling away on a pad of paper with her microphone recording anything she might miss. She wore wrinkled khaki pants and a tight red t-shirt that showed off freckled arms. Her auburn hair was tied back but several strands had escaped, making her appear dishevelled. Her article in the *Whig* that morning had made the first page and drawn reporters from Toronto and Ottawa like bees to honey. Canadian Press, *Globe and Mail*, *Ottawa Citizen*, and CBC were all present and accounted for. Two local television news crews were filming the media briefing, which would be broadcast online and across Eastern Ontario.

Heath managed to keep his serious, troubled expression plastered on his face even though Rouleau could sense his enjoyment at being centre stage, the limelight being something he courted. The proof was in his grey curls, freshly cut and styled an hour before, and the generous application of aftershave, a citrusy bouquet with a woodsy finish.

The CBC reporter, whom Rouleau recognized from the six o'clock news, shouted out, "How long before you call off the search for Violet Delaney?"

Heath pulled his reading glasses to the edge of his nose and focused the stare from his striking blue eyes over them directly into one of the television cameras. "We've got a crew from Ottawa helping with the search. We're giving it one more day. I'd like to commend my team for leading this tragic mission."

As if we're recovery troops in Afghanistan. Rouleau had argued against the TV crews being allowed to film on the Delaney property, but Heath had overridden him. "They need to show the public our people in action," he'd said. "People have a right to know what the team is up against."

The problem for Rouleau was that the footage was putting the spotlight on Ivo Delaney and narrowing the focus to him alone. His property had become a destination for gawkers with their own video cameras. Bennett had forwarded three home-made videos that he'd found on YouTube, all saying that Ivo Delaney had killed his family.

Marci raised her head. She waved a hand until Heath nodded in her direction. She got to her feet. "Marci Stokes. *Whig-Standard*. I understand that Ivo Delaney is under medical care. Can you confirm whether or not this is true?"

Heath looked at Rouleau.

"We're not at liberty to discuss this information," Rouleau said with more authority than he felt.

Marci kept standing. "Is Ivo Delaney your only suspect?"

"We're still working on gathering evidence. We've reached no conclusions at this point."

"But you've outlined the murders as a domestic situation."

Rouleau silently cursed Heath who was sitting like a doorstop next to him now that the reporter wanted some substance. "We haven't reached any conclusions at this point."

"Meaning you haven't got any real evidence?"

"We're not at liberty to discuss the evidence at this point in the investigation."

Marci took a long, slow look around at the other reporters then back at Rouleau. "You really haven't given us anything that we didn't already have last night." She made a disgusted face and sat back down. The two television cameras were fixed squarely on her.

Heath rallied. "We are giving regular updates as we do for all major cases. That'll be all for now. We'll call another press conference to update you when we've news to impart."

The irony of what he just said appeared to be lost on him. Rouleau stood and a technician came over to remove the microphone from his shirt. Heath stood next to him while his microphone was also removed.

"That went well," Heath said under his breath, "until the Stokes woman. Who's feeding her information?"

"No idea."

"Well find the leak and plug it before she becomes a problem. I'll meet you back at the station." Heath turned and strode past the reporters toward the door.

Rouleau checked his messages and waited for the room to clear. Gundersund and Stonechild were on their way back to the station. He texted that he'd meet them in the office after lunch. Woodhouse had also checked in. Still no sign of Violet Delaney's body in the creek — more like river with the nonstop rain and spring runoff.

He looked around. The reporters had gone, including Marci Stokes. He had a bit of time before he had to meet up with Gundersund and Stonechild. He'd take the small window to grab lunch downtown. He exited city hall and headed southwest on Ontario Street until he reached Market. He took a right and walked a block to King Street East then turned left. From there it was a short walk to the Pilot House on the corner where he and his father had spent many a pleasant lunch hour. A cool wind was blowing off the lake. Fat drops of rain were sprinkling down by the time he reached the bright blue awning that stretched above the door of the Pilot House.

He took a table near the window and the waitress came right over to take his order. He asked for a pint of Guinness and the cod and chips. It was only then that he cast an eye around the small pub and spotted Marci Stokes sitting at a table against the far wall. She was huddled over her cellphone, clicking away with both thumbs. Most of her hair had escaped its elastic band and hung tangled around her face. He looked away and then back. She was scowling and looked ready to take a go at somebody. Before he could look away a second time, she raised her head and looked directly at him. She waited until the waitress had delivered his beer before she picked up her own drink and walked over. She slid into the empty chair without being asked.

"Heath likes the camera," she said. "You not so much." She was older than she'd looked the night before in the darkness on the highway. Mid-forties he wagered. Fine lines rimmed her eyes and mouth.

He took a drink. "Goes with the job. You appear ready to kill somebody."

"Just responding to an email from my New York ex-editor at the *Post*. He's a pompous ass."

"I gather he's not offering you your job back."

"On the contrary. Why he thinks I'd take it after all the shit boggles my mind."

The waitress brought over her meal, a club sandwich and fries. Marci picked up a piece and glanced at him. "Hope you don't mind if I dig in. Press conferences make me ravenous."

"By all means."

He watched her eat with an appetite that reminded him of Kala Stonechild. Both devoted their entire concentration to their food and seemed to think of nothing but for the time it took to devour everything on the plate. His fish and chips arrived as she was popping the last fry into her mouth. He felt like he'd just eaten a full meal watching her even though his stomach was rumbling. He ate a forkful of battered cod.

Marci pushed her plate away with a contented sigh. "This feels like the time for a cigarette, but happily I gave them up ten years ago. Still, there are moments like right now when I'd give an arm to have one.

"So you really have no evidence about what happened to Adele and Violet Delaney?"

"Nothing more than we updated you with this morning."

"Sorry about my grandstanding. I was trying to make a point to my colleagues."

"Letting them know that you'd beaten them to the story yesterday."

She shrugged. "If you like. You've probably heard by now that I have something to prove."

The rain was picking up speed and rivulets slid down the window. Wind rattled the glass. Rouleau thought of the officers searching the woods and river for Violet Delaney. He looked from the glass to Marci. "Why are you in Kingston anyway?"

"I got a major story wrong. My contacts made up the story to get paid and I didn't see through it. My bosses thought time in the wilderness would make me contrite."

"The *Post* editor?"

"Him among others. It doesn't help that he and I were a couple for six years. Say, are you planning on eating that coleslaw?"

He glanced down. "Would you like it?"

She scooped up the white paper container from his plate. "If you're sure." Her fork lifted the shredded cabbage and carrots to her open mouth before he could look away. She had straight white teeth with a sizable gap between the top front two.

She swallowed. "You wouldn't confirm that Ivo Delaney is under medical care but I hear he has mental issues."

"How do you know that?"

"One of the tellers at the bank where he works. She has coffee with him now and then because they were in high school together. He confided in her."

"Did she say what the issues were?" If so, Marci was one step ahead of his team.

"Depression brought on by low self-esteem. He tried to kill himself in his late teens. He was hospitalized and put on meds."

"You didn't share that with your colleagues this morning."

"No. I thought I'd run it by you first. I'm not entirely without scruples, Detective."

"Good to know." He knew this information would have the public screaming for Ivo Delaney's blood. Heath would cut off the investigation or seriously scale back the money he was willing to put into it. "Can you keep this to yourself for the time being?"

She tilted her head and studied him with intelligent grey eyes. "There'd have to be something in it for me. A trading of information might benefit both of us. I can wait to file this story if you promise to give me a scoop ahead of the other media."

"Who else on the force is feeding you information?"

"No fair, Detective. I won't divulge my source but I can say that they don't have the full picture."

He thought over her offer. He didn't want Ivo Delaney skewered before the investigation uncovered all the facts. "All right. I'll let you know when we've got something concrete."

"And I'll do likewise."

He ate the last of his fish and drank a last swallow of beer. He had no desire to head outside into the rain but signalled for his bill. "I guess I'll be seeing you around."

"I guess you will."

She'd pulled out her phone and was back furiously typing with her thumbs as he stood at the bar waiting for the waitress to make change. Probably letting her ex-partner-slash-editor know exactly what she thought of him. Rouleau thanked the waitress and pulled his coat collar up as far as it would go. Then he stepped outside into the slanting rain and wind.

CHAPTER THIRTEEN

The team gathered in his office at two o'clock. Woodhouse and Bennett arrived first and got the visitor chairs. Stonechild and Gundersund found places to lean against the wall.

"Interesting to hear that Violet Delaney is not their biological child," Rouleau said. "Although I'm not seeing how this information fits into recent events unless it played on Ivo Delaney's mental state. Any theories?"

Stonechild looked around at the others. "I think we need to give this some consideration. Maybe check out Adele's life in Montreal. Gundersund and I found it peculiar that Adele's sister in Gananoque said they had no knowledge that Violet wasn't Adele's child."

"You'd probably have to go to Montreal. When would you make the trip?"

"Tomorrow. We know the bar where she worked before she moved to Kingston so we can start there."

Gundersund wasn't looking as enthusiastic as Stonechild. Rouleau made eye contact. "Your thoughts on this, Gundersund?"

"Bit of a stretch," Woodhouse interrupted. "Biological parents take four years to come here to kill the kid and the woman who adopted her from them? Out of the blue?"

Gundersund rubbed his fingers across the scar on his cheek. "I guess it won't hurt to check out Adele's past so we can rule it out as a motive for her murder."

Woodhouse snorted quietly into his coffee cup.

"Good smoked meat in Montreal," Bennett said. He spoke to Gundersund, "I could go with Stonechild if you want to keep working here."

"That's all right." Gundersund shot Bennett a searching look but kept his body turned away from Stonechild.

"We can take my truck," she said. She also kept her eyes safely pointed away from her partner.

Rouleau was not unaware of the tension but chose to ignore it. "As Woodhouse and Bennett reported, yesterday a child's pink rain boot was found floating farther down the river. Still no sign of Violet's body. The search has been called off until the water levels subside or someone happens across her."

"What about the search of their house?" Gundersund asked.

"Forensics is still going through it as well as Ivo's vehicle and his office at the bank. I haven't heard that they've turned up anything yet. That leaves the interview with Ivo, who is still sedated and under doctor's care. When we're able to interview him, I'll take the lead. Anything else?"

Nobody spoke.

Rouleau continued, "Bennett and Woodhouse, keep digging into Ivo Delaney's life and let me know what comes out of the search of his property. Gundersund and Stonechild, I'll want you to check in tomorrow from Montreal. As always, keeping everyone informed is a priority." He paused as he weighed the value of keeping the information that Marci Stokes had given him about Ivo's medical condition from them. The unofficial source made him hesitate. His phone rang, making the decision for him. He signalled for everyone to leave before picking up, then leaned back in his chair and looked out the window at the falling rain.

"Dad, how's the research going?"

His father sounded as if he was in the same room. The strength had returned to his voice which boomed across the miles. "I'm having a whale of a time in the Archives. I should have made the trip to Ottawa sooner." His father launched into a detailed account of his days spent searching through old documents while Rouleau tried to picture him happily ensconced in a library reading room with documents and books piled around him. Rouleau turned back to his desk and opened a folder, listening to his father with one ear while he skimmed through a report. His dad was spending most of his time alone and was making up for hours of silence. After ten minutes, he appeared to run out of steam. Rouleau tuned back in.

"That sounds great, Dad."

"It's been good all right. Which brings me to the reason for my call."

Rouleau knew what was coming. *Frances.* He headed his father off. "I can't make it to Ottawa this week, Dad. We've not made much headway on the murders. I'll come as soon as I can. No, I'm quite aware that the clock is ticking. I'll call you tomorrow if I can. Yeah, I know."

He hung up and got out of his chair to stand in front of the window. This was turning into the rainiest April on record. Rain and storms from one end of the month to the other. The heavy grey sky and early darkness matched his mood. It felt like the entire world was weeping for his ex-wife. Something he could not yet bring himself to do.

He worked at his desk until late afternoon. He had a report to complete before the end of the week and had promised Heath's assistant Vera that he'd get it done on time. The bureaucratic part of his job was the part that he liked the least.

The rain had mercifully stopped when he finally stood and looked out the window, at least for the time being. The abrupt end to days of rain should have lifted his spirits, but it didn't. He stretched and tried to ease the kinks from his shoulders. He'd finished the report and sent it by email to Vera but thought he'd drop by her desk to make sure she got it. He wouldn't mind some human contact and Vera liked to chat about inconsequential things.

He was surprised to see Stonechild sitting at her computer in the outer office, her face lit from the glow of the screen. She was clicking on the keyboard. A notepad filled with writing and a pen were on the desk in front of her.

He walked over and stood behind her. "Still at it?"

She turned in her chair and smiled. "Just finishing up. I've been researching Adele Delaney's past life in Montreal. It's taken some digging and phone calls."

"And?"

"She lived downtown and worked at the Chez Louis on Rue Sainte-Catherine. I tracked down the owner and he agreed to speak with us tomorrow. He also gave me the name of another waitress who was friends with Adele. She's not working at the bar any longer. She wasn't home when I called but I left my cell number."

He pointed to Gundersund's desk. "Did he make it back from court?"

"No, but he texted me that he hadn't testified as of four o'clock."

"Will you need Bennett to go with you tomorrow? Sounds like Gundersund will have to return to court."

"I can make the trip alone."

"I suppose that's an option." The research into Adele's past was a long shot at best and likely not worth the time of two detectives. "I'll make a phone call since you'll be entering another police district, not to mention province. I'll get word to you with a contact name before you leave. Have a good evening."

"I will. Thank you, sir."

Rouleau stopped at the door and turned. Stonechild was already hunched over the screen again, silently mouthing the words in front of her as she read. He wondered if she'd forgotten about Dawn, probably waiting alone at home for her to return. Stonechild's personnel file had been sparse but he'd been around her long enough to know that she was a loner. She'd grown up in foster homes and he had no doubt of the impact. He watched her a moment more before deciding this was not his call. There were depths to Stonechild that he would never understand, but he had to trust that she would do the right thing by Dawn if given time. He had to hope that Stonechild would find her way to becoming a parent when she had no past experience being mothered. Right now, the loner part of her was winning. He knew how easy it could be to let work take the place of family and intimacy.

During their marriage, Frances had come to know it too.

Kala was glad to see that the rain had stopped when she stepped outside the station. The air felt damp and the clouds still hovered, but at least she wasn't going to get wet walking to her truck. She climbed inside and drove slowly through downtown toward the waterfront before turning west out of the city. She'd sent Dawn a text to let her know that she was on her way. No response back, but no cause for worry. Dawn liked to walk Taiku when she got home and was probably not looking at her phone.

Gundersund's car wasn't in his driveway when she drove slowly past his property. She craned her neck to look at his house. It stood closed off and silent in the paling daylight. The trees and bushes were laden with buds that would open when the spring sun finally broke through long enough to heat up the earth. She figured a few more weeks and the trees would be in full leaf. She turned her attention back to the road. Gundersund should have been home by now. Perhaps he was having dinner in town with Fiona.

A few minutes later, she turned into her driveway. Her heart lifted when she saw Gundersund's Mustang parked off to the side. She was unhappy with herself for even caring that he was at her house and not out with his wife. She shouldn't have cared at all what he did or with whom. But still, she felt a lift in her spirits to find him there.

She parked next to his car and walked around the house to the back deck. Nobody was sitting outside, which didn't surprise her since a cool breeze was coming in off the lake. She climbed the steps and opened the back door. Gundersund looked up from the kitchen table where he sat reading the newspaper, his long legs stretched and crossed at the ankles. His eyes studied her warmly. Taiku and Minny galloped in from the living room to greet her. She bent to rub their heads, all the while looking at Gundersund. "Where's Dawn?"

"Upstairs doing homework. She's trying to get it finished before I take you both out for supper."

"Supper?"

"You've forgotten, haven't you?"

It was then she noticed his tan suit jacket over the back of the chair and grey dress pants. His curly blond hair was damp from a recent shower.

Kala slapped a hand against her forehead. "The art show."

"The opening is tonight. Dawn told me that you'd agreed she could go and you would come as well."

"That's right. I did. Do I have time for a quick shower?"

Gundersund checked his watch. "I can phone and move our dinner reservation half an hour."

"I won't be long."

She took the stairs two at a time, undoing her shirt as she went. She poked her head into Dawn's room on the way by. "We'll be going in about fifteen minutes." She noticed Dawn was wearing a blue blouse and white slacks. "You look very nice."

Dawn looked down and back up at Kala. "My best clothes. Mom got them for me at a second-hand store in Ottawa."

"Well, she has good taste. You look lovely."

Kala continued on to the shower, a guilty thought hovering on the edge of her conscience. She didn't care about fashion herself, but perhaps she should have paid attention to Dawn and her wardrobe. Most teenagers cared about clothes as far as she knew. Dawn had never asked for anything, but she had never offered. Had she been negligent?

She showered quickly and searched through her closet until she found the green wrap dress she'd bought the year before. She'd seen the dress on a mannequin in a dress shop on Richmond Road in Ottawa and for some reason gone into the store and tried it on. The sales girl had talked her into buying it, saying the colour made her skin glow. It may or may not have been true, but Kala liked the way the dress made her feel. She'd never gotten around to buying shoes to go with it, but her knee-high leather boots would do. She left her hair loose to dry.

Gundersund and Dawn had their jackets on and were waiting in the kitchen when she finally ran down the stairs. Gundersund didn't say anything when he saw her, but Kala thought she saw approval in his eyes.

"You look great," Dawn said. "I've never seen you in a dress before."

"It's as rare as a moon landing," Kala smiled. She grabbed her leather coat from the hook to cover her embarrassment. She hated knowing that people were looking at her. "Let's go eat. I'm starving."

Gundersund took them to the Lone Star restaurant on Ontario Street. The interior was Mexican-themed and casual, a long bar running the length of the main room. Dawn surveyed the crowded tables and busy bar with wide eyes. The hum of voices and clinking of dishes made for a party atmosphere. A pleasant hostess with bouncy hair led them to a table at the back of the main room and told them that their server would be right with them. Once seated,

Gundersund told Kala and Dawn to order whatever their hearts desired. The evening was on him.

Dawn silently read the menu and glanced at Kala enough times that Kala felt her discomfort.

"Would you like me to choose for you?"

Dawn nodded. She leaned in toward Kala and whispered, "I've never eaten this kind of food before. We didn't go to restaurants."

Gundersund looked over their heads at the soccer game on one of the televisions above the bar. A muscle jumped in his cheek, the only indication that he was listening to their conversation.

Kala whispered back, "I've only had Mexican food a few times myself."

Gundersund waited a few moments before he waved over the waitress. He smiled at Dawn and tapped the table with his menu. "Ladies, if you would allow me to order nachos to start and fajitas to share. We can go chicken, shrimp, or beef."

Dawn said, "We like chicken, right Kala?"

"Chicken works for me."

The waitress took the order and the menus and said their meal wouldn't be long.

"I have a work proposition for you, Dawn," Gundersund said. "Minny could use a walk after school before I get back from work. If you could stop by and take her to your place on your way home, I could pick her up later. I'd be willing to pay, say, sixty dollars a week."

Dawn's eyes opened wide. She looked at Kala. "Could I, Kala?"

"If you want to, I don't see why not."

"I love Minny ... almost as much as Taiku."

Gundersund laughed. "Minny's pretty fond of you too. I have a spare key that I can give you now. Knowing Minny isn't dancing around the house waiting for me to come home will be a big relief. For Minny especially, if you get my meaning." He reached into his pocket and pulled out a key on a Snoopy key chain. He dangled it in front of Dawn.

Dawn laughed before reaching for it and Kala smiled at Gundersund. "Thank you," she mouthed.

After the nachos were devoured, Gundersund demonstrated how to pile the chicken, sour cream, guacamole, onions, and peppers into a tortilla shell with a final topping of salsa. "The bigger mess you make eating one, the better." He lifted an overflowing fajita to his mouth and bit into it. Sour cream dripped down his chin.

Dawn watched him for a second before biting into her own. "Where have you been all my life?" she asked the fajita before taking a second bite.

Kala laughed. "I'll bet we could make these at home."

"Maybe on the weekend?"

"Possibly." Kala thought about the case and the uncertainty of her hours. "Let's see how the week unfolds." She immediately regretted her words. Dawn nodded but the brightness disappeared from her face.

Gundersund jumped into the silence. "I happen to have some Mexican blood flowing through my veins and would be happy to give cooking lessons when called upon. Enchiladas are my specialty."

"Are they as good as fajitas?" Dawn asked.

"In danger of boasting, some call my enchiladas better. Perhaps we need a cook off. The two of you can attempt fajitas and I'll supply my enchiladas. Dawn can be the official taste tester."

Dawn looked at Kala and the excitement was back in her eyes. "Maybe, when your work is finished?"

"I promise," Kala said. She felt the tension ease again from her stomach. "As soon as we have a free evening when we can spread out and make a mess in the kitchen. Although I have to say, Gundersund, that I cannot detect any Mexican in your lineage."

"An honorary affiliation bestowed upon me after one weekend in Puerto Vallarta where I consumed copious amounts of tequila."

They finished eating, and while the conversation didn't flow exactly, Kala felt that Dawn was relaxed and enjoying herself. They decided to walk the three blocks to the art gallery once they stepped outside and found that it wasn't raining. A breeze from the lake was welcome after the warmth of the bar and the air felt drier than it had for days. By the time they reached the second block, the moon had peeked out from behind the thinning bank of clouds. Kala sensed a better day coming tomorrow, although she'd learned that Kingston weather could be fickle.

"Here we are," Gundersund said, pointing to a narrow storefront sandwiched between two limestone buildings. A carved wooden sign above the door said MYSTIC GALLERY. "The first art show of the spring season."

Inside, the rectangular room was brightly lit and warm. Forty or more well-dressed people crowded into the narrow space. They gathered around the wine bar or stood chatting in groups while they looked at the vibrant paintings covering the dove-grey walls — expansive vistas of woods, sea, and sky; detailed close ups of trees and plants. Dawn stood stock still next to Kala, taking in the people and scanning the artwork on the first wall. Kala looked down at this girl she considered her niece, not by blood, but by the fact that she and her mother had made a childhood pact to become cousins. She was getting better at reading Dawn's emotions from the way she held herself and the expression in her eyes. Kala touched her arm.

"Would you like to go have a closer look? You can take as much time as you like."

Dawn looked up at her with brilliant eyes and a quick smile. "Okay." She immediately scooted over to a painting of a giant redwood, slipping into a group of people.

Gundersund came up behind Kala and handed her a glass of red liquid with raspberries floating on top. "Fruit punch," he said. He sipped on a glass of beer and looked at Dawn over the rim. "She's enjoying herself. I'll introduce her to the artist once she's had a chance to roam around. That's Colin Hall right over there."

Kala turned to look at a tall man dressed in a white suit and black shirt. He was as bald as Rouleau except that Colin had a goatee. He looked slightly younger than Rouleau, probably in his early forties. She turned back to Gundersund. "How do you know Colin?"

"He lived next door. He was like my older brother growing up."

Gundersund frowned as he saw Fiona break away from the group surrounding Colin and start toward them. Her red silk dress hugged her curves like butter. "Oh no," Gundersund said under his breath.

Kala felt as if she'd been caught with her hand in the cookie jar. Fiona had a smile on her face but her eyes weren't happy. She stopped in front of Gundersund and reached up to hug him. Her white wine slopped on the arm of his suit jacket. She let go but kept close to him. "Fancy meeting you both here. I was just saying to Colin that I thought you'd come, Paul. I didn't know you were an art aficionado, Kala."

"I'm not especially."

"Paul, the Reynolds are over there and they've been asking for you." She placed a firm hand on Gundersund's arm. "Please excuse us for a moment, Kala. These are old friends of ours in from out of town. I won't keep your partner long."

Gundersund shot Kala an apologetic look before letting Fiona lead him away. "Have a look around. I'll be back soon," were his parting words.

Not if Fiona can help it. Kala nodded and smiled to let him know that everything was fine. She should have guessed how this evening would end.

She took a sip of punch and looked for Dawn. She'd moved in front of a painting of Lake Ontario that had to be five feet high and stood staring at it oblivious to the adults crowding in around her. Kala kept one eye on her and crossed to the bar to get her a glass of fruit punch.

Nearly an hour later, Gundersund met Kala and Dawn at the door on their way to the cab that Kala had called. He looked sheepish and less than pleased. "I'm sorry. I got tied up with some people I hadn't seen in a long time. Let me take you home." He looked for a place to set down his wine glass.

Kala almost felt sorry for him. He had no idea how Fiona had worked him. Kala shook her head. "No, you stay and enjoy yourself. The cab is outside and I need to get Dawn home. Tomorrow is a school day."

"Thanks Gundersund," Dawn said. "I really had a good time."

He bent down so that he was at her level. "But I wanted to introduce you to the artist, Colin Hall."

"It's okay. We already met him. He said that I could come back anytime."

Kala opened the door. "See you later, Gundersund. Thanks again for a lovely dinner."

"I'm back in court tomorrow," he said. "Will Montreal wait a day?"

"No, but Bennett has offered to come with me." She wasn't sure why she'd said that. It wasn't as if she wanted Bennett to go with her.

She followed Dawn out of the gallery and into the cab waiting at the curb. After making sure Dawn was buckled in, Kala glanced out the back window. Gundersund was still standing in the door watching them as the cab merged into traffic on Ontario Street.

CHAPTER FOURTEEN

The call came when Kala was waving goodbye to Dawn as the school bus pulled away. She almost didn't answer after she saw whose name was on the screen, but thought better of it by the third ring. Bennett might have some information that she needed to know when she started interviewing people in Montreal. She put the phone to her ear. "Yeah? Got something for me, Bennett?"

His voice was loud and cheerful. "So happens I do. My company all the way to Montreal and back."

"I told Rouleau I'd be fine on my own."

"He decided you could use me riding shotgun. You're to swing by the station and pick me up. If you'd like me to be the chauffeur, I'm okay with that."

"I'll drive. Be ready in fifteen."

Shit. She dropped the phone back into her pocket and started back up the driveway toward her truck. The sun was weak but promised to gain strength over the course of the day. Already, blue sky showed through the patchy cloud cover like backwash in a watercolour painting. The evening of art appreciation appeared to have made an impact on her. The change in weather was the only good thing about the morning so far.

She got into the front seat and slammed the door. Cutting across town to the station was going to add time to the trip and she'd promised Dawn she'd try to be back by nightfall. The headway they'd been making over the week could topple if she wasn't careful. Leaving the kid alone too much wasn't going to help anything. Gundersund would be checking in on Dawn to pick up Minny after work, so that was something at least. Maybe she should think about hiring a housekeeper against Dawn's protestations. That way she could work late without guilt pricking at her conscience.

As she drove across the city toward the station, she thought about how little supervision she'd had growing up. It hadn't hurt her any. She'd turned into a fully functioning adult. She passed Princess and turned left onto Queen, giving wide berth to a man in a suit biking to work. Who was she kidding? The years between high school and college were not ones to be proud of. She sure didn't want Dawn to follow in those footsteps.

Bennett was waiting for her in the parking lot, leaning against the hood of his car. He wore faded blue jeans and a black jacket, pretty much the same as she had on. Aviator sunglasses hid the blue eyes she knew would be bright and shiny. He was a morning person, an admittedly charming grin on his square-cut face, dimples on display. He was also a mind reader, pulling a cardboard container with two large coffees and breakfast sandwiches from behind his back where they rested on the hood. He climbed in the passenger side and handed her a coffee and sandwich.

"Almost worth having you along," she said, accepting both.

She gulped down the food and set her coffee in the cup holder before putting the truck into drive. She'd take Highway 401 all the way into Montreal. Bennett had been around her enough to know not to engage in conversation until they were well on their way.

"Where are we heading first?" he asked once they'd passed the last Brockville exit.

She pulled into the outside lane and passed two transports before responding. "Adele Delaney worked at a bar called Chez Louis downtown on Sainte-Catherine. Her maiden name was Dufour. I made contact with the bartender, Philippe Lebeau, who said he'd be there at noon, so we'll start with him. He gave me the name of a waitress by the name of Lana Morris who had worked with Adele. Apparently, they were good friends. I called her and left her a voice mail but she hasn't called me back. We'll try tracking her down after we speak with Lebeau."

Bennett was on his phone. Kala glanced over and saw that he'd brought up a map.

"Looks like there's a few sketchy bars in the area," he said.

"We might find that Adele had an interesting past before she settled down with Ivo."

"I like a woman with an interesting past."

She stole another glance to see if he meant anything by that, but he had his head down studying the map. She let his comment pass.

They made good time on the 401 and took the auto route 20 past Beaconsfield and Pointe-Claire. It was closing in on noon as the road angled north past Westmount.

"Turn left on Rue Guy," Bennett said pointing at the next intersection. "Then hang a right on Rene-Levesque."

They kept going past the university and turned left on Berri and right on Sainte-Catherine. The street was flanked on both sides by dull yellow and red brick buildings with tired storefronts — pawn shops, drycleaners, restaurants, low-rise apartment buildings with wrought-iron balconies, mom and pop shops. The section of town was depressing. It felt to Kala like a place where hope came to die.

Chez Louis was in a two-storey building that took up the entire block on the corner of Rue Sainte-Catherine Ouest and Rue Peel. The Z and U were burned out on the red neon sign on the front plate glass window so that it read CHE LO IS. Kala figured you could tell a lot about a business that didn't care if its signage was kept up. The bar would be known by the regulars and outward appearances wouldn't matter. The owner wasn't going out of his way to attract a genteel clientele. The windows were darkened so that you couldn't see the interior. Speckles of light glinted from flecks of stone in the pink-coloured stucco.

"I wonder what we're going to find inside," Bennett said in a deadpan voice. He pointed. "Parking spot over there."

"Thanks." She pulled a u-turn at the intersection and cut off a van. The driver leaned on his horn. His middle finger was in the air as he sped by.

Bennett shook his head. "Welcome to the hood."

"Hard to believe this is where Adele chose to live when she left Gananoque. From a small-town place of beauty on the water to concrete and brick." Kala eased the truck into the parking spot. "Michel Prevost should be waiting for us inside the bar. He's a detective on the guns and gangs squad."

"So you've gone through the channels for the interviews."

"Rouleau called in a favour. Prevost should also have insight into Chez Louis and its crime connections."

Bennett paused with his hand on the door handle. "Woodhouse thinks this is a wild goose chase, but I want you to know that I disagree. Even if nothing turns up, I like that you've got us covering all the bases."

"Some creative use of clichés there, Bennett." What was he really telling her? To watch her back with Woodhouse, but he was on her side? If he knew how little she cared about the station politics or Woodhouse's opinion of her, he wouldn't have bothered. She did a shoulder check before opening her car door, then looked back at him and smiled. "Time to get this show on the road."

The inside of the bar was no surprise: a cavernous room with a long bar across the front wall, utilitarian dark wooden tables and chairs, a stage and dance floor toward the back of the room. The place reeked of stale beer and cigarette smoke that had embedded itself in nooks and crannies over the decades. Lighting was minimal and the blackened windows gave the sense of being cut off from the rest of the world. You could start drinking in the morning and it would feel like the middle of the night. Kala had lived in the Northern Ontario versions of this bar once upon a time. She liked to think of that period as the lost years. Luckily, it had lasted just long enough for her to know that she never wanted to go there again. Silent flat screen televisions were placed at strategic locations on the walls, high enough for patrons to have to crook their necks to watch whatever sports event was playing. At the moment, a Vegas poker game was filling in air time until something better came on. Men sat over bottles of beer at three tables. The waitresses were chatting in the corner. They were young and buxom with low-cut tops and black miniskirts. Their straight hair trailed down their backs.

A large man with dark curly hair sat with his back to them at the bar. He turned his head, then stood as they approached. He held out a hand and she took it. "Inspector Stonechild. I'm Michel Prevost. Good to meet you." His English voice was deep, the words carefully formed but still thick with a French accent. His eyes were black and assessing.

Kala held out a hand. "Good of you to meet us. This is Constable Andrew Bennett."

Prevost shook both their hands but spoke directly to Kala. "Philippe Lebeau is in the back getting beer. He said to call him when you are arrived."

Bennett started for the door next to the bar. "I'll get him."

Kala took the stool next to Prevost. His cologne was musky and a pleasant contrast to the room. "I appreciate you coming out."

"Anything for *mon ami*, Jacques Rouleau. How is he, by the way?"

"Good. You two go way back?"

"Back to a murder case fifteen years ago. Let's say that I wouldn't be sitting here next to you if not for Rouleau. So, any word on the missing child?"

"No. We think she was drowned in the river behind their house. We've found various bits of her clothing on the trail and in the river."

"*Désolé. C'est horrible, ça.*" Prevost shook his head. His black eyes filled with regret for the little girl he'd never met. Kala felt herself warming to this bear of a man. "By the way," he added, "I've got my people searching for that other waitress, Lana Morris. Rouleau mentioned that you are looking for her."

"Thanks for that."

The door next to the bar opened. A compact man in jeans and a black T-shirt exited ahead of

Bennett. Tattoos started at his knuckles and spread up both arms. A green pattern of crosses and snakes. The body art extended up the side of his neck, making Kala curious about what was going on under his shirt. She imagined he exposed his chest every chance he got to show off his tats. He looked her up and down with the practised look of a ladies' man. He reminded her of a puffed out rooster, all cocky stance and flashy feathers.

"*Salut.*" He slid in behind the other side of the bar and positioned himself between her and Prevost. "You have questions about Adele Dufour? I'll give you ten minutes. Then my lunch crowd will be pouring in."

Kala met Bennett's eyes. She could see disbelief mixed with humour. The pronouncement did seem overly optimistic. Kala pulled out her notepad. "Adele Dufour worked here for eight years, up until about four years ago, correct?"

"That sounds about right. She waited tables." He thought for a moment before adding, "Did a bit of dancing on the side."

"What kind of dancing?"

"We have strippers on Saturday night. Adele was a crowd favourite."

"Did she date any of the customers?"

Lebeau was silent for a longer moment before he lifted one shoulder in a shrug. "Nobody special. From what I saw, she played the field."

"How would you describe her?"

"A good-time girl. She liked to party but she was an okay worker. Reliable and not too much into the drugs, which is saying something in this business. She preferred alcohol."

"You said that she was friends with another waitress." Kala glanced at Prevost. "Lana Morris."

"Yeah. They hung out sometimes."

"I phoned the cell number you gave me but she hasn't called back. Do you know Lana's address?"

"Nope. Sorry." He took out a rag from under the counter and began wiping the counter in wide circular motions. "I don't know what else I can tell you about Adele. She worked here but she never got close to anybody except for Lana. She hasn't been back in four years, not since she quit."

"Did she have any kids?"

"Adele? No way. That would have cramped her lifestyle."

"Was she friends with anybody else that you remember?"

"Nobody else. The girls come and go here. Adele was one of my longest but she made good money dancing and in tips. Like I said, the men liked her. I gave her Sundays and Mondays off and she was happy with that. Most bars don't give two days off in a row."

"Was she hooking?"

"No. Definitely not."

Kala looked at Lebeau until he raised his eyes to hers in what could be taken as a leer. "How do you know she wasn't?"

"I just know. If the girls are hooking, we don't keep them. Now, if that's all your questions ..." He pointed behind her and Kala turned. Several of the tables were now filled with men and the odd woman. The waitresses were handing out menus and taking beer orders. "I'll have to end it here. You're welcome to stay for lunch. I recommend the poutine."

"Yeah, thanks. If you remember anything, here's my business card."

He took the card from where she'd slid it on the bar and shoved it into the back pocket of his jeans. Then he winked at Kala and walked to the end of the bar where two waitresses lined up to place drink orders.

"Speaks perfect English," Kala commented to Prevost.

"He's fluently bilingual. Better for business. Would you like to stay and talk here?"

"If you've got the time."

"*Certainement.*"

They found a free table near the stage and gave their order to a waitress: three large orders of poutine, beer for Prevost and Bennett, ginger ale for Kala. Prevost waited until the waitress was out of hearing range. He leaned in.

"We've had our eye on this bar for some time. It's a well-known biker hangout. Lebeau has two cousins, Etienne and Benoit Manteau, who are well known to police and the owners of this establishment. Benoit currently is serving life in Millhaven for murder. He was transferred a few months back from Quebec's maximum security pen, Donaconna, because he was being threatened by opposing gang members also locked up in that institution. In not his best career move, Benoit made a hit on a Hells Angels member and word got around. He's been locked up for five years of a life sentence at this point in time. Etienne Manteau became the sole owner when Benoit received his sentence. The three cousins grew up together in Gatineau across the river from Ottawa. They are like this." Prevost tightened his hand into a fist. "Etienne Manteau might pay a visit while we are here. *Si on est chanceux.*"

They stopped talking as the waitress set down their drinks and cutlery. Kala looked across at one of the waitresses who'd been sending glances their way from the time they sat down. She looked older than the other girls, her eyes heavily made up in dark liner and aqua eye shadow. All the colour had been bleached from her hair until it was Caribbean sand-white.

"Don't look now," Prevost said, drawing Kala back. "Etienne Manteau just walked in and is talking to Lebeau at the bar. He's in the black leather jacket — long hair and beard."

Bennett was sitting in front of Kala, facing the bar. He looked past Kala's shoulder.

"And?" she asked him.

Bennett's eyes came back to hers. "He's got the macho look down. Women are probably lining up."

Prevost nodded. "They pass their women around from what we hear. There doesn't appear to be any lack of them."

Kala casually turned and let her eyes make a sweep of the room until they found Etienne. He was only about five eight but broad shouldered. "We should probably call him over for a chat."

Prevost stood. "Let me do the honours."

Bennett said to Kala, "Remind me not to apply for a transfer to this neighbourhood."

"I don't know. Life would never be dull."

Etienne Manteau was laughing at something Prevost said as he reached their table. They both sat down and Prevost made the introductions.

Etienne was still smiling when his gaze came to rest on Kala. He had searching brown eyes that appeared to miss nothing. His smile tightened. "I understand that you are here to find out about Adele. We are in shock with what has happened to her. Nobody deserves that." His accent was more noticeable than Lebeau's but didn't interfere with meaning. Kala marvelled at the ability of people to slip from one language into another so effortlessly.

"No. Nobody deserves what happened to her. Can you tell us what you know about Adele from her time working here?"

"Never missed a shift, that one. She kept to herself, but we liked her."

"I understand she danced as well as served tables?"

"*Mais oui.* Most of the girls try dancing. It brings in extra money in tips."

"Was she seeing anybody in particular?"

"She dated, but I couldn't say. She liked a party. She had a friend by the name of Lana. Another waitress, but Lebeau must have told you that."

"Yes, he did. Why did Adele leave?"

"No idea. She was at work one night and gone the next. No notice. She never comes back. *Et maintenant* ..." He spread his hands wide.

"Your brother's in Millhaven for murder."

Etienne bowed his head in acknowledgement. "He is, but he is my brother always."

"Have you visited Benoit in Millhaven?"

Etienne's eyes latched onto her face. "Why do you ask?"

"Just making conversation. You implied that you are standing by him."

"It's tougher to get there now. I was supposed to go a few weeks back but couldn't. I need to book a new time."

"Was Adele working here when your brother was charged with murder?"

Etienne frowned. "Odd thing to ask. I think maybe, but I am not sure. She might have gone by then. I never thought about the two things together."

"Well, here's my number if you think of anything else." Kala slid a card across the table.

Etienne picked it up and stood just as the waitress appeared with three heaping plates of French fries topped with cheese and gravy. "I see you've ordered the house specialty. I'll leave you to enjoy." He stood and tapped Prevost on the shoulder. "*À la prochaine,* Prevost."

"*À la prochaine.*"

"You two friends?" Bennett asked after Etienne had rejoined Lebeau at the bar.

"Let's say that our paths cross … often. We are like *un chat et une souris*. A cat and mouse. We play a game that so far he is winning. But I think the cat wins in the end. It is always this way."

"As long as you are the cat and not the mouse," Kala said. "Sometimes it can be hard to tell when you play with the likes of these people."

"*Eh bien*. You have hit the nail." Prevost picked up his fork. "They weren't lying about the poutine at least. Everything else these men say, take with a shaker of salt. Now, *bon appétit*."

Kala visited the washroom before they left. She half-hoped that the waitress with the bleached hair would follow her in so that she could discretely ask her some questions, but this didn't happen. As a Hail Mary, Kala left her business card in each cubicle and a few by the sinks. If any of the waitresses was too shy to come forward, maybe they would reach out when they were away from the probing eyes at Chez Louis.

CHAPTER FIFTEEN

Kala and Bennett were crossing the street to her truck when Prevost called to them. Kala turned around and saw Prevost waving his cellphone in the air. She waited for a car to zip by before crossing back to his side of the street.

Prevost met her on the sidewalk. "My team's tracked down Lana Morris. She's living ten minutes from here in a first floor apartment on Sherbrooke. We can head there now if you've time."

Kala's spirits jumped a notch. "I'll follow you over."

Prevost pointed. "My car's just over there."

Once on Sherbrooke, the drive became a series of stops and starts as they hit red light after red light. They passed stores and restaurants and entered a residential area lined in low-rise apartments. By the time they reached the three-storey apartment building where Morris lived, Kala's jaw was sore from clenching. Not for the first time since they entered Montreal, she was happy to be living in a smaller city with fewer traffic headaches. She turned left at the next set of lights and started slowly down the side street looking for a parking spot. Cars were wedged in like sardines. Sun reflected off their windshields.

"Where do they expect visitors to park in these neighbourhoods?" She craned her neck to read the signs that limited parking to people with passes.

Bennett pointed to a space between two cars. "Just park there. If you get a ticket, Rouleau can pay out of his budget."

"We haven't much choice." It took her a few tries to manoeuvre her truck into the tight space, but she managed.

Bennett whistled. "You're one impressive woman. I can't name many who could wheel in like you."

"Thanks … I think."

Prevost waited for her and Bennett on the sidewalk in front of a yellow brick apartment building with wrought-iron balconies. Even though the building faced a busy street, it was well maintained and Kala imagined the rent wasn't cheap.

Kala turned to Prevost. "That was quick work, finding Lana."

"The surprise is that Lebeau and Manteau didn't know where she's living. They have a network." He shrugged. "Maybe they just didn't care enough to find out."

They started up the walkway together. Bennett brought up the rear. "I'll let you do the talking," Prevost said. "My source tells me that her first language is English." Responding to Kala's stare, he added, "We've checked into her documentation."

"Ah. Did you call ahead to let her know we're coming?"

"*Mais non*. I thought surprise might be the best way to get her to talk."

They entered the hallway and Kala knocked on unit number two. She could hear music thumping from behind the door. She knocked again, louder this time. She was rewarded by the music being turned down and footsteps. The woman who opened the door resembled the other waitresses from Chez Louis — tall, well endowed, and long, blond hair — although her features were sharper and older than the girls in the bar. Life appeared to have taken its toll in the papery lines around her eyes and mouth and the brittle dryness of her overly bleached hair. She was still attractive though and in good physical shape. She tilted her head and regarded Kala over the chain lock that she'd left in place.

"Yes?"

"Lana Morris?"

"Yes?"

Kala held up her police identification. "I'm trying to find out information about Adele Dufour. I understand that you were friends with her when she worked at Chez Louis. Philippe Lebeau sent us to speak with you."

The chain scraped out of the lock and the door opened wide. Lana stepped aside to let them in. "Has something happened to Adele?" she asked as Kala moved past her.

Kala stopped and turned. "I'm sorry to tell you that she's been murdered. We found her body on the highway just outside of Kingston."

Lana frowned. "My God." She pointed down the hallway. "That way to the kitchen."

Kala glimpsed the back of a man's head slumped against the back of the couch on their way by. Cigarette smoke drifted in a plume above his head.

The kitchen had a large dining area with an island separating the stainless-steel appliances and granite countertop from the glass-topped table where they all took seats. Kala took a moment to study Lana's face while they settled in. The lack of emotion gave her pause. If Lana had been a friend of Adele's, Kala would have expected something more than one feeble exclamation at hearing the news of her murder. Lana's eyes, rimmed in dark eyeliner, weren't meeting anyone else's. Sweat beaded on her forehead. Lana glanced at Kala and then lowered her eyes again.

"When did this happen? Who would want to murder Adele?" Lana's questions were oddly out of sync with the flatness in her voice.

Kala studied her expression. She couldn't detect any grief or even surprise. She said, "That's what we are trying to find out. How well did you know Adele?"

"Very well at the time, but we didn't keep in touch after she quit Chez Louis. She told me she wanted to move somewhere smaller."

"Was she dating anyone?"

"Nobody in particular. She dated but not exclusively. She didn't hang out with the other girls, just me. She liked to workout, party, and sleep."

"You both danced at Chez Louis. Did you dance at other clubs?"

"A few times, but mainly at the Louis. And before you ask, we weren't hooking. Bikers hung out there, but not so much after Benoit get locked up. Etienne changed course. He wanted to run a clean operation."

Interesting. Kala still couldn't get Lana to meet her eyes. "Do you know if Adele was ever pregnant?"

"Adele? No. She told me that she didn't want kids."

"And you?"

Lana gave a short sharp laugh. "No thanks. I hate kids."

"Is there anything more you can tell me about Adele? What kind of person was she?"

"She liked to party hard and work hard. She got tired of it though. Last time we spoke, she said that she missed the small-town life." Lana paused and appeared to be searching for something more to say. "I was sorry when she moved away."

"Did you find it odd that she never made contact again?"

"Not really. We were good friends but I understood. She wanted a new life and the best way to do that is to cut off the old one. I wished her happiness even if I wasn't in it."

Kala tried one more time. "So you didn't know that she married and had a daughter?"

"Are you kidding me? I never would have guessed she'd end up saddled with a family in a million years. When I knew her, that wasn't in our game plans."

Prevost stood apart from them speaking into his cellphone in rapid French. Bennett looked back up at the apartment building and appeared to be searching the windows for Lana Morris. They were outside on the sidewalk and Kala was getting fidgety. It was time to get back to Ottawa. Dawn would be arriving home from school soon. She was about to suggest to Bennett that they get moving when Prevost slipped his phone back into his pocket and sauntered over to them. He smiled at Kala as he stopped next to Bennett.

"I find her story that Chez Louis is a changed bar interesting. She might think this is so, but our sources say something is going on. We will not stop our watching of them. You Anglos have that saying about a leopard and its spots, *n'est-ce pas*? But this is our concern, not yours. Is there anything else we can do for you?"

"Only if you find out something that involves Adele Delaney and helps to explain her murder."

"My ears will be on the alert, you can be certain of that."

"Do you believe them when they say that the girls weren't hooking?"

The side of Prevost's mouth rose in what passed as a smile. "I think these people stretch the truth to hide what they are really up to. If they weren't being paid, they were still making the rounds with the bikers. My guess is that money changed hands. It is often this way with the strippers. The Manteau brothers were no angels."

Kala nodded. "I thought as much." She looked across the street at an old man on a scooter. He was zipping down the side of the road, a small white dog on his lap. She kept watching him as she mused, "We believe that Adele Delaney's daughter Violet was not her biological child, although Adele let everyone, even her husband, think that she was. I can't get past this feeling that whatever happened is about the child."

Prevost's black eyes studied her. "I have found that the thing that sticks in your mind often is for a reason. You should follow your gut. Rouleau would tell you this also."

She smiled and extended her hand to shake his warm one in a final farewell. "You and I are on the same page it seems, Prevost, because I can't seem to make myself do anything else but. Even when I know I should be going down the easy path, I have to take the hard one. I have to know the truth."

Prevost held her hand a moment longer than necessary. "If ever Rouleau retires, I will get you a job in my unit. It wouldn't be long for you to love Montreal."

She looked over at Bennett who was starting across the street toward her truck. "Thank you, again," she said. "I'll keep your offer in mind, but for now I'm calling Kingston home."

Chapter Sixteen

From where he sat in the main office, Zack Woodhouse watched Rouleau reading a report at his desk. Rouleau had left his office door open but was unaware that Woodhouse had returned from the useless search at the Delaney property. Woodhouse took a drink from the can of Coke he'd picked up on the way in before opening the antique cars website. He liked to check out the cars for sale at least once a day. He needed parts for his Austen Healy but would consider trading it in if a model in better condition showed up. He clicked on a few links and read car descriptions without taking any of it in. His mind was chewing over the best way to reveal what he'd found to Rouleau.

Kala Stonechild needed to be brought down a few pegs, that was one thing he knew for sure. Waltzing into the station like she was God's gift to policing. He didn't consider himself a bigot, so the Native part didn't bother him. Live and let live he always said. No, he wasn't anywhere close to being narrow-minded. What bugged him was the fact she hadn't paid her dues and had Rouleau and Gundersund fawning all over her like a couple of lap dogs. As for Bennett, the guy was thinking with his dick.

It wasn't right. She had them eating out of her hand, getting the best assignments while he was stuck doing the crap grunt jobs. You wouldn't catch Stonechild tramping around the bush looking for a drowned kid, not when she could spend the day in Montreal on a useless wild goose chase that they all knew Rouleau agreed to just to humour her. Shit. Somebody had to save the rest of the team from themselves.

Woodhouse enlarged a file he'd minimized on the bottom of his screen. The face of a much younger Kala Stonechild filled the monitor. Her eyes were staring straight into the camera as if daring it to take her on. Her hair fell in two braids to her shoulders and she was sitting on a curb in front of an underpass. She wore ripped jeans and a stained buckskin jacket. Her feet were bare and dirty. An older man with grey hair to his shoulders and a beard that went halfway down his chest was standing next to her. His clothes weren't much better. He held a sign that read *Hungry. Please spare some change.* Woodhouse scrolled up to the headline: "Homeless Problem Growing on Sudbury Streets." He scanned the article even though he'd read it through several times. The two heroes of the piece were homeless, both Native, both alcoholics. Somehow, the reporter had thought it a good idea to name them.

Kala Stonechild and Charlie Two Feathers. Shit. If he hadn't named them, Woodhouse would never have found the article. It was dated ten years earlier.

"So how'd it go at the Delaneys?"

Woodhouse jumped and clicked off the screen with one jerk of his hand. Rouleau had snuck up on him like a stealth bomber. Woodhouse belched and felt the Coke fizzing in his nose. He tried to keep the guilt he felt out of his voice.

"Yeah. They called it off until the water levels have a chance to go down. They figure a few more weeks and they'll give it another try unless the kid's body washes up somewhere and a local spots her. I was about to file my report in the system."

Rouleau frowned. "This will just prolong the heartache. Well, good work, Woodhouse. You can file the report tomorrow if you want. It's been a long day."

"Thank you, sir. I might just do that. Say, any word from Stonechild and Bennett?"

"Nothing yet."

"I guess I'll call it a day then."

Woodhouse thought over his next move. Should he hit Rouleau with Stonechild's sketchy past now or wait for a better moment? Would there ever be a better time? The problem would be explaining how he'd found the article. Rouleau was no dummy. He'd figure out pretty quickly that Woodhouse had been on a search. While Woodhouse hesitated, he caught sight of trusty Vera trotting into the office in her tight purple skirt and high heels, hips swaying like a pendulum. Everyone knew how she got *her* job. The only thing Woodhouse found offensive was that Heath was dating Vera's cousin too. The three of them must get up to quite the weekends. Both women were real lookers. Too good for Heath. Vera's eyes flicked over him before she stopped in front of Rouleau.

"A call just came in from Kingston General Hospital. Ivo Delany is doing better and they say you can see him if you keep the visit short."

"Terrific." Rouleau's face brightened. "Hopefully he'll have some answers for us." He took a step towards his office but stopped and looked back. "You want to come with me, Woodhouse?"

Woodhouse's first thought was did he have a choice? His second thought was that this was the kind of opportunity he'd been waiting for. His evening in front of the tube with a couple of beers and a pizza could wait. Stonechild's past could sit on the back burner a while longer. "Sure thing."

Rouleau nodded and kept walking. "I'll just get my coat. We should probably take our own vehicles so you can head home when we're done."

Ivo Delaney had checked himself out but had agreed to wait to speak with Rouleau before going home. He sat alone in the waiting room under the glow of the television set anchored near the ceiling. His wide shoulders slumped forward and his chin appeared to be resting on his chest. He was as defeated a man as Rouleau had ever seen.

"I'm glad you're feeling well enough to go home," Rouleau said as he sat down next to him. Woodhouse took a seat across the aisle, a little to one side so that he was out of Delaney's line of vision. Rouleau nodded at Woodhouse to take out his notepad before turning his body to face Delaney. "I know this is a terrible ordeal that you're going through."

Ivo slowly raised his head. "I just don't know what to do anymore." His large hands were clasped together between his knees. "My life may as well be over." His head bobbed once. "But I know I have to keep going … for Adele and Violet."

"Can you tell me what the doctor has been treating you for?" Rouleau knew that Ivo would have to give this information freely. He wouldn't be able to get it easily otherwise.

Ivo didn't speak for a while. When he did, his voice was resigned. "I suffer from depression. Since my teens. It's chemical. If I stay on the medicine, I do all right."

"And have you been taking your medication?"

"Faithfully. I was fine until this." He took a gulping breath. "Losing your entire family could depress anyone."

"I understand. Were you depressed about anything before Adele and Violet went missing?"

"No."

"How were you and Adele getting along the day she went missing?"

Ivo flinched as if struck. This time, the pause was longer. Rouleau exchanged looks with Woodhouse. Ivo sighed deeply and said, "We were getting along as we always did. She seemed distracted the last week or so, but she told me that it was nothing serious. Just spring fever. She was planning to visit her sister for a few days in Gananoque. Violet was excited to go."

"Distracted how?"

"I don't know. I'd find her staring out the window. She seemed to have lost her appetite and was roaming the house during the night. I think she just needed a change of scene. I encouraged her to get out of the house for a while. She could be a recluse if left alone."

A nurse in pink scrubs entered the waiting room and walked over to them. "The doctor said just a few minutes so Mr. Delaney isn't tired out." Her voice softened. "We've got a volunteer here to take you home, Mr. Delaney."

Rouleau answered for him. "We won't be much longer."

"I'll be back in two minutes to get him." She glanced again at Ivo as if assessing his condition before she left them. The squeaking of her rubber-soled shoes disappeared down the hallway.

Rouleau tried a new tack. Time was getting short if he was going to get to the bottom of the Delaney family relationships. "When you met Adele, did she already have Violet?"

"Violet is my daughter. Maybe not biological, but she's my child in every other way."

"I don't question that. Your wife's autopsy has shown that Violet was not your wife's biological child either. Did you know that?"

Delaney dropped his chin to his chest again and closed his eyes. His large body swayed back and forth in the seat. Rouleau placed a hand on Delaney's arm "Should I call for the nurse?" He looked over at Woodhouse and signalled for him to get her. Woodhouse began to rise.

Delaney's body shuddered and then was still. He was still sitting upright. He lifted his head and opened his eyes, turning until he faced Rouleau. He looked a bit like a bird, his neck elongated, his eyes pinkish around the edges and bulging out of their sockets. "I don't need the nurse. I just need my own bed."

Rouleau was vaguely aware of Woodhouse hovering at the end of the row of chairs and then sitting down again. He kept his eyes locked on Delaney's. Some struggle was going on within their blue depths that needed time to resolve. Rouleau was aware of rubber shoes squeaking in the hallway and getting louder. He'd almost given up hope of getting anything more from Delaney that evening when Delaney began to speak in a voice so low that Rouleau had to strain forward to hear.

"She kept the secret all of our married life. I think she would have kept it forever if but for the school registration. They need a birth certificate, you see. Violet doesn't have one. Adele needed my help to figure out how to come up with the paperwork to get Violet into kindergarten. That was why my wife was distracted this week."

"Did she tell you who Violet's biological parents were?"

"No. She refused to say anything about her birth. I didn't like to push." His eyes squeezed shut. "Maybe I should have been more supportive. I was just so angry. She lied to me for three years and I was scared we'd lose Violet if the truth came out. I should never have gotten mad at her because now I've lost them both."

The nurse stepped around Rouleau and spoke to Ivo quietly, helping him to his feet. She said, "We'll just be getting Mr. Delaney home and settled. You can save any more questions for tomorrow."

Ivo staggered back a step and Rouleau steadied him. The nurse smiled grimly at Rouleau and wrapped an arm as far as she could around Ivo's waist. They started down the hallway, Delaney towering over the nurse. She let go of his waist but kept a firm grip on his arm. The volunteer who held onto Delaney's other arm was an older man with a pleasant face. Rouleau watched them get on the elevator without comment.

Woodhouse pushed himself to his feet. He scratched his protruding belly. "That sounded like a confession to me. He got angry and killed his wife and kid when he found out she'd been lying to him."

Rouleau gave the idea serious consideration. Woodhouse was quick to make a judgment, but in this case he had good reason. "Might have gone down that way. Trouble is we're going to need some evidence. A good defence lawyer would have that vague confession in shreds within seconds."

Woodhouse scowled. "I know what you mean. The courts have justice all arse backwards. The guy's smart enough to play the nutbar card. He's setting us up in case we get some evidence to nail him."

They followed in Delaney's footsteps toward the elevator. "No message from Stonechild while we were interviewing Delaney?" Woodhouse asked.

Rouleau glanced at him. Woodhouse's face was expressionless, suspiciously so. He reached inside his jacket pocket and pulled out his phone. He scrolled the messages. "Not yet."

Woodhouse appeared to be searching for words. "She's a bit of a wild card, isn't she?" he said finally.

"How do you mean?"

Woodhouse shrugged. "I don't know. Just that she doesn't strike me as all that dependable." He hit the down button and the elevator door slid open. "What do you know? First time I haven't had to wait half an hour."

They rode to the lobby in silence. Rouleau filed away Woodhouse's comments about Stonechild but let them rest for now. He knew that officers like Woodhouse had difficulty accepting women officers as their equal. Kala Stonechild's singular modus operandi and taciturn personality would make her a bigger target for the old boys' club. He doubted she would care, but others might. Heath for one. He wanted a team that showed well in public.

They left the hospital through the main doors and walked toward the parking lot. The sun was going down, casting long fingers across the pavement and reflecting off car windshields. Rouleau caught a movement in a red car at the end of the first row. He squinted and took a step forward to see past the sun's glare. Marci Stokes lifted a hand.

"I'll leave you here," he said to Woodhouse. "See you in the morning."

"Sure thing." Woodhouse looking over at Marci's car. He mock saluted her before walking past.

Marci lowered her window at Rouleau's approach. "Got time for a drink?" she asked. Her copper hair was tied back with an elastic but still managed to spill around her face. Her eyes shone in a stream of sunlight. "I might have something of interest to share."

"How about the Merchant?"

"I'll meet you there in ten." She smiled up at him and turned on her car. He stepped back as she pulled away.

She'd picked a table that looked out over the sidewalk in the smaller room to the right of the entrance. A waitress was delivering a beer as Rouleau arrived. He waited for her to depart and sat down across from Marci. She lifted her glass of vodka and soda into the air at eye level and said cheers before taking a long drink.

"So what have you got?" Rouleau picked up the beer and tilted the glass in her direction as a way of saying thanks.

"You do understand that this is a fair exchange deal."

"I'm coming to that conclusion. I haven't anything earth-shattering to share with you, but when I do you will be my go-to journalist."

She appeared satisfied. "I've done a bit of digging. Ivo Delaney used to have a sister named Olive. She was a year younger than him."

"Was?"

"The Delaneys owned a cottage north of Kingston on one of the many lakes. The family used to spend their summers there. The father was a bit of an oddball scientist and taught at the university. The mom stayed home and raised Ivo and Olive. Actually, Ivo's name used to be Egor, and the last name was spelled Dellaney, with two Ls. Anyhow, when Ivo was fourteen and Olive thirteen, they went out boating on the lake one evening after supper. Ivo came back alone after dark. Olive's body was found washed up on shore two days later."

Rouleau took a second to take in her blunt revelation. "I have to tell you that none of this came to light when we did our background search."

"I'm not surprised. This was twenty years ago and the story didn't make much of a ripple beyond the people at the lake, if you excuse my pun. I happened to find a source who was one of their neighbours." She held up a hand as if stopping traffic.

"Don't ask me how. He said that after the drowning, the family moved to Toronto. Ivo must have moved back as an adult, and that must have been when he changed his name."

"Was Ivo ever investigated for killing his sister?"

"Nope. It was ruled an accident. His story was that they moored the boat and she went for a swim. He fell asleep and when he woke up, she hadn't returned. He searched around for her until it got dark and then returned to the cottage."

"He's been treated for depression since he was a teenager."

"I would say there's a direct link to his sister's death."

Rouleau drank from his glass and thought over Marci's story. "Where are the parents now?"

"His father died of cancer last year. His mother sold up and moved out west somewhere. Nobody seems to know how to get hold of her."

"I can get somebody on that. Do you have her first name?"

"Helen. Her last name still has two Ls."

Rouleau raised a hand to signal the waitress. "Let me return the favour before we head out." Marci had drained her drink and he gulped down the last of his beer.

"I wouldn't say no."

Replenished, Marci leaned back and studied him. "Are your eyes really that peculiar jade green colour or are you wearing contacts?"

"Real."

"Damn. What I wouldn't give. I used to think if I had something like piercing green eyes, I'd be happier. My boyfriend would have left his wife for my green eyes. You ever been married, Rouleau?"

"Once. My green eyes didn't keep her from leaving me."

"Sorry."

"Me too. So are you planning to return to New York and take that job your old boyfriend is offering?"

"Thinking about it. Also thinking that returning to my old situation might be the stupidest thing I could do to myself. I'm starting to like Canada. The people are friendly and the killers are a different breed than I'm used to."

"How so?"

"Less obvious." She lifted her glass and drained half of it in one go. "Well, time to go file my story about the rise in vandalism on university campus. I'll bide my time a while longer on the Delaney story until you get me a few more facts."

"I'll be in touch when I have something. Thanks for keeping this information quiet for now."

"My pleasure."

He stayed to finish his drink after she left. The bar was getting busier and he had no wish to be alone. His father had left two messages over the course of the afternoon. Time was running out if he was going to see Frances while she could still recognize him. His dad said nobody knew what was keeping her hanging on.

Rouleau finished his beer. He'd pick up some takeout food on his way back to the condo, although he didn't feel like eating. He paid the tab and exited the bar. Night had fallen while they were inside and a breeze had come up off the lake. He pulled up the collar of his jacket and started walking slowly back to his car, parked two streets over. He'd have to call his father back and make excuses for another day's grace. The Delaney case needed his full attention at least until then.

And he needed one more day before telling Frances goodbye.

Kala opened the back door and tiptoed into the kitchen. The clock on the stove read ten-thirty so Dawn would be long asleep. She heard the click of a dog's toenails on the hardwood floor in the living room and Taiku was soon at her side. She rubbed his ears and spoke quietly to him before lifting her eyes and looking into the living room. A light was on and Gundersund was stretched out the length of the couch, Minny lying on his legs.

Kala smiled as the guilt at having left Dawn alone so long lifted a bit. She'd checked her phone messages after dropping Bennett off at the station and a new worry kept her from being completely at ease. Dawn's teacher and social worker had called a meeting for the following day at four o'clock at the school. They might just want to check in to see how things were going, but likely the intent behind the meeting was something more serious. The doubt would be enough to keep her on edge until she knew for sure.

She walked into the living room and over to the couch. Gundersund would have made a fine Viking warrior back in the day, with his too-long blond hair and high cheekbones. The scar on his left cheek added to the illusion. She stood over him for a moment, debating whether to get a blanket to cover him or to wake him up. She took a step back to get a blanket from the chair when his eyes snapped open. He had himself in a sitting position with an arm raised before she had time to say anything. Minny went flying off the end of the couch but landed unhurt.

Kala jumped back. Taiku whined and turned heel into the kitchen with Minny right behind him.

"Glad I wasn't a burglar." Kala plopped herself down beside him and began to laugh. "Your face … I wish you could have seen it." She clutched her stomach and doubled over with laughter.

"Very funny," Gundersund grumbled, but he was smiling. "I had it covered. I was ready to defend the fort if necessary." He lowered his arm and checked his watch. "You're later than I expected."

She straightened up and wiped tears from her eyes with the back of one hand. She didn't know if they were from laughing or being over tired. "Traffic was bad getting out of Montreal. An accident tied up a couple of lanes. Dawn asleep?"

"Yeah. I fed her some of that lasagna you had in the freezer and helped her with her math homework. She headed up around nine."

"Thanks for looking out for her. I sent her a text when I was stuck in traffic but she didn't say you were here."

"It was my pleasure. I like hanging out with her."

"Do you think she's settling in okay here, with me?"

"It's going to take time. I guess you know that, but I think she's happy enough. Any particular reason you're asking?"

Kala chewed on her bottom lip. "I'm meeting with her social worker and teacher tomorrow. I only got notice of it late this afternoon. Dawn didn't say anything happened at school today?"

"Nothing. I'd tell you if she had."

"I guess I'll just have to wait until tomorrow then."

Gundersund stretched and yawned. He got slowly to his feet and looked down at her. "I'll be heading out. Have you checked in with Rouleau?"

"Not yet. Any news here?"

"He and Woodhouse interviewed Ivo Delaney, who is now back home. We have a nine o'clock team meeting tomorrow morning."

"I didn't get much information in Montreal but a few things to share. They can wait until tomorrow."

"Good enough. There's some lasagna left in the fridge if you're hungry."

After Gundersund's footsteps had receded from the back deck and she knew that she was alone, Kala stretched out on the couch in the exact place where he'd lain. She rested for a moment and breathed in his scent, a mix of soap and the outdoors. He was a comforting man. A good man. She closed her eyes. She knew better than to depend on Gundersund's friendship forever, but she would allow herself to feel happy that he was here for her and Dawn now. For the first time, she realized that she didn't mind having a partner. She could even admit that she looked forward to seeing him. She just had to make sure that she didn't come to rely on him. She knew that if she did, she could expect the inevitable let down. Trusting someone to be there when push came to shove was a fool's game.

She sat up and swung her feet onto the floor. If the social worker wanted to take Dawn away, would that be such a bad thing? Already Kala was getting used to having her around, even looking forward to seeing her at the end of the day. If Dawn left now, she'd get over her leaving without much trouble. That might be for the best for both of them. She could go back to fending only for herself and Dawn would be in a home with somebody better suited to looking after her.

Kala reached over and turned off the lamp on the coffee table, then stood and called for Taiku to come. She made the rounds, checking that the doors were locked before they started up the stairs to bed. As Kala passed by Dawn's room, she stopped at the doorway and looked in. The blind was up and Dawn's bed was bathed in pale moonlight. She was sleeping on her back, her hair fanned out across the pillow, one arm bent over her head. She'd kicked off the covers, which lay half on the bed and half on the floor. Kala tiptoed across the room and bent to retrieve the blankets and tucked them around her. Dawn stirred in her sleep and her eyes fluttered, but her breathing remained deep and regular. Kala stood for a moment looking down at the sleeping girl. She looked so young and beautiful in the silvery light, almost like a princess waiting to be awakened from a dream. Kala reached out and touched the smooth warmth of Dawn's cheek with her fingertips. Then she turned and silently walked back to where Taiku waited for her just outside the bedroom door.

CHAPTER SEVENTEEN

"Man, I hope that coffee's strong." Woodhouse grabbed a mug from the selection on the shelf and lined up behind Bennett. "When will I learn not to stay up half the night watching MMA fighting?"

"Are they still showing that garbage?" Bennett handed Woodhouse the coffee pot.

"Mixed martial arts is an art form. Pure poetry in motion. Two men in peak physical condition taking each other on with no holds barred."

"Not from where I sit. Two people kicking the shit out of each other is not poetic in any sense."

"All you wusses say the same thing."

Bennett shook his head and stepped around Woodhouse to take a seat next to Kala's desk. She looked up at him from her computer and smiled. "Getting a cultural lesson from Woodhouse, were you?"

"You might say that."

They were still smiling at each other when Rouleau and Gundersund walked into the office. Kala looked across the room and saw that Gundersund's eyes were going from Bennett to her and back again. Then he turned to Rouleau and continued talking as they headed over to where Woodhouse stood sampling from his coffee mug. They also poured cups and emptied the pot before walking together toward Rouleau's office. Rouleau called everyone to join them as he passed.

Kala followed Bennett into Rouleau's office and took one of the seats facing his desk. Bennett and Gundersund stood while Woodhouse slid into the seat next to her. Rouleau welcomed everyone to another workday before he reported on the interview with Ivo Delaney. He concluded with, "Bennett, I need you to locate the mother. We have to find out more about her son's mental state and the death of his sister. Her drowning is bearing a striking similarity to Violet's."

"Will do."

"Wouldn't he have drowned his wife too?" Kala asked. "I mean, why kill his daughter that way but not Adele?"

Rouleau thought for a moment. "Maybe she put up a fight. Maybe he wanted her to suffer."

Kala could see the logic, but did this fit with what she'd seen in Ivo Delaney? She wasn't altogether convinced but admitted that the news of his sister's drowning could be the game changer. He might very well be a cold-blooded killer when angry or threatened.

"If you don't agree," Woodhouse said, "is it because you found some other suspect in Montreal?"

Kala knew his question was meant to make her look incompetent. Rouleau nodded at her to tell them what she'd uncovered.

"When Adele lived in Montreal, she waitressed in a dive bar and stripped on Saturday evenings at that same bar or another one down the street. Nobody knows why she quit suddenly or where she got Violet. I plan to do some more research today. I'm going to start checking adoption agencies, although it was probably a private adoption, which will be more difficult to track down."

"I think Ivo lost it when he found out she hadn't given birth to the kid." Woodhouse looked directly at her. "He didn't like being lied to for nearly four years. Nothing more than that."

Gundersund said, "Still, it would be nice to tie up the loose ends."

"I'd like someone to head back out to the Delaneys' and interview him today," Rouleau said. "Are you done at the courthouse, Gundersund?"

"I'm on standby in case I'm recalled, but hopefully they won't need me again."

"Can you take this on? Stonechild can go with you."

Kala nodded. She could do the research anytime, at home later today if necessary. Seeing Ivo again would help her to get a better perspective on his state of mind. Adele might even have shared something with him about Violet's parentage that he'd share with them if asked the right questions.

Rouleau picked up a file on his desk. "Good. Well, looks like everyone has some work to do, so report in as you go. Have a good day everyone."

This time Stonechild agreed to drive together with Gundersund to the Delaneys'. He supposed it was because it was early in the day and they'd be heading back to the station when the interview finished. She seemed on edge whenever she didn't have her own wheels, almost as if her escape plan was compromised.

"Nice spring day," he commented as he turned onto Division Street. The sky was blue with a fila-ment of wispy white clouds off to the west. "No rain in the forecast for a few days."

"We could use the break. It felt like the mon-soon season was never going to end." She slumped back against the headrest. "I didn't sleep well last night. I'm tired today."

"Yeah, I didn't sleep that great either." He didn't tell her that Fiona was waiting for him when he left her the night before and arrived home. Fiona upstairs in his bedroom with a bottle of red wine and wanting to talk about their separation. It was almost one in the morning before he convinced her to leave. Her parting words were that she was going to fight him on the divorce because she knew it was a mistake.

"How do you want to approach this?"

"Sorry?" he tuned back into Stonechild's voice.

She was looking at him with a quizzical expression on her face. "I said, how do you want to handle our interview with Ivo?"

"I think you should do the questioning. I'll stay in the background. He seemed to trust you last time and we can only hope that he'll feel comfortable enough to start spilling his guts. If he is as ill as we believe, he could be ready to get things off his conscience."

"Okay."

They settled back into silence, more companionable than awkward. This past week they'd become friends again. He knew it was because he was helping her with Dawn, but getting on Stonechild's good side had been the furthest thing from his mind when he spent the last few evenings kid-sitting. He felt for Dawn and he liked her. While Stonechild struggled with her new responsibilities, he felt good helping the two of them out at home. Stonechild and Dawn would find their way given time. Right now he wanted to talk to Stonechild about his issues with Fiona. She might have advice on how to deal with a wife who wouldn't take no for an answer. She also might open up to him more if she knew he wanted a divorce. On the other hand, knowing that he was free might make Stonechild run in the other direction.

He took Princess Street through downtown and turned left at the harbour. The water level remained high under the bridge heading out of the city. He thought of Violet and the odds of finding her body with the swelled creeks and rivers. He hoped the rain would hold off for a while and give them a chance to locate her. He didn't like thinking of her out there alone, even if her soul had long left this earth. She needed to be brought home.

They passed ten minutes of silence and a steady stream of oncoming traffic before they turned into the Delaney driveway. He rolled halfway up the drive and parked behind two cars parallel to each other taking up the width of paved space. A ginger-haired boy about four years old sat on the front steps, watching them get out of the car.

"There's the neighbour's son," Stonechild said. "Sammy Lockhart. Catherine must be inside with Ivo."

"Did you find out if she's married?"

"No. She's a single mom."

Gundersund thought for a moment. "It could be another avenue to explore."

Stonechild paused. "An affair, you mean?"

"Has anyone checked her out?"

"Just the basics. We can add a background search to the list, but I have to say that in appearance, Catherine is no match for Ivo's wife, although she's a freelance writer and seems intelligent."

"She might be better suited to him. One never knows what's going on behind closed doors."

"We can do some probing today."

The boy had scampered inside the house by the time they made it to the front door. Gundersund studied Catherine Lockhart when she answered their knock. Her face was wide browed and pleasant; creamy white skin with red cheeks like a milkmaid in a British movie. The stress of the week appeared to be wearing her out by the dark circles under her eyes. She nodded to Gundersund but spoke to Stonechild. "We came by to check on him. I've had such a time trying to convince Sammy that Violet isn't here anymore."

Stonechild kept her voice warm and low. "It's good of you to be here. We know how difficult this has been for you and Sammy and Ivo. We have a few questions for Ivo today so having you here is a huge help."

Gundersund was learning to appreciate how adeptly Stonechild managed the line between empathy and police work. She never said anything without a reason. Woodhouse could take a lesson. He followed a bit behind her as Catherine led them into the kitchen at the back of the house. Sammy was already sitting at the table with his back to them. Ivo looked up from where he sat, holding with both hands onto a cup of coffee that rested on the table in front of him. Sunlight streamed into the room from a large window over the sink, surrounding Ivo in a golden glow. The word demented popped into Gundersund's mind when he studied Ivo's dishevelled appearance and red-rimmed eyes. He looked like a man skirting on the edge of sanity.

Stonechild took a seat kitty corner to Ivo. Catherine put her hands on Sammy's shoulders.

"Time for us to go to the grocery store, Son. We'll be back within the hour, Ivo."

Sammy shrugged off her hands and got out of the chair. "Can I get some ice cream this time?" His voice was petulant and demanding at the same time.

"If you behave as you can. We'll see."

"I'll be-be-have-have." He jumped past her and shot down the hallway.

Catherine sighed heavily. "We won't be long. Ivo's out of bread and milk and I thought I'd get something to make a meal for him." She spoke as if he wasn't in the room.

"We'll wait until you return," Stonechild said. She met Gundersund's eyes briefly and he could see that she was biding her time and would question Catherine later. He signalled that he was going to slip into the background as they'd agreed and crossed over to the counter out of Ivo's line of vision. From his vantage point, he could see Ivo's face and Stonechild in profile.

Stonechild sat silently beside Ivo for several minutes until Gundersund felt his legs cramping from holding himself in one position. He wondered at her tactics, but in the end her patience paid off. Ivo tipped his head toward her.

"I didn't kill my wife. I sure as hell didn't kill our daughter. Violet was my daughter no matter who …" His voice broke and Gundersund watched Stonechild place a hand on his forearm resting on the table.

"Did Adele ever speak of anyone from her past who might have worried her or done something to her that made her frightened?"

Ivo thought. "No. She always said that the past didn't matter, only the future. It was just this last week that I thought something was wrong. She didn't want to talk about it, that is until she told me that Violet didn't have a birth certificate and couldn't register for school. She admitted that she hadn't gotten Violet by the regular channels."

"How did she get Violet?"

"A private adoption, she told me. I asked her about paperwork and she said that there wasn't any."

"Did she say whether Violet was born in Montreal?"

"No. She didn't want to talk about it."

Stonechild was silent again. Gundersund shifted positions and waited. When she resumed speaking, he too felt himself being lulled by the calm spell she was weaving around Ivo Delaney. "We've learned of your sister's drowning when you were teenagers. Can you tell me about that?"

"Olive?" Gundersund could hear genuine surprise in Ivo's voice. "She drowned but it was an accident. We were out in the boat and she went for a swim. I dozed off and when I woke up, she was gone. Why are you asking me about this? Adele and Violet didn't even know her." He seemed to see something in Stonechild's eyes. His voice rose. "You can't believe there's a connection." He half stood from his chair, but lowered himself when Stonechild reached out again and gripped his arm.

"We have to look at all the pieces and put them together as best we can. You've said that you've had difficulty with depression since you were a teenager. You didn't tell us about Olive." She spoke mildly, without judgment. Ivo responded by sinking back into the chair and blinking, once, twice, three times until his eyes closed.

"My parents blamed me. I blamed myself, not for killing her, but for not saving her. Her death marked every waking minute of my life until I met Adele. She didn't care about my miserable past. She made me happy. Do you know what it's like, officer, not to have any hope left that you'll ever be happy again?"

"I've known my own despair, Ivo." She spoke so quietly that Gundersund almost missed what she said. "We both know that words don't help, but believe that you will be happy again. We'll find what happened to Adele and Violet and knowing will help you to accept. Remember what you said. You have to go on for both of them. They wouldn't want you to give up. Are you in contact with your mother?"

"No. She wants it that way. She moved to the Okanogan Valley when my father died. I know because she called me to tell me about his death and to say that she was moving out there. He didn't want any contact with me when he was alive and she said she had to respect that. I'm still hoping she'll change her mind."

"I hope that for you too. For both of you." Stonechild turned in her chair. "Gundersund, would you make some hot coffee? Ivo's has gone cold and I think we could all use a cup while we wait for Catherine and Sammy to come back."

"Coming right up."

He got busy filling the pot with water from the tap and measuring coffee grounds from the canister next to the machine while Stonechild kept up her conversation with Ivo. She didn't find out anything else useful, although Ivo looked slightly more together by the time Catherine and Sammy tromped into the kitchen with three bags of groceries. Stonechild rose from the table and left it to Gundersund to speak with Catherine while she helped Sammy unpack the food. She'd already convinced Ivo to go upstairs to have a shower.

Catherine led Gundersund into the living room so that her son wouldn't overhear. "I've thought and thought about anything that might help, but there's nothing. The last week I saw Adele and Violet, we met for playgroup twice and then the outing to the plant nursery. Adele begged off stopping for ice cream on the way home, saying she had a headache. That was really the last time I saw her."

Gundersund asked, "Did she speak about her life before she met Ivo?"

"No. She said she lived in Montreal and has a much older sister somewhere in the Ottawa Valley, but she never talked much about her life before Ivo and Violet."

"Did you find it odd that she had so few friends?"

"Not really. We both like the solitary life, so I understood her desire to be alone for the most part."

"Did she share anything about her relationship with Ivo?"

Catherine grinned unexpectedly. "She laughed about his bumbling ways, but only fondly. I came to believe that she genuinely cared for him." The humour left her eyes. "You probably find them an unlikely match, as did I, but I never saw any animosity between them. Ivo adored her and he doted on Violet. He's lost the only people he was close to, as have Sammy and I. We're going to have to stick together to get through this. I see that now. Adele wouldn't want me to leave Ivo alone. He really has nobody else."

CHAPTER EIGHTEEN

Kala set a mug of tea onto her tray next to an egg salad sandwich and bowl of vegetable soup. She paid at the cash and found a spot at the end of a long table away from the handful of other cops lingering over a late lunch. Gundersund had been called back to the courthouse as they were leaving the Delaney property so they'd driven downtown together and she'd caught a cab back to the station. The one time she didn't take her truck and of course she'd needed it. What was it that British people called that? *Sod's law.* It had been a classic case of Sod's law.

She dipped her spoon into the bowl and raised a brimming scoop of hot soup to her lips. The cafeteria made good soup, she'd give them that. Maybe she'd cook a pot of black bean soup for Dawn on the weekend. Homemade soup always felt like comfort food. It could warm the empty places and fill your belly. She might even teach Dawn how to make bannock to go with it.

Kala lowered the empty spoon and checked her wristwatch. Two-thirty. She had to be at the school in less than three hours. Dawn would be waiting for her in the library and they'd drive home together after her meeting. As the time got closer, she found herself getting more and more anxious. Schools had never been her favourite place to spend time, that is until college. She'd attended several grade schools and high schools during the foster years and had always been an outsider. School had mirrored her life, bouncing from one family to the next and never being part of any of them for long. The only good thing was that she'd found school easy and had earned a scholarship out of high school. She hadn't pursued higher education for five years after graduation but that was a story for another day.

Her phone rang as she was finishing her lunch. She swallowed the last bite of the sandwich before answering. "Officer Stonechild. Can I help you?"

"Kala? It's Jacques's father, Henri Rouleau. Sorry to bother you at work."

"No bother, Mr. Rouleau. Is everything okay?"

"Yes. Everything is just fine, but please call me Henri. Did Jacques tell you that I'm in Ottawa?"

"No, he hasn't. Are you having a vacation?"

"No, I'm doing some research for my latest book."

She listened with a smile on her lips as he spoke about his work and the cruel spring weather that was at last turning a corner. He had even gone for a long walk that afternoon along the canal and spotted crocuses and daffodils in some of the gardens. He'd had an early lunch at the Café Ritz with a table looking out over the bike path and ribbon of water beyond. Finally he got to the reason for his call as Kala knew he would given time. She listened carefully to what he told her and promised to do what she could to help him. They signed off with his invitation to drop by for supper when he returned to Kingston. Kala sat for a moment afterwards and turned his request over in her mind. She knew it had been difficult for him to ask and she'd agreed without considering all of the implications.

The noise of a tray and cutlery hitting the floor jarred her from her thoughts. An officer in uniform had dropped his full tray of food in front of the cash register and others had jumped up to help clear the mess. Kala picked up her own tray and walked it over to the counter, carefully stepping around the coffee and smashed plate of shepherd's pie and salad that had exploded as if shot from a cannon. The cashier appeared from behind the counter with a broom and all seemed in hand so Kala didn't offer to help clean. As it was, she'd have to hurry if she was going to finish compiling the list of adoption agencies in Montreal. She needed to allow enough time to cut across town to Dawn's school to deal with whatever the teacher and social worker were going to throw at her. Everything else would have to go on the back burner for the time being.

The two women sitting across from Kala were as she'd expected. The social worker, Tamara Jones, was just like some of the social workers she'd dealt with throughout her childhood. Young, earnest, and driven by the need to make a difference. When they'd first met, Tamara told Kala that she'd been on the job less than a year, straight out of university. Kala could see that the job, the burn out, the depressing reality, hadn't ground her down ... yet. She had no doubt that it might take another year or two, but the day would come when Tamara Jones woke up wondering what the hell she was doing wasting her life.

The teacher, Mrs. Zelasko, was a foreshadow of what young Tamara Jones would morph into twenty years from now. Mrs. Zelasko's cynical brown eyes let you know that she had seen it all and wasn't about to suffer fools. She was plumply turned out in a long blue skirt, red shirt populated by dogs playing musical instruments, white tights, and solid-looking clogs — a school teacher uniform that would blend into comfortable motherliness for her students. The pre-adolescents wouldn't feel that Mrs. Zelasko was attempting to compete with their budding self-awareness and narcissism. She'd hide her own needs and desires behind the shield of teaching and appear to them as bland as vanilla pudding.

Mrs. Zelasko took the lead in the conversation as Kala knew she would.

"Thank you for making time to meet with us today. I thought the three of us should discuss how Dawn is settling in. Have you anything to share with us at this point, Officer Stonechild?"

"Dawn continues to meet with Dr. Lyman ..."

Tamara interrupted. "I have the doctor's report

here. She says that Dawn is quiet and introverted and not yet talking about her mom, Gil Valiquette, the robbery, or their arrests."

"I'm not surprised." Kala said voice sharp. Why did everyone feel that talking about problems and feelings was the only indicator of emotional health? She added, "Dawn is a private person, which I respect."

Tamara's limpid blue eyes glistened brighter. "We can't get better unless we share what we are going through. Surely, you see that?"

"I do, but I also think we have to give Dawn room to come to grips with some of what she experienced on her own. She knows we're here for her. I really believe that she will share when she's ready."

Tamara kept her gaze steady on Kala. "Dr. Lyman indicated that she wants you to go in for some sessions. Are you willing to do this?"

"Of course." She knew what would go on the report if she said anything different.

Mrs. Zelasko pulled back control of the interview. "Dawn is also having difficulty fitting into the classroom. She doesn't take part in anything if she can help it and hasn't made any friendships with the other girls." She paused and looked meaningfully at Kala.

Kala stared back and prepared herself for the real reason they'd summoned her to this meeting. By the intrusive look in the two sets of eyes fixed on her like headlights, it wasn't going to be good.

Mrs. Zelasko's voice took on an even more sombre tone. "It gives me no pleasure to tell you that

Dawn stole another girl's iPhone yesterday morning. The phone was found in Dawn's bag after I became aware of the problem. One of the other students saw her take it from a desk and put it there." Her mouth formed into a straight line of disapproval. Tamara's mouth opened and shut twice before she pursed her lips together.

"Are you sure it was Dawn?"

"Without question. However, when confronted, she refused to deny or admit to the theft. This is most disturbing in and of itself. I work very hard to have my students own their mistakes, accept responsibility, and change their behaviour moving forward. Dawn has chosen to do none of these things.

Kala had no idea how to respond. Filling the empty space, Tamara ignored Mrs. Zelasko's frown and jumped in to change the subject.

"How is Dawn settling in with you?"

And this is the crux of the interview, Kala thought. *How I respond is going to determine Dawn's future with me.* She felt a slow-burning anger spread through her gut like gasoline. Anger at the situation. Anger at the fixed hand that she and Dawn and Dawn's mother, Lily, had been dealt long before any of them had been born. But anger wouldn't help Dawn now. She forced herself to speak in a pleasant tone.

"Dawn is doing very well at home. She's opening up to me and is extremely happy. We both are. I have to say that I am having a great deal of difficulty believing that she would steal. It is completely out of character. I promise that I'll speak with her and get to the bottom of what is going on. If she needs to apologize to the other student, I'll do my best to make her see the importance. I'm going to phone Dr. Lyman when we leave here today and set up that appointment."

Tamara nodded and a delighted smile spread across her face. She even spread her hands and raised them into the air as if giving thanks to God before clasping them together. "Excellent. We were worried that Dawn hasn't had a chance to develop a sense of right and wrong, what with the life she's led with her mother and her boyfriend. Even her father is in prison for goodness sake. You need to instil this because you are such a good role model. I have to tell you, Officer Stonechild, that your profession and standing in the community are two factors that we considered when agreeing to place Dawn with you."

"And I take my guardianship seriously."

"Good then." Mrs. Zelasko ended the conversation with these two words. She stood and smoothed the wrinkles in her skirt at the same time. "Dawn is waiting for you in the library. Please contact me once you've spoken with her and we can work on an action plan together. I'm sure the other students will accept her apology once they see real contrition."

Kala knew the system well enough to have learned the words she must say. "Thank you for this team approach to helping my niece." She rose too and shook both of their hands. "I will most certainly be in touch."

She was rewarded with quick smiles before

both Mrs. Zelasko's and Tamara's expressions eased and they closed Dawn's file in their minds for the moment. They could now resume their personal, after-school lives believing that they'd made progress helping a troubled child get on the path. Kala was not fooled by their easy acceptance of her promises. They'd be watching and judging her. One misstep and young Tamara Jones would swoop in and move Dawn to a new foster home with the uncapping of her pen. Twenty-three years old with the power to change lives. She was the child care system dressed up in a navy suit from Banana Republic.

Kala smiled at them each in turn but the smiles stopped short of her eyes. A determination had replaced the anger. The system would do to her niece what it had done to her over her dead body. She bid them a good evening and headed into the hallway.

Mrs. Zelasko had given directions to the library on the other side of the first floor. Kala set out and the familiar hallways took her back about ten years. The corridors were lined in green lockers and the air had that peculiar school smell of rotting fruit, gym socks, and floor wax. Only a few students lingered. Most had caught their buses home an hour before. A janitor was mopping the hallway in circular motions and she tiptoed across the wet stretch of tile to push open the library door.

She found Dawn alone, sitting at a computer with her back to the door. Sunlight from the tall windows along the far wall brightened the rows of books arranged in parallel formation. The librarian was nowhere in sight. Kala silently crossed the carpeted floor until she was standing behind her niece. Dawn's head was bowed and a book rested in her lap. When she finally looked up at Kala, she jumped slightly and grabbed at her heart. Almost instantly, the startled look gave way to relief. "Hey Kala." She reached down and picked up her knapsack from the floor next to her chair and shoved the book she'd been reading into it. This time when she looked at Kala, her eyes gave nothing away. She stood and pushed the chair under the desk. "Can we go home now?"

"We can in a minute. Just one thing before we leave."

Dawn slung the knapsack over one shoulder and straightened her back. "What?"

"Put your bag on the chair."

Dawn hesitated. A look of defiance crossed her features but she did as she'd been asked. She flung the bag onto the desk and faced Kala again. Her shoulders slumped. She let her head drop until she was looking at the floor. "You believe them."

"No. I want to hear what you have to say."

"You say that now."

"I mean it. I want your side."

"I didn't take her iPhone."

"Well then, I believe you didn't take it."

Dawn looked up. "Just like that, you believe me?"

Kala reached out with both arms and pulled Dawn toward her in a tight hug. They stood locked together as the seconds ticked by. They stood until Kala felt Dawn's rigid body soften and relax into her own. Only then did Kala say, "You and I are in this together. Whatever has happened, whatever is coming, we are in this together. Do you understand me?"

Dawn's head bobbed up and down against her chest.

"I will fight for you." Kala lowered her face and kissed her on the forehead. "You are worth more to me than all the other kids in this school put together." She let Dawn go and reached around her to pick up her knapsack. "Now let's get out of here and go home to Taiku. You can walk him down by the water while I make us something good for supper. Then maybe you can tell me what's going on."

Sammy Lockhart finished his rice pudding and pushed away his bowl. He'd told his mom that he hated rice pudding but she'd taken away his empty plate and dropped the bowl on the table anyway. She'd sprinkled the yucky pudding with brown sugar and he'd decided to have a taste. One taste led to another and he'd ended up licking the bowl until he could see his face shining from it.

He climbed down from his chair. His mother was sitting at her desk in the living room working on her laptop. She'd been working on a story all day. He remembered what she'd said at breakfast.

"I need to get this story finished by tonight to

make the deadline. You're going to have to entertain yourself today I'm afraid, buckaroo."

He'd done his best to keep out of her way. She hadn't had much work lately and wouldn't let him buy anything good at the store. That was because they didn't have any extra money. He knew that because he heard her telling her sister how worried she was on the phone the night before when she thought he was sleeping. The little bees of worry had been humming in his stomach ever since.

So he tried his best to be good. He'd built a fort out of couch cushions and a blanket she'd given him and hid inside with his Lego for most of the morning. After lunch, he watched two movies and then played with his toy cars in the front hallway. She'd stopped working long enough to make him a hotdog but had taken hers back to the computer.

Sammy got up on the sofa and craned his head back to look up at the sky. It was still blue and he could see the sun high up. He turned and looked at his mom. She had an unlit cigarette in her mouth and was twirling her hair around and around with her fingers. She always did that when she was thinking.

He jumped down and slipped past her. At the doorway to the kitchen he stopped and looked back. He thought about telling her that he was going outside to ride his bike, but she'd begun typing again. He shrugged. His black rubber boots were on the mat by the back door. He sat down and pulled them on and then unlocked the back door. He stepped outside and shut the door so that it didn't slam.

His bike was right where he'd left it next to the back shed. He picked up a stick and poked it in the holes under the steps for a while. He knew a raccoon was living under there. Or maybe it was an otter. He wasn't sure, but he knew it was something big. He'd like to get it out and make it his pet. He lost interest after a while and looked over at his red tricycle. He was almost too big for the bike, but he still liked riding it up and down the driveway as fast as he could go. His mom said she was going to get him a two-wheeler as soon as she got some money ahead. Maybe he'd get it after she got paid for this job she was working on.

It took him a few minutes to lug the bike across the lawn and around the house to the top of the driveway. One of the pedals hit his leg and made a scratch. He rubbed it for a second but then forgot about the sting when he got on his bike and started down the little hill, being careful not to scrape his mother's car. She'd said the car had to last another winter at least even if the driver door didn't lock any-more and rust had made little holes along the sides.

He pedalled hard and liked the feel of the wind in his face. "Yippee!" he screamed and kept pedal-ling as hard as he could until he reached the trees on his right. That was when he had to brake so that he wouldn't keep going onto the road. He slowed and drove his bike in a wide arc back toward the house. His feet started moving in slower and slower circles. The pedals slowed until the bike came to a stop. He stared across the driveway into the trees.

A man was standing in the shadows watching him.

Sammy remembered his friend Violet and the worry bees started buzzing louder in his tummy. He got his feet back on the pedals ready to pump his legs as hard as he could, to get back up the hill to his mommy. The man took a step toward him. He was smiling and called out his name.

"Sammy, I want to talk to you."

Sammy hesitated. Only friends knew his name was Sammy. The man was saying something and he listened. He wasn't sure if he should go over to the man like he asked. Sammy looked back toward the house. The front door had been flung open and his mother was standing on the front steps. She had one hand over her forehead and she was looking down the driveway.

"Sammy, you get back here right now!" she called.

"Coming, Ma!" he yelled back, relieved not to have to make a decision. He looked over to where the man was standing, but the space was empty. The man had disappeared back into the trees. Sammy squinted into the shadows but couldn't see any sign of him.

He slowly started to push his feet against the pedals to build up speed to make the hill and get back to where his mom stood, waiting with her hands on her hips. When he was closer, he could see the unhappy look on her face. Something told him not to mention the man standing in the trees. Her face was red enough already. By the time he reached her, his legs were tired and he was panting. She grabbed onto his arm and gave him a shake.

"You never go outside without telling me again, do you hear me, young man? I was worried sick when I realized you weren't in the house. Now get inside and into your pajamas. You are going straight to bed."

He didn't think about the man again until his mom had tucked him into bed and gone downstairs to finish writing her story. Only then did he wonder about what the man had told him.

Sammy closed his eyes and tried to see the man's face. He'd been wearing a black ball cap and a black jacket and all Sammy could remember was his smile. A wisp of a memory tickled in his head. He'd seen the man somewhere before. But where?

Maybe the man knew what happened to Violet and had come to take Sammy to see her. That might be how the man knew his name. He must be a friend. Sammy rolled onto his side and closed his eyes. Maybe the man in black would be back tomorrow. He might even take Sammy to find Violet because it was getting *really* boring waiting for her to come home.

CHAPTER NINETEEN

The next morning, Kala drove into work early, stopping at the Tim Hortons drive-through to pick up a bagel and large coffee. She took a second to enjoy the sun rising over the strip mall — looked like another nice day was shaping up, and she was sorry to be spending it indoors. She carried on to the station and ate at her desk while she checked her email. The most urgent answered, she printed the list of adoption agencies that she'd saved in a file the day before. As soon as the clock struck nine, she began calling.

Her limited French seemed enough to get by, especially since most of the people who answered the phone switched to English as soon as she began speaking French. By twelve o'clock, she'd gone through the entire list of agencies without learning anything of use. Nobody had placed a baby with Adele Dufour in the time period provided. She doodled on a notepad while considering next steps. Woodhouse would tell her to bark up another tree. She looked across at Gundersund who was talking on the phone. They were alone in the office. Bennett and Woodhouse were spending the day at Ivo Delaney's bank, interviewing his coworkers.

She stood up and stretched and started toward Rouleau's office. The door was open but he wasn't inside. Gundersund called to her.

"Vera came and got Rouleau an hour ago. He and Heath went back downtown for another news conference."

She turned. He'd hung up the phone and was leaning back in his chair watching her. "I was hoping to speak with him." She walked back to her desk and sat down. "What're you working on?"

"Tracking down Delaney's mother. I just spoke to her."

"And?"

"If I had to guess, I'd say she's one bible-thumping, God-fearing woman. She talked a lot about sin and judgment day."

"Man. Just what Ivo Delaney must have needed growing up after his sister drowned."

"She said that her husband never forgave Ivo, although she did after years of going to church. Still, her husband cut off contact with Ivo and she feels that she has to respect his wishes even in death."

"See, I don't get that. People who play the forgiveness card but don't act on it. Where I come from, we call that hypocrisy."

Gundersund grinned. "Where I come from too. Say, you want to get some lunch? I can fill you in on what Mrs. Delaney said about Ivo over a sandwich."

"When's Rouleau due back?"

"He figured by one-thirty if all goes well."

"We could text him to meet us at the Merchant."

"I like how you think, Stonechild. I'll send him a text now and we can be on our way."

They snagged what had become their regular table in the smaller room to the right of the entrance. Gundersund checked his messages and Kala read the menu. Gundersund talked while reading. "Rouleau has to head back to the station. He says he'll meet us there later."

"Did he say how the press conference went?"

"Not really. He didn't have much to report so I imagine not that great."

The waitress came over and they ordered drinks and cheeseburger platters. When she left Kala asked, "So what did Mrs. Delaney have to tell you about Ivo?"

"She said that he was a loner, never any friends to speak of. From what she said I gathered that their daughter Olive was the shining star. She was popular and pretty and did well in school. The Delaneys pinned all their hopes and dreams on her. Olive and Ivo were close until she began high school and started hanging around with a new group of friends. Mrs. Delaney said that Ivo was jealous. She calls him Egor, by the way. The name she gave him at birth. She said that the day of the drowning, Olive was planning to leave the lake and go to an overnight party with some girlfriends. Ivo sulked about it all morning but seemed to rally toward lunchtime. He talked her into going for the boat ride around the bay later in the afternoon. They had no proof that it wasn't an accident as Ivo said, but Mrs. Delaney and her husband always believed that he'd done something that caused her death. She suggested that he'd left Olive in the middle of the lake and took the boat back to shore where he waited until she was gone. Olive wasn't a strong swimmer."

"If Ivo didn't admit to anything all those years ago, I don't think we'll get him talking now."

"No. I wonder if Adele was planning on leaving him. If she was, that could have triggered the same reaction as when he felt that Olive was ditching him for her new friends."

"Didn't Adele's sister say that Adele wanted to visit with Violet the weekend before they went missing?"

"That's right. Adele was disappointed that she had to wait another week because Leanne was busy."

Kala tried to piece it together. "So Adele was not close to Leanne, but all of a sudden she couldn't wait to visit her. A week later, Adele and Violet are dead. Tell me that's just a coincidence."

Gundersund didn't respond while the waitress set down their drinks and plates of food. "Ketchup?" he offered Kala before loading up his French fries. He took a bite of his burger. "So, maybe Adele Delaney was trying to take a vacation from Ivo."

"Or maybe she was going to use her sister's place as a launching pad to get away from Ivo permanently." Kala picked up her burger. "This smells good. I didn't realize how hungry I am."

"Don't let it get cold."

They dug into their food, putting the case on hold by silent agreement. Gundersund finished eating before she did. He took a swallow of beer before asking, "How'd your interview go with Dawn's teacher?"

"Good." She dropped the French fry she'd been holding back onto her plate and pushed it away. She could feel his gaze upon her. She raised her head and looked across at him. "Okay, not good. Dawn isn't fitting in and some girl said that Dawn stole her iPhone."

"You're kidding."

"I wish I was. When I tried to talk to her about it last evening, she brushed me off. She said she didn't steal it and she wasn't apologizing."

"What did you say?"

"That I'd back her up. I know she's not a thief."

Gundersund looked thoughtful. After a few moments, he shook his head. "No way she took an iPhone. Half the time she doesn't remember to charge her own phone and told me that she's not a big fan. Besides that, she's a good kid."

Kala leaned forward. "So what do I do, Gundersund? I have no experience with this shit."

"It was another girl who accused her?"

"Yeah, backed up by some girlfriends."

"Could be this girl is trying to control the group. Maybe she feels threatened. Let me talk to Dawn and see if I can get anything more out of her."

"I'd appreciate that. Why can't life ever be easy?"

"I wish I knew. The important thing is that she knows you believe in her."

"I one hundred percent back her up, but I can't help worrying that with all she's been through with her parents ... well let's just say that they weren't the best role models. I have the tiniest, niggling doubt in the worried part of my brain that she did steal the phone and it's a cry for help. I've called her shrink for a one-on-one. Just waiting for a call back."

"It's good not to be blind where kids are concerned. I think you're going about this the right way, if my opinion counts for anything."

"Did you have a normal family growing up?"

"I did. Two parents, a brother, and dog."

She felt her face burn remembering that he'd told Dawn his brother had died in a car crash. She tried to keep her voice light. "Well, I might need you to tell me what normal is now and then." She smiled and pretended not to see the sadness that came and went in his eyes.

"No family's perfect, Stonechild, but I should be able to draw on my parents' example. They're good people and solid. I might take you to meet them some day."

"I think I'd like that."

CHAPTER TWENTY

Rouleau arrived back at the station with Heath after the press conference. Heath was in a jovial mood. He'd liked the questions from the media, which had been benign at best. Marci Stokes had been conspicuous by her absence.

"Still some national media attention kicking around." He ran a hand through his greying curls. "We should be able to hold their attention a few more days until the arrest. I hope my promise to them that we're close to charging someone won't be misplaced."

"The team is being thorough. It's prudent to wait until we've gathered as much evidence as possible before we charge Delaney. So far, most is circumstantial. Forensics came up empty, as you know."

They stopped walking at Vera's desk. She smiled at Rouleau. Her long blond hair was clipped back with blue sparkly combs in the shape of butterflies. Her amber eyes regarded them both as she handed a folder to Heath. "Your wife called half an hour ago. She wonders if you'll be home for dinner."

Heath's smile faded. "Thanks. I'll give her a call." He took the folder. "Let me know when you're ready to make that arrest," he said to Rouleau and headed into his office, shutting the door behind him.

Vera shook her head. "He's got to make a decision," was all she said.

Rouleau chose not to respond since Heath's affair with Laney Masterson was none of his business. The fact that Laney was Vera's cousin gave her a stake in the outcome and maybe the right to an opinion. "See you later, Vera. I'll be in my office if needed."

He spent the afternoon reviewing the forensics and reports on the Delaney file. Nothing new popped out at him except the feeling that Ivo Delaney was looking more and more guilty. He also confirmed to himself that they didn't have enough evidence to charge him. He pondered a strategy for getting Delaney to confess. Gundersund had said that Delaney seemed to connect with Kala Stonechild. Perhaps this could be exploited. His door was open and he looked into the outer office. Gundersund and Stonechild were busy at their desks. Woodhouse and Bennett had come and gone. He looked at his watch. Going on five and time to call it a day. As he watched, Gundersund grabbed his jacket and headed for the door. Stonechild stood and put on her jacket too but instead of heading for the door, she crossed the floor to his office.

"Do you have a minute, sir?"

"Of course. Come and take a seat."

"This won't take long." She settled herself in the chair across from him. "I just got a call from a possible source in Montreal. She's a waitress at Chez Louis. I think it's one of the older ones who was watching me quite closely when we were there. Anyhow, she didn't want to give her name or talk on the phone. Her English and my French aren't great. I convinced her to meet me in Ottawa tomorrow around ten and was hoping you could go with me, you know, to help with the translation."

"Seems like a long way to go for dubious information."

"I know, but she said that she had something we might find of interest."

Rouleau thought it over. He knew from past cases that Stonechild had good instincts. He also knew that she'd go her own way if she believed she was onto something no matter what he said. Gundersund had to hang around for a court call back. Bennett's French was weak, and Woodhouse ... well, Woodhouse would balk at a trip to Ottawa and make Stonechild's life miserable.

"I guess we could take a run in the morning. Where are you meeting her?"

"She's driving so we agreed to meet in the east end at St. Laurent shopping centre at the A&W in the food court. She said that she may as well make it a shopping trip while she's there. I could pick you up around seven thirty."

"Okay. I'll meet you out front of my building at seven thirty."

"Thank you, sir."

He watched her leave while he thought about a trip to Ottawa. He could use the time to strategize with her about how to approach Ivo Delaney with the objective of getting him to confide in her. Besides being a chance to brainstorm with Stonechild and plan next steps, a short road trip would get him out of the office for a few hours and feel part of a spring day. It seemed like a win-win.

Dawn was sitting outside on the bottom step of the deck in her backyard when Gundersund rounded the corner. She held a ball in her hand that she threw across the expanse of lawn. Minny and Taiku chased each other across the yard and Taiku let Minny get to it first. As they bounded back toward Dawn, Taiku spotted Gundersund and both dogs changed course to greet him. He gave them each a good rub on their sides with both hands before joining Dawn on the step.

"Hey," he said, sitting down.

"Hey," she replied. She took the ball from Minny's mouth and the dogs cavorted around the lawn in front of her waiting for another throw.

He tried to read her mood but could not. Her hair hung in two long braids but her bangs were long enough to hide her eyes as she hunched over and bounced the ball on the flagstone under her feet.

"Kala said to tell you that she's not far behind me. She had to talk to Rouleau for a few minutes."

"Okay."

"How was school today?"

She turned and looked sideways at him. "Have you been talking to Kala?"

He held up a hand. "Guilty as charged. She's worried about you."

"I can handle it."

"But the question is, handle what?"

"Handle the girls in my class." She heaved the ball across the lawn and the dogs galloped after it.

"Is there anything Kala or I can do to help?"

"No."

Gundersund tried to think of a new approach but he was coming up empty. "We're here, you know. You don't have to go through this alone."

"I know."

"You're getting good at the short answers." He smiled at her. "If you need to talk and figure out how to handle these girls, I'm here for you."

"Good to know." She smiled back at him. "Really, everything is okay."

"So you say."

They watched the dogs racing toward them. Taiku had the ball this time and dropped it at Dawn's feet. She picked it up and bounced it on the flagstone while the dogs waited. This time she stood and threw it toward the end of the property.

"You have a good arm."

She looked down at him. "I play baseball at

school during recess." She looked ready to say something else but stopped. She looked toward the side of the house. "I hear Kala's truck."

He looked in the same direction. The sound of an engine and tires on the pavement abruptly stopped. "Well, I'm going to take Minny and head home. Thanks again for taking care of her after school."

"I like doing it."

He waited until Stonechild walked around the corner and had her moment being greeted by the dogs. She kept walking toward them and looked at Gundersund with a question in her eyes. He shook his head ever so slightly. They'd agreed that he'd come ahead to see if Dawn would open up to him.

"Stay for supper, Gundersund?" she asked without giving anything away.

"No, I have to head home, but thanks."

"Another time. Rouleau and I are heading to Ottawa first thing to interview a waitress from Chez Louis, so I won't be in the station until one or so."

"I've been called back to court so might not see you at all tomorrow." He whistled for Minny and started toward the side of the house. He would have liked to stay but Fiona was coming by on his request. He wanted to start the paperwork to make their separation official and knew it wasn't going to be an easy discussion. But it was a discussion they needed to have.

She was late … again.

Piss me off, Woodhouse thought. He checked his phone again for messages before signalling to the barmaid for another rum and Coke. For the third time, he swivelled his head to look around the Holiday Inn bar. Nobody he knew had entered since his last check, for which he gave thanks. He reminded himself that he'd picked this meeting place precisely because nobody from work ever came here.

Did she think he had all night to hang around waiting for her to show?

Seconds after his drink arrived, she walked in the door looking as unkempt as usual. Her copper hair was half in and half out of a ponytail and her blue cotton shirt looked as wrinkled as the linen blazer that topped it. She dropped her oversized straw bag onto a vacant chair and sat down in the one opposite him.

"Sorry I'm late." Her breath came out in a rush. "I was interviewing someone and couldn't find a way to end it."

"No problem. It's not like I haven't put in a long enough day already."

The waitress appeared with a glass of clear liquid with lemon wedged onto the top and set it in front of Marci Stokes, who looked steadily at Woodhouse until the waitress left.

"I took the liberty," he said. "It's not like you've ever ordered anything but vodka soda."

"Am I that easy to predict?" She picked up the glass and tipped it in his direction. "Cheers."

"Yeah, cheers." He didn't bother to drink.

She settled in like a little bird worming into a nest. Well, maybe a big bird. She wasn't exactly a fragile-looking woman. He leaned back in his chair and looked up at the television over the bar. They had it locked on the golf channel. He wasn't a big fan of golf. Too slow and boring. Old men walking around a big lawn hitting a ball at a flag. What was the excitement in that?

Marci rattled the ice cubes in her glass and set it down. "So why have you brought me here when I could be back in my hotel catching up on my sleep?"

"I was hoping you had something for me tonight."

"Nope. My day has been uninformative at best."

"I hear through the grapevine that you missed Heath's press conference. Where were you?"

"Do you seriously think I'm going to account for my whereabouts to you, Officer Woodhouse?"

She'd put enough emphasis on his name so that he couldn't miss the disrespect. Woodhouse smiled. He liked sparring with her since he knew that he held the trump cards. His old partner Ed Chalmers had taught him well. He'd been the master at manipulating the media. "Feed them enough so that they think you're onside, all the while you're getting information out of them. That's how you get ahead in this world," Chalmers liked to say. Well, he'd fed Stokes enough about the case to keep her onside and now it was time to use her. He slid a folded paper across the table. "Have a look at that," he said.

She picked it up with one hand and flipped it

open. He watched her eyes skim across the article before moving back up the page to stare at the photo. "Is this who I think it is?"

"Yeah. Kala Stonechild. Not a very pretty sight, is she?"

Marci cocked her head to one side and looked at him. "Let me get this straight. One of your own was a homeless drunk before she joined the force. I say before because of the date on this article and how young she looks. Why are you sharing this with me?"

"Oh, I think you know. Someone like Stonechild isn't good for policing. For one, she could be blackmailed by people she consorted with in the past. Who knows what criminal activities she got up to in those years? She showed a lack of character and judgment. You don't ever outgrow those traits. The public has a right to be informed who's taking care of their law and order."

"Does Rouleau know about this?"

"My guess is no. I happened to have a look at Stonechild's resume and she didn't have anything on it about this period of her life. She never talks about herself. Now I know why."

"I thought resumes were protected."

"They are. But where there's a will ..."

Marci swallowed the last of her drink and picked up her bag. She tucked the article into it. "Okay. Let me sit on this for a bit. I have to work an angle. I'm guessing you don't want anybody to know where this came from."

"Not if we're going to keep doing business."

"Yeah, understood. Well, thanks for the drink. I'll be in touch."

"And next time, maybe I'll have something bigger for you about the Delaney case."

She saluted him with her fingertips. "I'll be waiting."

After she left, he called the waitress over and got her to change the channel to wrestling. He asked for a menu and ordered another rum and Coke. He might as well settle in for a while since he had nowhere to be and no food in the fridge. Call this a little celebration for himself for getting Stonechild removed from the force in the not too distant future. He deserved a steak dinner for all his dogged legwork tracking down her past. Rouleau would never know how Stonechild's misspent youth came to light, but he'd be happy to have her gone once he found out how she'd hidden the worst of her past from him — of this, Woodhouse was certain.

Catherine Lockhart sighed as she asked Sammy for the fourth time to get into bed. He'd been bouncing off the walls all day, ever since she'd punished him for going outside without her permission the evening before. Punishment had amounted to no television for the afternoon. In hindsight, the punishment hurt her more than it did him. Normally, he watched two half hour shows while she made supper. Tonight he raced around the living room like a cat on crack.

"Sammy, don't make me ask you one more time," she said to her son, who was sprawled out on the floor playing with a Lego car. "Get into your bed ... NOW."

"Alright. Alright. You don't have to yell!"

He got up slowly and spun around a few times before finally climbing into bed, but he didn't lay down. He got onto his feet and jumped up and down all the while grinning like a monkey. She reached up her hands and caught him around the waist until he stopped bouncing. He dropped to his knees and she pushed him into a prone position and pulled the covers up over him snugly. She lowered herself into a sitting position on the edge of the bed.

"What has gotten into you tonight?"

"Nothing. Will you read me a story?"

He looked up at her with the pleading look that always won her over. She waffled while she thought about the work waiting for her downstairs. If she didn't finish the revisions that the magazine editor had requested this morning for end of day, the article wouldn't make the publication deadline. "I can't, but after tonight I promise we'll spend some time together doing whatever you want. I promise." She reached across him to turn out the bedside light.

"I want the light on."

"You always sleep with it off."

"I want it on."

"Well, if you're sure." She straightened and looked down at him. She could always come up and turn the lamp off when he was asleep. He was looking around the room as if searching for something.

"What is it?" she asked.

His eyes landed on her. "Will you stay for a bit?"

"Just for a bit. Close your eyes."

"Okay."

He reached over and held onto her hand. She couldn't remember the last time he'd done that. She watched him longer than she should, reluctant to break this unexpected physical bond with her son who was growing up much too fast for her liking. Soon, he'd be spending all his free time out of the house with his friends and moments like these would be only fond remembrances. His breathing started to slow and his hand relaxed in hers. She lifted his hand and gently laid it on top of the bedspread. As she did, his eyes popped open and he looked up at her with no recognition in his eyes.

"The man," he said. He lifted an arm and pointed past her.

Startled, Catherine turned to look in the direction of his finger, but there was no man in the open doorway. She turned back and rested a hand on the blanket covering his chest. She could feel his heart beating through the covers.

"There's nobody there. Go to sleep now." The panic in his eyes disturbed her and she was happy when he closed them again. He mumbled something else that she couldn't hear and she leaned closer.

"Violet," he said. "I saw him."

And then he rolled onto his side facing away from her. Catherine sat a moment longer trying to still her own racing heart. Sammy had been dreaming in the space between waking and sleeping. She knew that, but should she read any significance into his words? Would he remember in the morning?

When she was certain that he was fast asleep, she pushed herself from the bed and stood. She looked over at the lamp but decided it wouldn't hurt to leave the light burning. He might wake up and she didn't want him frightened. Violet's disappearance must be affecting him more than he'd let on.

She crossed to the window and reached up a hand to lower the blind. As she did, she looked out into the backyard. A wind had come up since supper and dark shadows swayed with the movement of the tree branches. She pressed her face against the glass and stared toward her garden at the back of the property. The shadows were thicker and she imagined someone crouched near the raspberry bushes. She squinted and looked again. Of course, nobody was there. Why would there be? Her gaze travelled back to the shed and the circle of brightness from the backdoor light before she stepped to the side and pulled down the blind with a snap.

Enough of this fanciful nonsense, she told herself. *Those edits aren't going to correct themselves while you stand here scaring the bejesus out of yourself.* She started toward the stairs pulling a cigarette out of the pack crushed into the pocket of her sweater. She'd have just one to calm her nerves even though she'd promised herself not to smoke after supper. Just one cigarette wouldn't be a terrible crime. She'd smoke it before she settled into her computer and got to work — right after she double checked that all the doors and windows were locked up tight.

CHAPTER TWENTY-ONE

The wind nearly tore the handle out of his hand as Rouleau pulled the truck door open. He managed to tuck himself inside the cab and yanked the door shut with both hands. He turned to look at Stonechild.

"Feels like a hurricane out there."

"And the rain should start late in the afternoon. What do you say we just head south until we hit ocean?"

"Don't tempt me."

She put the truck into gear and they were soon on the 401 heading toward Brockville. The truck was buffeted by the wind but not enough to make driving difficult. Low grey clouds scudded across their line of vision through the front windshield. The clouds were thicker on the eastern horizon, a sign of what was headed their way.

Stonechild pulled off at Brockville for coffee, after which they headed north on the 416 a little farther on. She was making good time, slightly over the speed limit but not enough to get pulled over. Their conversation was light and sporadic, each seemingly content to ease into the morning. When they passed the exit to North Grenville, Rouleau brought the conversation around to the investigation.

"What are your thoughts now on Ivo Delaney?"

Stonechild glanced at him before looking back at the road. "Not sure. He's unstable by all accounts. He might have cracked when he found out Adele had kept such a big secret from him."

Rouleau couldn't tell from her face and flat voice whether or not she believed her own assessment. "I need you to take another stab at getting close to him. We haven't any real physical evidence, although maybe enough circumstantial to try to get prosecution to take it on."

"Okay. Although he's denied everything so far. I suppose that's to be expected."

"The majority of people who kill will deny it to high heaven. I can't recall too many who admit killing someone unless cornered by evidence, and even then …" He sipped coffee through the plastic lid. The coffee was too hot and bitter but a familiar part of highway travel. "Did you get a name for the waitress we're meeting?"

"She called herself Émilie. It may or may not be her real name. She wanted to make sure nobody found out she was speaking to us."

"Odd."

Stonechild glanced at him again. "Doesn't fit with Delaney killing Adele and Violet. Why would this waitress go out on a limb to tell us anything?"

"I guess we'll soon find out."

St. Laurent shopping centre was at the far end of the city. Traffic was heavier the closer they got to the city core. The highway passed over the downtown and Rouleau could see the famous canal off to the left where tourists came from all over the world to skate. Frances had dragged him out on more than one wintery evening. She'd skated the canal's length at least once every year.

"Penny for your thoughts, sir?" Stonechild had turned her head to look at him with her unfathomable black eyes.

"Just thinking how simple life feels in Kingston. Not near this much traffic."

The St. Laurent Centre's concrete parking lot was filled with cars even this early in the morning. Stonechild drove slowly on the first level until she found a space. She backed in and turned off the engine.

She rested her hands on the steering wheel for a moment. "Let's hope Émilie shows."

"Did you get the feeling she might not?"

"She seemed skittish, although maybe it was just my poor French." Stonechild turned her head sideways and smiled at him before opening her door.

They took the escalator to the third floor and located the A&W in the food court directly in front of the Hudson's Bay store. Predominantly mothers and kids were seated with drinks and fries in front of them, although not all of the tables were filled. Stonechild took a walk around the perimeter but reported to Rouleau that she didn't see the waitress.

"May as well get something to eat," Rouleau said. "What would you like?"

"A coffee and a Teen Burger would be great."

"Coming right up. Sit somewhere conspicuous."

He placed their order and joined her at the table a few minutes later. Still no sign of the waitress. They ate quickly, as if they'd been starved and this was their last meal. Stonechild matched him bite for bite. He swallowed the last of his coffee before loading the tray with their wrappers. "I'll get rid of this."

"I'll keep an eye out for her."

He crossed over to the counter and dumped the trash into the can and then slid the tray onto the counter. He turned in time to see a platinum blond woman sit down in the seat across from Stonechild. She was wearing a barely buttoned green blouse with a silk scarf tied loosely around her neck. From his vantage point she looked late thirties. She was attractive but as he approached he could see that her expertly applied makeup helped hide flaws — lines around her mouth and pale blue eyes, and acne scars on her cheeks and forehead.

He sat down next to Stonechild and extended his hand. In French he said, "Hello, my name is Jacques Rouleau and I work with Officer Stonechild. How are you?"

Their conversation continued for a while in French while Stonechild sat, in the dark as to what was being said.

Rouleau turned toward Stonechild. "Did you get that?"

"You're going to need to translate."

"Right. She has something to tell us that she thinks will be of interest."

He spoke with Émilie at length. Her French was quick, her accent from the Gaspé region as far as he could discern. When she finished answering his questions, he looked directly at Stonechild who'd been listening closely without appearing to comprehend much. Now it was Émilie's turn to watch silently.

"How much of that did you understand?"

"She lost me after *je suis*."

"What she just told me is incredible. If we are to believe Émilie, Adele snatched Violet as a newborn from a home fostering the kids whose single mothers are in prison. There was never any adoption."

"I can't recall a story like this in the news. It would have been what, three to four years ago? Surely, this story would have made the national papers."

Rouleau asked Émilie more questions and she responded with what seemed like a reasonable explanation.

"She says that the abduction made the Quebec papers for a few weeks but quickly died away. There wasn't a great deal of interest since the mom was in prison for a violent crime. She was in for selling drugs and beating up a teenager who tried to take off without paying. She hurt him quite badly. Not much public sympathy for her. The file was never closed but it was felt that the father had taken Violet.

The mother wasn't in a position to put up much of a fuss."

"Lovely. And who's the father?"

"Well, this is where it gets really interesting. The mother, whose name is Cécile Simon, worked at one of the bars where Adele used to strip. They knew each other, but not well. Cécile was apparently sleeping with the older Manteau brother — Benoit. She was considered his property."

Émilie cut in and spoke in her rapid-fire French to Rouleau. He asked her a few questions before translating for Stonechild. "Émilie says that Etienne and Philippe let you find Lana Morris and prompted her ahead of your visit as to what to tell you. Lana barely knew Adele Dufour. Émilie isn't certain why they misled you but said that these are secretive, tough men. She says that she is actually the one who was closest to Adele. Etienne warned Émilie not to speak with you before your visit to Chez Louis with Bennett."

Stonechild thought for a moment before she asked, "Did Émilie know that Adele had taken the baby?"

"She says that she suspected but was never completely certain until she read in the paper that Adele had a three-year-old daughter. Adele quit her job a few weeks before the baby was snatched and told Émilie that she was heading to her hometown. She never revealed where that was. She kept her private life private and made up stories about her childhood, depending on the day. The cousins tried to track Adele down at one point but she'd disappeared without a trace. Émilie says that the cousins tried to get her to tell them where Adele came from, but Émilie honestly didn't know. It seems that she and Adele agreed when they first became friends that they would not share anything about their pasts with anyone at work. You might say that Adele set up her own disappearance from the very start."

"Perhaps the cousins found her nonetheless."

"Perhaps, but there's one final twist."

"What's that?"

"Cécile Simon was released from Joliette prison over a year ago. She stayed with a stripper acquaintance of Émilie's in Montreal for a few months after she was released. Cécile told this woman that she had a good idea who'd taken her kid and she was going to make them pay."

"Where's Cécile now?"

Rouleau ran a hand across his bald pate. "Émilie hasn't kept in touch with her." Rouleau gave Stonechild a sideways smile that felt like a grimace. "Looks like the suspect pool just widened. I'll give Prevost a call and let him know that you'll be making another visit to Montreal."

Émilie signalled that she was leaving. She took a look around the food court, as if to assure herself that nobody had followed her.

Stonechild said, "Ask her if the women were expected to turn tricks with customers."

Rouleau spoke quickly in French and Émilie scowled. She replied in a few words before standing and backing away from the table. They both watched her strut away from them on her stiletto heels, her only objective appearing to put distance between herself and them.

"She said she wasn't going to talk about work. She'd said enough."

"She's picked a tough life," Stonechild said. Rouleau was surprised by the sadness in her voice.

"She appears to have chosen it of her own free will."

"Yeah. We'd like to think so."

"I'll just make these phone calls. Prevost should be able to get in touch with Cécile Simon's parole officer."

"And I'm going to get another burger. Want one?"

"Thanks, I'm good."

Michel Prevost's phone went directly to voice mail. Rouleau left a message to call him as soon as possible. He then checked in with Gundersund.

"Case wraps up today and I'll be released from testifying again." Gundersund sounded tired. "Sure, I can make the trip to Montreal tomorrow."

Rouleau tucked his phone back into his pocket and looked across at Stonechild. She was fully engrossed in eating her second burger. He smiled at her enjoyment whenever she tucked into a meal. She must have felt his eyes on her because she ran her tongue across her top lip and looked over at him. She tilted her head. "Problem?"

"No, just can't reach Prevost. I think we can head back to Kingston and you and Gundersund can head to Montreal tomorrow once Prevost has a chance to track down Cécile Simon."

"Is he done with the court case?"

"He just told me that the case ends this afternoon."

"If he'd rather I can always take Bennett."

"I'll run the idea past him."

They were back in the truck and pulling onto the Queensway when Stonechild cleared her throat. She kept her eyes on the road and her voice soft. "We have time."

Rouleau took a second to understand what she was talking about. "You've spoken to my father." He also kept his eyes straight ahead, not trusting himself to look at her.

"He's waiting for us at the hospice." She merged the truck into the three lanes of traffic. "Your call."

Rouleau leaned his head back against the head-rest. The clouds were now so low and black that he couldn't understand why it wasn't raining. Almost as if his thoughts had been heard by the universe, several large raindrops splattered against the windshield. Rouleau closed his eyes and saw Frances's face. She was looking up at him from the crook of his arm. They were stretched out on the couch and one of her hands rested on his chest. Her eyes were bright and happy. Her lips were lifted in the sideways smile that made his heart leap.

"Okay," he said finally. He blinked away the image but the feeling of release remained. The rain was streaking down the window with increasing intensity and Stonechild turned on the wipers. "It's time."

CHAPTER TWENTY-TWO

Gordon met Rouleau and Stonechild outside the door to Frances's room. Rouleau extended his hand and Gordon shook it firmly. Rouleau wasn't surprised by the change in his ex-wife's new husband. He expected that he had much the same pale look of quiet desperation and grief. Rouleau introduced Stonechild to Gordon and they exchanged handshakes.

"Frances is in and out of consciousness now." Gordon's voice trembled but his eyes didn't waver. "I was just going for coffee so would appreciate if you sat with her for a while. I might even take this opportunity to get some lunch."

"Of course. Take all the time you need."

"Your father was by earlier. He should be back in an hour or so. Frances's sister and mom have gone for lunch."

Rouleau looked at Stonechild. "You could go shopping and come back for me later if you like."

"I might go for a walk." Her eyes gave nothing away but he took strength from them nonetheless.

Gordon reached out and squeezed Rouleau's arm before he set off down the hall.

Rouleau entered the room alone. The air was warm and still, muted light from the window the only illumination. Bouquets of flowers filled every available surface, the smell not unpleasing. His eyes swept the room until they found Frances lying in the middle of a single hospital bed, her hands folded above the sheets. Her breathing was shallow and raspy, but she was breathing on her own. He was relieved not to see tubes and machines hooked up to her. She wouldn't have wanted that. He somehow crossed the floor and stood looking down at her face, so porcelain white that he was afraid to touch her. He sank into the chair at the head of the bed, never taking his eyes from her. His face was level with hers.

"I'm here, Franny." He reached through the bar that was there to keep her from falling out of bed and rested his hand on top of both of hers. He willed her to wake up but her eyes stayed closed. "I wanted to come earlier, but you know how hard it is to … say goodbye to you, my love." He sat for a while watching her breathe in and out. Her hair was cropped even shorter than the last time he'd seen her and had gone almost completely grey. He shifted in his seat and pulled out a thin paperback from the inside pocket of his jacket with his free hand. "I kept that T.S. Eliot book you liked so much and have been carrying it around … close to my heart. I don't read aloud as well as you but thought you might like to hear those poems you used to read to me after supper."

He managed to get the book opened to "The Love Song of J. Alfred Prufrock." He held the book so that he could see her face as he read. He thought he saw her lips part but he couldn't be sure. "Let us go, then, you and I. When the evening is spread out against the sky." He stopped and willed the moisture to leave his eyes. He continued on, surprised at how the words were imprinted in his memory. He could say them without reading. How many nights had he taken comfort from these poems after she'd left him? "For I have known them all already, known them all — Have known the evenings, mornings, afternoons. I have measured out my life with coffee spoons."

He glanced at her face again. Her eyes were open and watching him, the smile on her lips for real now. He stood and leaned closer, kissing her forehead.

"I knew you'd come." Her voice was papery thin.

"Always."

He found the ice chips and held her head while she captured some in her mouth. "Read ... more," she said.

He settled in, finished the first poem, and flipped to her favourite. "April is the cruellest month, breeding Lilacs out of the dead land, mixing Memory and desire ..." He stopped reading, lowered the book to his lap.

"I love you, Franny. Never stopped. I wanted you to know."

She smiled up at him. Such love and kindness in her gaze, he felt the connection to her that he thought he'd lost when she'd told him it was over. What he'd felt for her had never been over.

"Stay with me," she said. She reached out her hand to his. Her words were slow and laboured. "I'll know you're ... here." Her eyes fluttered closed.

"I'm not going anywhere," he said. For he knew that she was at peace and would soon give in to the cancer that had destroyed her body. The reason he'd held back from coming might have been selfish but he'd wanted her on this earth just a few more days. He'd known that she wouldn't give in until she'd seen him one last time.

But now, it was time he let her go.

It was still early when Kala reached the Division turnoff into Kingston. She'd made the trip back alone after Rouleau said that he'd be spending the night with his father in Ottawa. Henri Rouleau had thanked her for her small role in bringing his son to the hospice. Kala knew that he would have faced the death of his ex wife in his own time. She hoped that this way would bring Rouleau closure, even if seeing her was the more difficult route.

She drove past the station and carried on toward Princess Street. The rain had tapered off just past Merrickville but was still spitting down, making the roads shiny and slick. If the rain didn't stop soon, they'd be into summer before they'd have a chance of finding Violet Delaney's small body. Cutting west through the university, she reached Dawn's school a few minutes before class ended for the day. She circled the block and found a parking spot a short distance from the main entrance. She got out and walked toward the front.

Dawn's bus driver was standing on the sidewalk talking to two other drivers. He recognized Kala and she let him know that she'd be driving Dawn home. She stepped back so as not to intrude on his last minutes of peace before the kids came pouring out of the school.

At exactly five after four, the front doors swung open and the grade seven and eight kids started pouring out. The noise level rose from zero to ten, shrieks and laughter punctuating the garble of voices. Kala watched closely for Dawn but she was one of the last, trailing behind a group of girls, head down, knapsack swung over one shoulder. Kala's heart caught at the sight of her aloneness in the crowd of boisterous adolescents. She called out.

"Dawn! Over here."

Dawn's neck snapped up and her eyes brightened when she saw Kala standing next to the fence. She started running toward her, jacket flapping and rain glistening on her face.

"I thought you were in Ottawa."

"I got back early. I was hoping you and I could run some errands on the way home. I've let the bus driver know you're with me."

"What about Taiku and Minny?"

"They'll be fine for another hour or so."

They walked past the bus and Kala noticed Dawn glance over at the group of girls standing just outside the door. The four girls had long hair, tight jeans, and striped shirts. The tallest one had blond hair and a pretty face. They stared at Dawn as she walked by before the tall one said something and laughter erupted.

"Are those the girls?"

"Girls?"

"The ones giving you trouble."

"Nobody's giving me trouble, Kala."

Kala looked at her but let the moment pass.

She drove back downtown and parked one street over from Princess. Dawn had shared little about her day but Kala hadn't pressed. When they were on the sidewalk, Dawn looked confused. She asked, "Are we getting groceries?"

"No. I need a new pair of jeans and thought you could use some too."

Dawn walked silently beside her. They reached the entrance to the Gap. "I hear this store has a good selection." Kala held the door open.

Dawn looked inside but hesitated. "Are you sure we can afford this?"

You're breaking my heart. "We can afford this."

They entered the store and Kala looked for a young salesperson to help them. She lucked out with a cheerful eighteen-year-old girl named Laura who took Dawn under her wing. Before long, Dawn had tried on several pairs of jeans and tops, her face shining as Kala and Laura wrapped her in compliments. Laura chatted to her like best friends and their laughter was like spring sunshine to Kala's ears.

When Dawn finally emerged from the dressing room in her own well-worn clothes, Kala was finalizing the sale. Dawn walked over to stand next to her.

"Aren't you trying on clothes too, Kala?"

"Not today." Kala smiled at her and handed over two bags. "You looked so good in all the jeans that I bought a few pairs and the tops to go with them."

"You didn't need to do that."

"It was my pleasure."

They walked back to the truck, taking their time and looking in the store windows. Dawn became more and more quiet as they walked. When they reached the truck, Kala unlocked Dawn's door first and slid the parcels inside on the floor. Dawn clambered in behind them and Kala walked around the back of the truck to the driver's side. She climbed in, put on her seatbelt, and put the truck into gear. As she made a right shoulder check and put on her turn signal to merge into traffic, Dawn turned her face toward the side window. She wasn't quick enough though for Kala to miss the tears on her cheeks. Kala reached over and touched Dawn's shoulder.

"Is everything okay? What is it?"

Dawn took a moment to answer. Her voice came out a strangled wail. "I don't know." She rested her forehead against the glass, keeping her body turned away from Kala.

Kala waited a moment but when Dawn didn't make any move toward her, she took her hand away and did a final shoulder check before easing the truck out of the parking spot and into traffic. She'd give Dawn the space she needed and hoped patience would win out. She could think of no other way.

The ride home was a silent one. They were almost at the turnoff to Old Front Road when Dawn finally rolled her body back around and rested her head against the back of the seat. She looked straight ahead and said, "Thank you, Aunt Kala."

Aunt. Kala darted a glance at her. "You don't need to thank me. I just wish I knew how to make everything better." She'd told Dawn when she took her in that she considered her family and Dawn had made it official with one word. The tightening in Kala's chest eased a little.

Dawn turned her face toward Kala. Her eyes were hard and dry. The small crack into her pain had been closed off with the finality of a door slamming. When she spoke, her voice was light and eager, completely at odds with what had just happened. "Do you think we should stop to get Minny on our way by? I'll bet she misses her walk with Taiku." She stared at Kala as if nothing else was on her mind, her eyes daring Kala to contradict her.

It felt like time had fallen away and Kala was looking in a mirror.

You've taken on the role of keeping the peace. You've learned how to pretend that everything is okay when your world is falling to pieces around you. You've learned to hide your fear.

She tried to keep the sadness from her voice, tried to match Dawn's lightness. "Only if Gundersund's car isn't in the driveway."

"Okay."

Kala glanced once more at her niece before turning onto the side road. She was thankful in a way that Dawn had pulled back because she was more comfortable with silence. Defences and walls kept a lot of nasty things at bay, including pity, something she hated more than life itself. She'd never put any stock in talking through feelings or blaming her childhood for current problems. Rehashing what happened from every pathetic angle seemed like a big wallowing waste of time. But now she had someone other than herself to consider. For the first time, she could admit that stoic denial might not be working. Her aversion to introspection was going to have to change if she and Dawn stood a chance.

She was finally ready to subject herself to Dr. Lyman if it meant getting them through this together.

CHAPTER TWENTY-THREE

They met Michel Prevost in the lobby of the tiered red-brick office building on René-Lévesque Boulevard a few minutes after ten the next morning. It was just over three hours from Kingston to Montreal so it had meant a six-thirty start. The twelve-storey office complex was south and west of Chinatown and a few blocks from the Old Port of Montreal. The lower level contained businesses and a daycare, and hooked onto the Hyatt hotel. A fountain in the centre of the busy lobby featured a circle of spouting water under a high ceiling of purple and yellow glass blocks.

When Prevost shook hands with Gundersund, Kala saw that they were practically the same height, but there the physical resemblance ended. Prevost carried more weight than Gundersund, and while Gundersund had shaggy blond hair and blue eyes, Prevost's black curls and dark features spoke to Kala of a Mediterranean heritage. Both men had watchful eyes and relaxed body language that Kala knew could be deceptive for those who equated extroverted behaviour with competence. She'd take either man backing her up in a dicey situation anytime over flashier numbers.

Prevost spoke first. "Cécile Simon's parole officer works on the troisième, that is the third étage. She's expecting Cécile at eleven thirty and wants to speak with her before calling us in."

"Where should we wait?" Kala asked.

Prevost pointed to a coffee shop visible beyond a supporting column. "I will be getting a text when it is time for us to join them. Let us get some coffees."

They walked over and Prevost ordered in French. He paid before Gundersund and Kala could stop him. They each took a cup and added cream at the counter and then sat at a table near the entrance.

"Have you dug up anything further on Cécile?" Kala asked, sipping from the cup. As coffee went, this was bitter and strong. The cream hadn't diffused the muddy blackness by much.

Prevost nodded. He took a drink from his cup and grimaced. "Merde that's terrible. Must have been sitting all morning."

"Tastes okay to me." Gundersund shrugged.

"Gundersund always drains the pot at the station long after its best before." Kala grinned at him.

Prevost's eyes swung between the two of them. He seemed to confirm something to himself because he gave Gundersund a small smile before addressing Kala's question. "It is like this. Cécile Simon is a woman with violence never far from the surface. She can be charming one minute but ferocious the next if someone crosses her. She had a corner of the drug trade in an east end neighbourhood before she was busted. The Manteau brothers were tight with her. We hear that one of them is father of her missing child. Word on the street is that it is Benoit, the one in prison."

Kala said, "So she's as tough a customer as the Manteaus."

"It would appear that way. In this case, two like-minded people were attracted to each other."

Gundersund set down his empty coffee cup and looked at Prevost. "Was Cécile's sentence linked to Benoit's in any way?"

"Not that we know. Cécile was busted for trafficking and assaulting a teen for not paying up. She got four years but was released last winter after serving half her sentence. The kid recovered and was scared to press charges, but we had witnesses to his beating. Benoit is in for murder. He ordered a hit on a rival gang member again over drug distribution. We found no evidence that the crimes are linked. Excuse me." Prevost pulled his phone out of his inside jacket pocket. He read the text message. "Bon, she is ready for us." He glared one more time into his coffee cup before pushing it away. "Another thing. Cécile grew up with an English father and speaks English if you want to take the lead in the questions."

"Great. We will." Kala stood. Gundersund and Prevost followed her out of the restaurant and they headed together to the elevators. People looked at them as they walked by, and Kala could imagine why. Gundersund and Prevost were big men and she walked between them as if they were her body guards.

The parole officer, Odette Landreville, met them outside the elevator. She shook hands with each of them before leading them through the security door and into a meeting room. Cécile Simon was standing next to one of the chairs, arms folded across her stomach. She looked at each of them as they walked in, her gaze lazily hovering over each of the men, but coming to rest on Kala. Her eyes were a light shade of blue, much like a washed out sky, and hard as marbles in a narrow, fox-like face. Kala had pictured a more imposing figure than the slender woman in front of her. Yet, she'd known helpless looking women who'd terrorized their children and spouses. Cécile's eyes were calculating, without kindness, and no doubt windows to her soul. Kala's sixth sense kicked in and a shiver started between her shoulder blades and rippled down her back.

"Let us all sit down." Odette extended a hand toward the table.

They arranged themselves so that Kala was directly across from Cécile with Gundersund and Prevost on either side of her. Odette took the seat closest to Cécile and sat back looking over the three officers, assessing them with experienced eyes. Her middle-aged face and grey hair told Kala that she'd been around this business a long time and was likely not far off retirement.

Kala spoke directly to Cécile. "Thank you for meeting us. As Mme. Landreville has told you, we're here about your daughter, and let me say that we are very sorry about the circumstances." She was going to say death but held back since they hadn't located the body.

Cécile looked at her, hands folded in her lap. She played with a silver ring on her middle finger as she spoke. "I only had her a few months before they put her in that home. When she was abducted, there was nothing I could do from inside." Her voice hardened. "Fucking Adele Dufour. My kid's name was Pauline, by the way, before Adele turned her into a fucking Violet."

"Did you know that Adele had taken your daughter?"

"How could I fucking know?"

Odette put a hand lightly on her wrist. "Cécile," she said calmly. "We know that you are angry, but these officers are trying to find out what happened to Pauline. Please show them courtesy."

Cécile stared defiantly at Kala before dropping her eyes. "Yeah," she said but her voice was sullen.

Kala continued. "We understand that you spoke of knowing who had your daughter and that you intended to get her back. Is this true?"

"I suspected everyone while I was in jail, but no, I didn't know for sure. I said that I was going to find out who had my daughter and get her back. I certainly didn't know where Adele had disappeared to four years ago or that she'd taken my daughter with her. She never talked about where she came from.

Cagey, wasn't she just? We danced together in a strip bar and sometimes the girls went out afterwards for drinks or something to eat. We weren't bosom buddies or anything."

"Did Adele know you when you were pregnant?"

"Yeah. Adele was around when the kid popped. She even covered a few of my shifts when I had to go to court. Adele had already quit by the time I was locked up. I thought she'd left town before Pauline was taken and didn't even think of Adele as a possible suspect for a long time. I mean, why would I? How could I possibly know that she'd hung around after quitting Chez Louis and stolen my two-month-old baby?"

Kala asked, "Who is your daughter's father?"

Cécile tilted her head to look sideways at Odette before answering. "Benoit Manteau. He didn't know where she'd been taken either." She swung her face back toward Kala. "Not that he could have done much to get Pauline back from his prison cell."

"How did Benoit feel about being a father?"

"He didn't get to meet her because he didn't make bail. His trial was going on at the same time as mine, oddly enough. I guess now we'll never have a chance to find out if he would have been a good father." Cécile pulled the silver ring off her finger and bounced it up and down in the palm of her hand. "What Adele did to me is unforgivable. She stole my baby, for Chrissakes. If I had killed her, and I'm not saying that I did because I didn't, it would have been with good reason. In a way, you could say that her husband gave her what the lying, two-faced bitch deserved."

"Have you been to Kingston since you were released from prison?"

Cécile darted a look toward Odette then back at Kala. "No."

"Do you keep in contact with Benoit or Etienne Manteau, or their cousin Philippe Lebeau?"

"I talk to Benoit by phone, maybe once a week. I check in with Etienne now and then to see if he's found out anything about who took my kid, but so far nothing. He'd been trying to find out since she disappeared. Philippe has tried to help but he heard nothing. The provincial police, the Sûreté, were fucking useless. I don't even think they gave a crap if they found my kid or not."

Odette interrupted the flow of questions. "Cécile is working to make a clean break from her old life. I'm encouraging her to avoid Chez Louis and the other bars where she worked, as well as the toxic people from that time. She has a job in a restaurant chain and our goal is for her to work up to assistant manager."

Cécile kept talking as if Odette hadn't spoken. "Even if I had known that Adele took Pauline and where they were living, why would I have killed my own daughter after waiting so long to find her? I'm the victim here. You can't turn it on me."

"The thought of Cécile Simon as a mother chills the blood." Gundersund swivelled on the bar stool to take another look around Chez Louis. He reminded Kala of a bird surveying the landscape for predators. Almost automatically, her eyes travelled around the room, following the same arc as his.

The lunchtime crowd hadn't arrived yet and the waitresses were gathered by the kitchen talking. Émilie didn't appear to be working today. An Asian woman in a skin-tight dress and stiletto heels with straight black hair to her waist was leaning on the other end of the bar, talking to Philippe Lebeau, who was serving drinks. He was watching them over the top of her head but so far hadn't approached. He and the woman laughed about something and she put her hand on his arm. Prevost had gone to the washroom so Kala was content to wait for his return before she called Lebeau over. ZZ Top was singing about a sharp-dressed man from the loudspeakers in the ceiling at a level just below painful.

"This bar is a throwback to my college days," said Gundersund. "Although the clientele in the Kingston bars that I frequented might have been a cut above this place."

"Well, unless the clientele was strippers, bikers, and drug dealers, you spent time in bars of a higher calibre than Chez Louis."

"Yeah, our fun was definitely more innocent." Gundersund moved in closer so that he didn't have to speak so loudly to be heard over the music. "How about you? Did you spend any time in bars when you were younger, Stonechild?"

His tone was playful, but Kala wasn't sure where he was coming from. "I might have visited a few," she said. "I learned that alcohol and me don't mix very well."

Gundersund nodded as if understanding, but how could he? He had no idea how low an addiction could bring you. He'd never woken up sick and desperate, the day's only goal to get enough money together to buy another bottle before the shakes got too bad.

He looked over his shoulder and asked, "So, do you know who the girl is talking to Lebeau?"

As Kala adjusted her position to have another look at Lebeau, Prevost manoeuvred into the space behind their bar stools. "That's Etienne Manteau's chum Li Li. They've been living together almost two years. The word on the street is that she's tamed him, but their relationship could have something to do with her father Wang Tao's construction business and his nasty reputation. We've been keeping an eye on Tao for some time but he's not a man easy to nail down."

Gundersund looked at Prevost. "This just keeps getting better."

Prevost smiled widely. "I can confirm that we're never bored."

Kala was watching Lebeau and Li Li when Etienne Manteau entered through the main door. He stopped and took in the scene before walking over to them. He slid an arm around Li Li's waist and kissed her on the mouth. Lebeau stepped back and got busy wiping down the counter.

"Time to have our little chat." Prevost left them and made his way over to Lebeau and Manteau. He gestured to a table close to the bar and Kala and Gundersund got off their stools to join them. Li Li, who took Lebeau's place behind the bar, bent down and lowered the music volume, for which Kala was thankful. She felt the beginnings of a headache throb in her left temple.

Lebeau and Manteau took seats next to each other, with Prevost facing them and Kala and Gundersund on either flank. Prevost led the questioning this time.

"We've come to learn that Adele Dufour made off with Cécile Simon's daughter while she was in prison and that the child was Benoit's. We believe this was the same child who drowned behind Adele's house outside Kingston. What do you have to tell us about this kidnapped baby, which you conveniently didn't mention on our last visit?"

Lebeau cracked the knuckles on his right hand, the tattoos on his biceps flexing. "Perhaps you should ask Cécile. It was her kid."

Prevost regarded Etienne. "Was your brother upset about his child going missing?"

Manteau ran a hand up and down across his beard as his brown eyes looked past Prevost to Li Li at the bar. He pulled his gaze back to Prevost before answering. "I doubt it. He never met the kid. I never met the kid."

Prevost kept speaking to Manteau. "So nobody knew that Adele had taken Violet — or Pauline, as Cécile named her?"

"We didn't have a clue until we heard about Adele's death and her missing kid. Let's say that puzzle pieces started slotting into place when we saw Adele's photo in the news and heard she had a daughter the same age as Pauline would be. It's not like Adele was pregnant when she conveniently disappeared at the same time as the kid went missing."

"You didn't think this worth mentioning when we last met?"

Manteau shrugged. "What good would it have done since we knew nothing before the two of them were murdered by her husband. It's too late for Cécile and Benoit to have their daughter back."

"You're certain that Cécile didn't know Adele had her daughter for the past three, almost four years?"

Lebeau answered, "Yeah. She would have said."

Kala unfolded her arms and leaned on the table. "Do you not find it odd, Etienne, that your brother would father a child and then not care about what happened to her?"

Etienne's eyes swung over to her. He gave a half-smile. "My brother is hardly in a place to care. He never met the kid and so had no feelings for her one way or the other."

"And he wouldn't have wanted to make Adele pay for taking his child?"

"Maybe if he'd known, but he didn't know. None of us knew." Etienne's stare slid back to Li Li at the bar.

"So you keep saying." Kala sat back and tried to still the pain now pulsing behind her eyes. "You and your brother don't have any other children?"

"No."

"Have you ever wanted children?"

Etienne and Lebeau both laughed at the same time. Etienne's face reddened above his beard. "I have a couple of kids with different girlfriends. I pay them money to keep the brats out of my hair."

Lebeau shrugged. "Maybe, but I can live without them."

He and Etienne laughed again. Kala wanted to take her fist to both their faces. She knew that she had to disengage or this would become personal.

Gundersund held up a hand and said, "I hear you grew up together in Gatineau. You appear close."

"My parents had a house and Philippe would come over to hang out," Etienne said, "especially in the summer because of our in-ground pool." He punched Lebeau on the arm. "He was like a stray dog that we got used to having around."

"Yeah, while my mother entertained." Lebeau exchanged a glance with Etienne.

Prevost asked more questions but Manteau and Lebeau gave nothing else away. Kala finally signalled to Prevost that they'd had enough. Gundersund said that he was going to the washroom before they hit the road. Traffic would be light and they'd be back in Kingston mid-afternoon. Prevost pulled out his cellphone while Etienne and Lebeau discussed the beer order.

Kala walked over to where Li Li was sitting on a bar stool, one long leg crossed over the other. She wanted to find out if Li Li gave off the same nasty vibe as Cécile Simon.

"Do you work here regularly?"

Li Li shook her head so that her silky hair swayed back and forth, giving off a coconut scent as she moved. Her eyes were perfectly almond-shaped and her lips upturned. Glossed in red, they formed a pouty rosebud. "I spell off Philippe behind the bar on his days off and lunchtimes now and then, depending on his shift. I also work in my father's office." Her accent was Chinese, maybe Mandarin, but Kala couldn't be certain. "Philippe and Etienne will be having the afternoon off now that the beer order has been sorted out. They like having someone they can trust in charge of the till."

"How'd you meet Etienne?"

"Through a dinner meeting with my father." She smiled with small white teeth. Her black eyes invited shared confidences. "Being in charge suits Etienne. Benoit was a prick in many ways."

Kala began to ask what Li Li meant, but Etienne was suddenly next to her and slung his arm across her shoulders. Kala thought about getting rid of him but Gundersund was waiting by the front door, and if they left now she'd have the afternoon to herself until Dawn got home from school. Her head was making her nauseous and she needed to get out of this place before she couldn't function.

"Here's my card, if you think of anything else." She handed it to Etienne but realized even as she did so that the gesture was futile. No way would anyone in the Manteau inner circle be telling tales. She was quite certain they hadn't said anything truthful since the police walked in the door. Lying was second nature for the whole lot of them. Etienne took the card and tucked it into his pocket. He saluted her and walked toward the front entrance with his arm around Li Li's waist.

"They make a pretty couple, don't they?" Lebeau said as he walked behind the bar to get his jacket. He stepped back from behind the counter and over to where Kala was sitting. "Have you ever thought about dancing on stage?" he asked, his eyes running up and down her body in a look both suggestive and slimy. "You have a nice body ... for a cop. You move pretty good too. Nice hip motion."

Kala laughed. "Yeah, thanks. I'll keep it in mind in case if I ever take complete leave of my senses."

CHAPTER TWENTY-FOUR

Fred Taylor punched through a call to Woodhouse just before seven o'clock. When Woodhouse put down the receiver he scratched his belly and called over to Bennett, who was researching something on his computer. They were staying late because they'd taken the morning off to sleep in and get some personal stuff done. Rouleau encouraged flexible hours when working a case or when they needed them. Woodhouse couldn't argue with his management style.

"We need to head over to the Delaneys."

Bennett looked up. "Something going on?"

"Not sure, but Ivo Delaney just called in that somebody broke into his house while he was out." Woodhouse reached for his jacket that he'd flung on the desk when he'd returned from lunch. "Sounds unlikely, but we should go have a look. Might be another opportunity to get him to confess."

Bennett made a few clicks on whatever it was he'd been working on while he grabbed his jacket with his free hand from the back of the chair. "I thought Rouleau had a uniform watching the Delaney house."

"He did up until yesterday."

"Maybe somebody was waiting for an opportunity to break in."

Woodhouse wanted to believe that Bennett was more than just a pretty *GQ* face but he was becoming less convinced the more time they spent together. He spoke slowly as if Bennett wouldn't grasp what he was saying otherwise. "Ivo Delaney is doing everything he can to divert us from the fact that he killed his family. Having us believe he got broken into is just a ploy. Any idiot can see that." Woodhouse wasn't thrilled with the look Bennett gave him, but the guy was going to have to learn to accept criticism. Either that or keep his mouth shut so the stupid ideas didn't escape.

Bennett took the wheel without asking, as he did now whenever they went out on a call. Woodhouse had driven Ed Chalmers around when he was the junior partner, so it was only fitting that Bennett did the same for him. He'd made it clear to Bennett from the get go that his role was the secondary one. Being chauffeured around also gave Woodhouse time to look at websites and check his email. He opened up the latest *Whig-Standard* online and looked for Marci Stokes's article on Stonechild, but nothing yet. What the hell was the hold up? He'd practically handed her the text and all she had to do was give it the right outraged spin.

He looked out the side window. The rain had stopped for the moment but water glistened off the grass and had pooled in lower-lying areas. The countryside had turned into a bog. Flooding was affecting half the county. Brown, cold, and soggy. Man, he hated this time of year.

Bennett finally broke his silence when he pulled into the Delaney driveway. "I think we should go easy, maybe not push Delaney too hard."

Woodhouse slapped the dashboard with the palm of his hand as if he'd just heard a whopper. "Next you'll be telling me not to ask any questions about the murders in case I hurt his *wittle feewings*." He shook his head. "You really have to grow a set, Bennett. We're detectives, not bloody social workers."

"I'm just saying, the guy doesn't look like he can take much more."

"Not our problem. Where's your compassion for his dead wife and three-year-old kid?"

"It's there. I think we should wait to see what Stonechild and Gundersund come up with before we go at Delaney again."

"Yeah, I'll keep *that* in mind."

They climbed the driveway, Bennett holding back a few steps. Woodhouse rapped on the door and moved back. After half a minute and no sound of anyone moving around inside, he pounded on the door again. He tried the door handle just to be sure, but the door was locked.

"I'll check around the back," said Bennett.

Woodhouse nodded and tried to peer in the square of glass covered by a curtain. Bennett was at the corner when Ivo finally opened the door. The sight of Delaney's sunken eyes and white face almost gave Woodhouse pause, but then he remembered his dead wife and child. Who would speak for them if not the police? This guy didn't deserve his sympathy.

"We're here about a break in. Can we come inside?"

Delaney stepped back, leaving the door open.

Woodhouse waved his arm at Bennett to hurry up before following him inside. Delaney was already disappearing into his office by the time Woodhouse started down the hallway after him with Bennett close on his heels. They crowded inside the office and Bennett let out a low whistle. Papers and books were tossed about, the desk and bookshelves overturned and laying on their sides on the floor. The desk drawers had been emptied of contents and tossed against the wall.

Delaney stood just inside the doorway with his shoulders hunched and hands hanging at his sides while they surveyed the damage. He was everything Woodhouse despised in a man — weak, snivelling, and soft to the point of effeminate. Top that with his murdered family and Woodhouse had no compunction about bringing him to breaking point if that's what it took to make him own up to what he'd done.

"Anything taken?" asked Bennett. He took his camera out and started snapping photos.

"It's hard to tell. My bedroom's been gone through too."

Woodhouse pointed to the door. "Well, let's go have a look."

They trooped upstairs and met with the same mess in his bedroom and bathroom. The sweet smell of talcum powder filled Woodhouse's nose and he saw that a container of it had been dumped on the tile next to the tub. Bennett moved around the debris, taking more photos while Woodhouse asked questions and took notes.

"Where were you when this alleged robbery was taking place?"

"I went into work in the afternoon to take my mind off Adele and Violet. I might as well have stayed home because I couldn't concentrate. When I got back after six-thirty, this is what I found."

"How'd they get in?"

"I'd left the back door unlocked. Whoever came in left it wide open."

"Now why would you go out and leave your door unlocked?"

"We never lock it during the day. I never thought of it."

Convenient. "What did you think when you first saw that you'd been broken into?"

"That someone from the media was in here looking for something."

A slippery thought nagged at the back of Woodhouse's brain. He let his mind go back over their visit. The ah ha moment wasn't long in coming.

"Your front door was locked just now. Why would you have locked it and not the back door?"

"I didn't want anybody else to get in. I locked both doors after I saw this mess."

Woodhouse let the silence lengthen, long enough for Delaney to start looking uncomfortable. He kept his voice on the accusatory side. "Have you remembered anything else about the day your family went missing?" *Like the fact you killed them?*

Delaney looked confused for a moment, then his eyes focused on Woodhouse's. "I have nothing more to tell."

"A guilty conscience is a tough thing to live with," Woodhouse said softly. "You might want to rethink your earlier statement and take responsibility for your part in their deaths."

Comprehension crept across Delaney's face. He dropped his eyes from Woodhouse and looked down at the floor, his big shoulders drooping like a sail made slack from retreating wind.

Bennett picked that moment to straighten from where he'd been crouching near the bed taking photos. "I think I'm done here." He motioned toward Delaney. "Perhaps you can call someone to help clean up this mess."

"I can manage."

"We'll be close by if you decide to ease your conscience." Woodhouse snapped his notepad shut. He put his mouth near Delaney's ear. "Adele and Violet deserve that the truth come out. Their spirits'll never rest easy until you tell us what really happened."

They left Delaney standing by the door to the bedroom. As they clattered down the stairs, Woodhouse in the lead, Bennett stopped partway and said, "Do you think we should call the neighbour woman to come over and give him a hand? He seems ... I don't know. Unwell."

Woodhouse stopped too and looked up at Bennett. *Are you friggin kidding me?* He turned back around and kept going down the stairs. He said over his shoulder, "Nah. He'll figure it out. He's a big boy."

CHAPTER TWENTY-FIVE

Gundersund gathered the team in Rouleau's office at eight the next morning. He'd brought doughnuts and Bennett had been the first in and made a pot of coffee. They stood around Rouleau's desk taking a few minutes to ingest sugar and caffeine before recapping the previous day's activities.

"So we're up to speed," said Gundersund after Woodhouse finished his report on their trip to the Delaney house in the early evening, for what he called a wild goose chase. Gundersund looked at Bennett who was studying Woodhouse with thinly disguised dislike. "Anything to add, Bennett?"

"No."

"Rouleau is staying in Ottawa for another day. I'm keeping him informed as much as he needs to be. At this point, we haven't much new to trouble him with. What are your plans for this morning, Stonechild?" He didn't ask her what was on her mind even though he wanted to. She'd been quiet since she came into the office. Distracted, he'd say.

"I'm going to see about getting us an interview with Benoit Manteau in Millhaven. I put in a call last night and am waiting to speak with somebody."

"It's prudent to close that loop," said Gundersund, more for Woodhouse's benefit than Stonechild's. He knew that Woodhouse wasn't a fan of Stonechild's investigative style. Woodhouse believed the obvious was always the answer and the rest deserved only a cursory look — his biggest failing as far as Gundersund could see. He added, "And I'll be updating Heath this morning. I can come with you to interview Benoit Manteau if you're able to set something up for this afternoon, Stonechild."

She nodded. "I have a personal appointment at four but am hoping Millhaven can accommodate us closer to lunchtime. If not, we'll have to try for tomorrow."

He looked at Woodhouse. "What have you got on today?"

"We'll be finishing up interviews with Delaney's coworkers while we wait for the final forensics to come in."

"Great. We're promised the report on his vehicle and Adele's by end of day. The team continues to go through the computers and laptops, so hopefully we'll get something from them today too."

Woodhouse nodded. "If it plays out like it should, we'll be waiting for your call to bring in Delaney. Is that it?"

Gundersund thought for a second. "I got nothing else. Just keep in touch if you find out anything the rest of us should know."

Woodhouse signalled to Bennett to follow him out.

Gundersund watched Stonechild smile at Bennett as if telling him to keep the faith. Bennett smiled back before trailing out after Woodhouse. Gundersund felt his stomach tighten at this exchange.

Stonechild held back after the others left. It took her a few seconds to start talking. "I have to go into Dawn's school again."

"Has something else happened?"

"I'm not sure, but the social worker wasn't as friendly as last time she called."

"How was Dawn when you got home yesterday?"

"Fine. She'd made supper and then went upstairs to do homework. A typical evening."

Gundersund wondered how typical it was for a thirteen-year-old to spend every evening in her room doing homework, but he kept silent.

Stonechild seemed to sense something in his mood because she added, "I'll be calling her counsellor to set up an appointment for later in the week now that our case appears to be settling down. I'm trying, Gundersund. I just don't know if I'm who she needs to get through this."

"Don't sell yourself short. I think you're just what she needs."

She smiled at him but the smile didn't linger. "Thanks for the vote of confidence. I really hope your faith in me isn't misplaced."

* * * *

Gundersund would later remember how close together the two calls came. Two devastating calls, one expected and the other a complete shock. The first came through on his cell — Rouleau telling him that Frances had passed away that morning and he'd be staying in Ottawa a few more days until after the funeral. Gundersund had never met Rouleau's ex-wife but he knew by the odd comment that Rouleau had let drop that he was still in love with her. Her death would be hard for him to get over.

Gundersund looked over at Stonechild. She was eating an apple while reading something on her computer screen. He was going to have to let her know, let the entire team know. He always felt like time hung suspended at these moments just before breaking bad news, knowing that the person he had to tell would never be quite the same. The desk phone rang before he could get up from his chair. He picked up the receiver, planning to make quick work of the call, knowing that Rouleau had called Vera before him and word would spread quickly through the station.

In response to his abrupt hello, the caller didn't say anything, but Gundersund could hear raspy breathing and a strangled sound that made him lean forward and cover his free ear in an effort to hear better.

"Are you in trouble? Can you tell me where you are?" Why hadn't this person called 911? From the corner of his eye, he saw Stonechild stand and start toward him, a look of concern on her face.

"Are you there?" he asked again, louder this time.

At last a woman's voice made a discernible sound that sounded like a high-pitched shriek. "I found him. *Hanging*. You people did this. You drove him to it."

"I'm sorry, but I don't know what you're talking about. Can you tell me who you are?" He was vaguely aware of Stonechild next to him, bent over so that she could hear. He pulled the receiver from his ear and held it between them.

"He's dead." The woman's voice was lower now, in vicious control as she enunciated every syllable. "Ivo Delaney is dead. He hanged himself from the beam in their bedroom. Sammy and I found him when we came by to make lunch." She began sobbing then and Gundersund let Stonechild take the phone while he took out his cell. He listened to Stonechild's calm voice assuring Catherine Lockhart that they were on their way, while he placed a call to the front desk to mobilize a squad car and the ambulance. He and Stonechild wouldn't be far behind.

Stonechild finished speaking with Catherine at almost the same time as he completed his call. She stood motionless for a moment, the look on her face broken but quickly hardening into anger. She glared at him.

"How could we have let this happen?"

"Woodhouse and Bennett were with him yesterday because of the break in. They would have reported if he seemed suicidal."

"Bennett maybe. I'm not so sure about Woodhouse."

"You can't know that. This is an awful shock, but we have to work together. You have to step back."

Her eyes bore through him and it took an effort not to look away. He'd never seen this anger and pain from her before and he wondered for the first time what she was capable of doing when provoked. She had depths that he was only now glimpsing.

She was the first to look away. "I'll just get my jacket," she said, her voice even, revealing none of the emotion he'd just seen in her eyes. She ducked her head and said as she turned, "I'll take my own truck and meet you there."

"I'll just stop by Heath's office and will be right behind you."

He was in the parking lot before he remembered that he hadn't told her about Frances. He looked at the taillights of her truck pulling onto Division Street. "Dammit," he said out loud. He'd have to find a moment to tell her as soon as he got to the Delaney house because if Stonechild heard about Frances from somebody else, his lapse wouldn't be easily forgiven.

He reached his car and unlocked the door. How had the day gone from contained to disaster in the space of ten minutes? He slid inside and started the engine. For the first time, he thought about what Delaney's suicide could mean. If they were lucky and he'd left a note confessing to his family's murders, his death might be a blessing in disguise. Gundersund had almost convinced himself that this was how it would play out by the time he reached the outskirts of Kingston. Only the anger he'd seen in Stonechild's eyes kept him from fully believing in the possibility of a tidy ending to this whole ugly mess.

CHAPTER TWENTY-SIX

Gundersund parked on the side of the road behind two police cars and waited for Fiona to get out of her SUV. He'd seen her in his rear-view mirror pull in behind him.

"This is tragic," she said. She wore a black leather jacket and grey slacks, her hair pulled back in a pony-tail. She carried her medical bag in one hand and her cellphone in the other. It rang as they started up the driveway and she spoke a few words into it before tucking it back inside her pocket. They walked up to the house, past the ambulance and fire truck parked next to each other in the driveway.

"Have you heard if he left a note?" Gundersund asked.

"No, but I haven't heard that he didn't."

He held onto the hope as the officer standing outside the front door greeted them. Two firemen came out of the house and headed back toward their truck. Gundersund and Fiona stopped and put white suits and boots on over their clothing and shoes before stepping inside the front hallway. The light was greyish and damp, dust visible in the air. A second officer directed them upstairs.

Stonechild was already in the bedroom, standing next to the photographer, both also dressed in the protective white suits. Two paramedics stood talking in quiet voices next to Ivo Delaney's body, which they'd lowered to the floor between the bed and the window. The remainder of the rope still hung from the beam, but a length of it was wrapped around Ivo's neck and trailed on the floor next to him. A chair lay on its side not far away. His face was white and his eyes bulged from their sockets. His body looked big and awkward even in death. He lay on his back with his arms at his sides, palms upturned. He was wearing a plaid shirt and beige pants and he smelled of urine and sour body odour. It took all Gundersund had to keep looking. Fiona crouched to begin her inspection of the body.

Stonechild moved over to where Gundersund stood. "No note," she said. "Catherine Lockhart is in the kitchen waiting to be interviewed."

"I'll come with you. I'm not much use here."

Fiona looked up. "I'll see you before we leave." She had on her professional face but he knew suicides always upset her. Her sister had killed herself when she was sixteen. They'd formed a bond over dead siblings. In the end, it hadn't been enough of a reason to keep the marriage going.

"Yeah, I'll check in with you before we head back."

Stonechild didn't say anything on their way downstairs but he knew that she'd overheard the exchange with his wife. They found Catherine in the kitchen with Sammy. He was colouring on a pad of paper with a pack of crayons. He looked up at them as they entered, but went right back to colouring. A female officer was refilling Catherine's mug with tea and she smiled gratefully at Gundersund as they took seats at the table.

"I'll just take Sammy out to play in the backyard, shall I?" she asked.

"Don't wanna," Sammy said without looking up.

"Go with the policewoman, now, Sammy. I mean it." Catherine spoke without her usual energy and Sammy stared over at her. He looked puzzled but obediently put down his crayon and got up, racing ahead of the officer and yanking open the back door. "You can push me on Violet's swing," he said.

"If you like." The officer gave Gundersund one last smile before following Sammy outside, shutting the door behind her.

"What am I going to do with that boy?" Catherine looked at Stonechild. "Luckily, he was behind me and didn't see Ivo hanging. He's already having nightmares. All I need is for him to have walked in on that. I keep thinking, a whole family dead in the space of a week. Happy and alive last week at this time and now…. The speed and cruelty of their deaths has been truly mind-boggling."

"This must be very painful for you. We're sorry to have to ask you more questions." Stonechild's voice was kind and Catherine reacted with a loosening of her shoulders and the tight line of her mouth. Her eyes filled with tears.

"That's okay."

"When was the last time you saw Ivo alive?"

"Yesterday. Sammy and I've been coming by to keep his spirits up. I brought some soup and homemade bread for supper around eight o'clock because I was working on a story and time got away. Anyhow, I found him cleaning up from a break in. He was quieter than normal and seemed, I don't know, just empty. Drained. I helped him tidy for an hour before I had to get Sammy home to bed. I left him with the soup on the stove and he promised he'd eat."

"Did he say anything at all about Adele or Violet?"

"Nothing specific. He talked about them as if they were still alive, I remember that."

"How so?"

"Oh, you know, Adele likes this photo and Violet always takes this stuffed giraffe to bed, that kind of thing. I thought it odd but decided it must be part of his healing process. I think in hindsight that he'd already decided to kill himself and join them."

"But he didn't say anything that gave you cause to worry."

"No. He only said that the detectives who came to check into the break-in didn't believe him. They thought he'd made the mess himself to have them think someone else had killed his family."

Stonechild sat back and looked at Gundersund. He signalled her not to react before taking over the questioning.

"Let's go back a bit further. When was the last time you saw Adele and Violet?"

"I've already told the other officers."

"Perhaps going over it again might trigger things you forgot the first time."

"It was a week ago Tuesday. We went on an outing to Green's Plant Nursery on Highway 2, about half an hour from here. We made a day of it. Adele drove and we stopped for lunch at Country Kitchen, which is a family restaurant a few miles down the road. We got to Greens' around two o'clock after we stopped at the market to buy apples on the way, because Adele wanted to bake some pies for Ivo. Apparently, apple pie was his favourite. It had stopped raining for once but was chilly enough." She paused and stared at the floor. "We were going to stop for ice cream at the same restaurant on the way back but Adele said it was getting late and she wanted to get home. It wasn't even three o'clock but she seemed tired and complained of a headache. Then she cancelled playgroup the next three mornings, so I guess she'd been coming down with something. When she dropped us off, that was the last time I saw her. It's not like I didn't try to contact her all week. God help me, I thought because she kept not showing up at playgroup and didn't return any of my phone calls or emails that she was avoiding me. Finally, she took my call the day before they went missing. She said that she'd been sick all week but that she and Violet would meet us at playgroup the next day. When they didn't show up, I came to see for myself if they were okay. That's when I found her car in the driveway and the front door wide open."

Stonechild said, "Ivo didn't say that she'd been sick."

"Then maybe she really was mad at me for something. We don't have many friends living this far out of town and Sammy was missing Violet. Maybe I pushed too hard to get us together. I still don't understand why ..." Her voice trailed off. She picked up the mug of tea.

"Could Adele have thought that you had an interest in Ivo?"

By her reaction, Gundersund's question caught Catherine by surprise. She'd taken a sip of tea and spit it back into the cup, coughing and laughing at the same time. "You've got to be kidding me. Have you seen pictures of Adele? She was stunning and so full of life. Believe me, she did *not* look at me as competition for her husband. The idea is beyond ludicrous."

"People can imagine all kinds of things, whether true or not." Gundersund kept his voice non-judgmental. "And you've been here a lot since she's been gone."

Catherine reddened and opened her mouth without any sound coming out. "God, I could use a smoke," she said when she finally become capable of speech. She took a deep breath. "Look, Officer, I was just being kind. I had no designs on Ivo Delaney and we had nothing, absolutely nothing, going on between us. I was friends with Adele, not Ivo, and even that friendship was mainly because of our kids."

"We have to check out every possibility." Gundersund wouldn't apologize for doing his job. He looked at Stonechild. "Any other questions?"

"Not at this time. We're sorry again for all of this."

She was playing good cop to his bad but that's what made them an effective team. Keep the witnesses off balance with a soft touch before the hard questions.

Stonechild stood and they left the kitchen together, leaving Catherine as she pulled a pack of cigarettes out of her pocket. In the front door hallway, Stonechild stopped.

"She seemed genuinely shocked by your last question, but she protested a bit too much, did you notice?"

"Her protesting was rather vigorous. Maybe she feels guilt for stepping in to look after him with Adele so recently gone. She's been doing a lot of cooking for the guy and seemed to be here a lot."

Stonechild checked over her shoulder to make sure they were still alone. "She strikes me as lonely. It could just be that she's embarrassed that her acts of generosity were interpreted as cold-blooded self-interest. She's not at the top of my list for being a killer in any case."

"Nor mine."

"What do you make of her saying that Woodhouse and Bennett told Delaney they believed he ransacked his house to divert suspicion because he killed his family?"

"Hard to believe either of them would do that, even Woodhouse. Delaney might have come up with that on his own, especially if he did kill his family."

"Should we tell Rouleau?"

Crap. Gundersund hit his forehead with the palm of his hand. "I meant to tell you but we've been so busy. Just before this suicide call came in, Rouleau called. Frances died this morning and he's staying on a few more days until the funeral. I'm really sorry she's dead, and sorry for not telling you sooner."

"I guess we knew that was coming but it's never easy. Did he sound okay?"

"Tired but holding up, I'd say."

"Don't worry about the delay in telling me. I know this case took over."

"Thanks." He looked upstairs. "Say, I have to check in with Fiona. Can you hold on a few minutes?"

"Sure. I'll have a quick look in Ivo's office and then I'll wait for you outside."

"It's just that," Gundersund paused, "Fiona hates suicides. They get to her even if she doesn't show it."

"No need to explain to me." Stonechild gave her unreadable smile and started walking down the hall. "She's your wife after all."

He let her go without responding. He wanted to say wife in name only, but that somehow felt like a betrayal to Fiona. She still wanted the marriage to work, or so she was insisting. Until she agreed to the divorce, he didn't want to discuss their relationship, even with Stonechild. Maybe he and Fiona went so far back that they could never completely untangle their lives. They'd be friends eventually he hoped, but knew they couldn't live together anymore. He was going to have to be patient until Fiona came around to knowing this too.

Kala finished her search in Ivo's office and re-entered the hallway. She'd heard Gundersund's feet thump up the stairs and knew the coast was clear for exiting the house without running into him. He'd be up talking to Fiona and probably making plans to see her after work.

The same officer was outside and media had gathered in the driveway. A young blond reporter in a red trench coat was talking into a handheld microphone while a guy holding a TV camera on his shoulder filmed her. Three other media types hung around smoking cigarettes and chatting several feet away.

Kala started down the driveway, sticking to the side farthest away from the reporters. She was approaching the road when she heard her name being called. She turned to see the new reporter from the *Whig* running toward her. She'd seen the woman at the station but couldn't recall her name. Her copper-coloured hair was distinctive.

"Marci Stokes," she gasped as she stopped in front of Kala. She rested her hands on her thighs and bowed her head as she took a few deep breaths. "Whew. I need to get to the gym." She straightened up and grinned at Kala. "I'm with the *Whig-Standard*. I wonder if you could tell me what's going on inside the Delaney house. I'm hearing rumours of suicide."

"I'm sorry, but I can't comment." Kala took a step sideways to go around her.

"Officer Stonechild, isn't it?"

Kala hesitated. Marci Stokes's brown eyes were friendly, but Kala never trusted a reporter. They were always after a story. Media training had taught her that nothing was off the record. Ever. She said, "That's right." One more step and she was by.

"I've found an article in the *Sudbury Star* about your life before becoming a policewoman. I was hoping to have a conversation with you for my article."

Kala stopped and stood stock still. She turned slowly to face Marci Stokes. "What did you just say?"

"I'm writing a profile about you and wanted more background to flesh out the story. I was hoping you could share more about your history."

"You can't be serious. My life is not news."

"The *Star* article has a photo. You were homeless and somehow pulled yourself up to become a cop.

Readers would be very interested to know your life story and the way you changed everything around to get to where you are today."

"I don't suppose I could talk you out of writing this?"

"Not likely."

Kala's mind was scrambling at a hundred miles an hour. A great feeling of dread filled her. Tamara Jones had placed Dawn with her because of her upstanding character. A role model — that's what the social worker had called her. Now Marci Stokes was going to spread her sordid past all over the news in the name of a good, uplifting story. She had to think how to stop this woman from digging any deeper.

"We could meet at the Merchant this evening." The words were out before Kala gave them much thought.

Marci Stokes tilted her head and appeared to think the offer over. "I could do that. How's seven?"

"Yeah. Seven works."

Kala kept walking, not sure what she was going to do but knowing that she was going to have to come up with something fast. She still had to manoeuvre her way through the meeting with Tamara Jones and Mrs. Zelasko at four o'clock with no idea why they'd called her in. Before Gundersund had broken the news of Delaney's suicide she'd left a message with Dawn to call her back in the hopes that she could get a heads up on the school situation. She pulled out her phone and checked for messages. Nothing.

When she reached her truck, she looked back at

the Delaney house. Catherine Lockhart had nailed the tragedy on the head when she'd said how quickly this family's lives had changed. All three dead within a week — and barely anyone left to mourn them. She'd seen evidence of a good family in the photos and cozy lived-in rooms when she'd first entered their home. The house had had an aura of happiness, even with Adele and Violet gone. Their essences had felt alive to her that first visit, but not anymore. This time the house felt sad and empty, any lingering traces of the Delaney family driven out by Ivo's horrific end.

As she stood on the road, letting the grief she felt for this lost family ride over her, a gust of wind lifted her hair and cooled the heat on her face. She tilted her head way back and stared at the blue sky, the sun stronger than it had been all month. *Are you circling out there, Ivo? Are you with Adele and Violet and finally at peace?*

The wind buffeted the pine and balsam branches in the thicket of trees not far from the property line and rattled the wind chimes left hanging from one of the lower limbs. Kala squinted in the direction of the sound. She caught sight of silver chimes hanging from a hook with the wires attached to a top that looked purple from a distance. She jumped down the culvert and up the muddy knoll, skirting past a boggy patch until she reached the spot where she'd seen the swaying metal tubes. She reached up and lifted the chimes from the pine branch and held them up for a closer inspection. The ceramic top was handmade and the blur of purple up close was a mass of violets, each one meticulously hand painted. Inside the top, she found the words *for my Violet* painted in cursive gold lettering.

There had been love.

Very gently, Kala returned the wind chimes to the exact spot on the branch. The wind caught the chimes and their music began again. Somewhere up above in the pine tree, a cardinal trilled its throaty call. Compost and earth and damp leaves filled her senses. In the shelter of the trees she felt distanced from the activity going on just up the driveway. This place felt sacred. She bowed her head and said a silent prayer for Adele, Violet, and Ivo. She wished them safe journey to the other plane and rest for their tortured souls. When she finished her prayer, she closed her eyes and let the peace of the spot calm her.

When she opened them again and looked toward the house, Gundersund was standing on the front steps, looking toward the road, searching in the direction of her truck. As she watched, he lowered his hand from where he'd cupped it over his eyes to cut the sun's glare. He leaped down the steps and started down the driveway. He still hadn't seen her standing in the shadow of the tree. She turned and cut across the grassy incline toward her truck where she'd wait for him to make his way to her.

CHAPTER TWENTY-SEVEN

Mrs. Zelasko was dressed in a shapeless lime-green shift sprinkled with watering cans and dahlias, striped yellow and blue tights, and sturdy black clogs. Kala didn't normally notice someone's fashion choices except for identification purposes, but Mrs. Zelasko's wardrobe intrigued her. Surely, the offbeat clothes were deliberately chosen to give her some sort of psychological advantage over her pre-adolescent charges? The woman didn't strike Kala as daft, but these clothes made her appear kooky and untrendy. If not for the intelligence in her eyes and her no-nonsense manner, Kala might have been fooled by her appearance.

They'd been sitting looking at each other for five minutes, Kala at one of the student's desks and Mrs. Zelasko behind her own, when Tamara Jones finally came flying into the room, her brown hair spilling out of an elastic on top of her head.

"Sorry, sorry, sorry. I had to remove a child from a home and it took most of my day." She dropped a file folder onto the desk and squeezed into the seat across the aisle from Kala. The smile she beamed at them felt out of place after what she'd just revealed.

Mrs. Zelasko shuffled some papers on her desk. "Well, let's get started, shall we?" She looked directly at Kala. "Ms. Jones and I thought it would be a good idea to touch base on how things are progressing with Dawn. Getting right to it, has she admitted to stealing the iPhone, Officer Stonechild?"

Kala met her eyes without wavering. "She has not. I am of the opinion that Dawn didn't steal the iPhone and wonder if we should investigate other scenarios."

Mrs. Zelasko looked far from happy with this suggestion. "Giving in to a false version of events is not going to help your ..." she glanced down. "I suppose we could call Dawn your niece as she's begun referring to you as aunt. Anyhow, perpetuating an untruth will not help in the long run. I was hoping we could have Dawn apologize to the girl in a private meeting, which I would supervise of course. That way, Dawn would take responsibility and the girls could start afresh."

Kala looked across at Tamara. Her head was bobbing up and down in agreement and Kala knew that the two had discussed this beforehand and arrived at a plan to force Dawn to make restitution. They'd already made up their minds about her guilt.

Tamara's entire demeanor was one of earnest, well-intentioned concern. She asked, "Have you been to counselling with Dawn yet?"

"We have an appointment." Kala knew that she had to give them something. She hadn't set one up yet, but not because she hadn't meant to. She ventured on. "Perhaps we should wait until Dr. Lyman has a word with Dawn. We wouldn't want to impede any progress that she's been making by jumping the gun on this thing."

Tamara's face scrunched up into a frown. Mrs. Zelasko appeared to be thinking. When the teacher finally spoke, her words were measured. "I, that is *we*, were hoping to have this problem settled as quickly as possible. When are you meeting with Dr. Lyman?"

"She only has time for us later in the week. I could update you right away after our session."

"What do you think, Ms. Jones? Can this wait a few more days?"

Tamara tilted her head from side to side, her ears nearly touching her shoulders each time. "I guess we'll have to see if Dr. Lyman can get through to Dawn. Yes, I think this would be the best way to go. Have you noticed any change in her behaviour in the classroom, Mrs. Zelasko?"

"She's still keeping to herself, although I understand that she's been playing baseball at recess."

Tamara's face brightened. "Well, that is something to build on! How is she at home, Kala?"

"Good. Everything is going well."

Kala was tiring of this game of cat and mouse. They held most of the cards, but she also had a working knowledge of the social services system.

She'd spent her entire childhood in it, learning how to survive.

"Well, let's plan to meet this time next week." Mrs. Zelasko looked at Tamara. "Can I keep you for a minute after this meeting?"

"Of course, Mrs. Zelasko."

Kala wormed her way out of the desk and stood. "I'll be on my way then." She would leave them to it to plot their next moves.

Dawn was waiting for her in the library. She was reading a book at the long table facing the door. She jumped up and grabbed her knapsack when she saw Kala. "I was getting tired of waiting." They were in the parking lot before Dawn asked, "So? Am I being suspended?"

"Nope, but we're going to have to come up with a plan to keep Mrs. Zelasko and Ms. Jones happy. We can talk about it tomorrow. I'm going to pick up some submarine sandwiches for supper and then I have to head out for a meeting at seven. Will you be okay for a few hours on your own?"

"I'll be fine. Besides, I'm not alone. Taiku keeps me company."

They got into the truck. Kala leaned on the steering wheel and looked sideways at Dawn. "Do you like living with me? It's okay if you say no. I need to be reassured that you are where you want to be."

Dawn didn't look away. "I like living with you, Aunt Kala."

"Then we're good?"

"We're good."

Kala reached over and turned on the engine. "Well then, we'll just have to figure out what we have to do to keep you with me."

Perhaps it was a coincidence that Marci Stokes was sitting at the same table that she, Gundersund, and Rouleau had claimed on their previous visits to the Merchant, but the sight of her there gave Kala pause. What were the odds that the reporter would pick their regular table in a place this size? Marci had her back turned, typing away at something on a laptop. Her copper hair was pulled back with a couple of clips but looked untidy, as if she didn't care about her appearance. Kala watched her for several seconds from the doorway before crossing the floor and taking the seat across from her. Marci looked at her over reading glasses resting on the edge of her nose.

"Good, you made it. Drink?" She raised her glass and rattled the ice cubes to attract the waitress. "I'm having a vodka soda."

"Coffee would be fine."

"Coffee and another one of these." Marci slid her glass onto the waitress's tray. She closed her laptop and took off her reading glasses, setting them on top of the case. "You've managed to remain anonymous on the Internet aside from the one *Sudbury Star* article and some publicity around a couple of recent cases."

"What do you need to know?" Kala still wasn't sure which way to play this.

"Your childhood. We could start there." Marci pulled a small tape recorder out of her pocket. "Do you mind?"

"Can we talk off the record first?"

"If you like." Marci tucked the recorder back into her pocket. She sat back in the chair as the waitress set their drinks onto the table. When the girl left, Marci took a sip from her glass and watched while Kala added cream to her coffee. "So, what did you want to talk about, off the record?"

"I was wondering how you came across that article. It's not like it was recent or earth-shattering news."

"Just a regular scan on all the officers. We do them now and then to look for any ... issues."

Kala wasn't convinced this was how she'd found the article but would let it go. The fact was that Stokes had the story and it was time to do some damage control. She'd try some honesty mixed with pleading. "I might have had a rougher past than many, but I'm at a point in my life that talking about it to the public could harm me personally. You see, my niece is living with me and I'm trying to keep her from being moved into foster care. If this story about my past comes out, I'll likely lose her."

"Surely not. Yours is a story of triumph over terrible odds. We can emphasize the positive. You'll be an inspiration and role model."

"Not if my niece's social worker hears about this. She only let me have Dawn temporarily because she believes I've led a spotless life."

"The social worker can't be that naive."

"Fresh out of university and eager to save the world, one sad kid at a time. She's already put me on notice in several conversations, making it clear that my exemplary life is the only reason she let Dawn live with me. I'm attempting to make this a more permanent living arrangement, but I need the social worker to sign the papers."

"Why is your niece placed with you? How old is she?"

Kala's normal aversion to speaking about herself and her family conflicted with her need to win this woman over. "Dawn is thirteen. Her parents are both doing time for robberies. I'm all that's standing between her and life in foster care, not a system that I'd recommend to anybody."

Marci took another drink from her glass, never taking her eyes from Kala. She didn't say anything but Kala could tell that she was thinking things over. Kala took a drink of coffee while she waited. Her hand trembled and she wrapped both hands around the mug as she set it back on the table.

"How about I put the story on the backburner for now? If your situation with your niece changes, we can agree to meet again and you can give me more background."

A deal with the devil. Did she have a choice? "Yeah. Thanks for understanding."

"I'm not in this business to ruin a kid's life."

Kala took another drink from the coffee mug and thought about leaving. She reached around for her purse hanging on the back of her chair. "I should be going." She started feeling inside the bag for her wallet.

Marci waved a hand. "This is on me. I dragged you out. One more thing before you leave. We heard Ivo Delaney hanged himself today. Did he confess to killing his family?"

"I can't really say anything that's not been released publicly. I believe there's another press conference in the morning."

Marci smiled. "You really are a closed off person, aren't you? I guess I'll have to wait to question Rouleau tomorrow."

Kala stood and slung her purse over her shoulder. "He's in Ottawa but Captain Heath will be available."

"What's Rouleau doing in Ottawa?"

"A personal matter. Well, thanks again for the coffee and for hearing me out."

"I'll admit that I'm a bulldog with a good story, so don't think this is the last you'll see of me." Marci smiled again and opened her laptop. She was typing with her head down when Kala walked away.

CHAPTER TWENTY-EIGHT

Rouleau called her back shortly before eleven. She'd just checked that Dawn was asleep and climbed into bed when her cellphone buzzed on her bedside table. She turned the lamp on and checked the name before answering.

"How are you, sir?"

"Not too bad, Stonechild, all things considered. The visitation is tomorrow and the funeral will be the following afternoon. Frances asked for no fuss, but Gordon appears to need this ceremony to get through. Who am I to judge?"

"People find comfort in ritual."

"I suppose. I got your message. Gundersund and Heath have also been in touch."

He sounded sad and Kala hesitated. Should she tell him her concerns about the case or carry on without telling him? He read something of her mood in the silence because he said, "You're not convinced that Ivo Delaney killed them, are you?"

"I think we have loose ends."

"Heath is of the opinion that we don't need to waste any more resources digging into his past.

The case has cost quite a bit already with the river search, which will have to resume when the water recedes."

"We've been told to wrap things up, but ..."

"Did you have something left to do?"

"The warden at Millhaven got back to me late today, and I have an appointment to meet Benoit Manteau tomorrow morning."

"If I was to tell you to go ahead, I'd be countering Heath's directive."

"I'm sorry, sir. I didn't mean to put you in an awkward spot." He was silent again and she decided it was time to end the call. Rouleau didn't need this distraction when he was dealing with such loss. "I'll call the warden and cancel."

"No. I want you to go and interview Benoit Manteau. Like you, I'm not convinced of Delaney's guilt. He might well have killed his family but all of our evidence so far is circumstantial. What time is your appointment?"

"Nine-thirty, right after their breakfast."

"You're okay to go alone?"

"Of course."

She could almost hear the smile in his voice. He knew she didn't like having a partner. "I'll run interference if necessary. Give me a report afterwards. We'll go from there."

"Thank you, sir."

"Don't thank me. I want you to do a complete job before we close the file. Violet and Adele deserve our best effort."

Millhaven Institution housed approximately four hundred of the country's most violent offenders. Located in the town of Bath just outside Kingston, "Thrill Haven" was surrounded by a double thirty-foot razor fence with observation towers in each corner. Armed patrol vehicles with Colt Canada C7 rifles and parabolic microphones that picked up sounds from many metres away were on guard day and night. The three main living units and the segregation unit were bursting at the seams with the closing of Kingston Penitentiary; the packed units radiated out from a central axis so that offenders could be observed in their living quarters.

Kala had expected the thorough search of her person and belongings that she received after reporting to the security desk and signing the visitors' log. She passed through a metal detector and her bag was placed into a locker. Her phone and recording devices also were not allowed inside the prison. The Correctional Services victim liaison coordinator met her and led her through the locked gate and into the waiting room, inviting her to sit at a round table with seats bolted into the floor. Another male guard came out from behind a glass partition to greet her. The room had the chemical smell of the recently cleaned. The walls were painted a cheery green but there was no hiding the institutional feel of the place.

"Benoit Manteau has been a model prisoner and he knows the drill. He'll sit across the table from you and will keep his hands where we can see them. There's a microphone in the table top and I'll be listening in on your conversation. If I hear anything worrisome, the guards will step in immediately. Any questions?"

"None that I can think of."

She looked at the green walls for ten minutes before a side door opened and Benoit Manteau entered escorted by an armed guard. Benoit was wearing an orange jumpsuit and black shoes and he was smaller than she would have thought based on his reputation. His size wasn't the only surprise. Unlike his brother Etienne, he was beardless, grey hair shaved close at the sides and spiked on the top of his head. His eyes were black and hard; his skin permanently tanned. Kala was puzzled.

"You aren't the same race as your brother."

"That's what you came all this way to tell me?" Benoit set his hands on the table and one of his exposed wrists had a fleur-de-lis tattooed in green ink. His legs were spread wide under the table. "We have different mothers. Mine's Hispanic but lived in Canada her whole life. Etienne's not so much."

"Did you grow up with Etienne?"

"Yeah. His mother wasn't all that motherly as it turned out. Lucky for him, my dad was stable with a good job and my mother liked kids."

"Where did your cousin Philippe Lebeau fit into your childhood?"

"My father has a sister, Lou. She raised Philippe alone in an apartment building in downtown Hull, now called Gatineau. Her boyfriend took off right after he was born, so she made do on welfare when she didn't have work. We lived in the richer English-speaking part called Aylmer until we moved to Montreal in our late teens. Anyhow, Philippe was just at our place, you know after school, weekends. It got so my mother just set him a place at the table." Benoit laughed. "I used to get him to do my chores. He never wanted to go home to their dumpy apartment."

"Didn't his mother miss him?"

"What do you think? She was seventeen when she had him and not ready to play house from what I remember."

"You're forty now and Etienne and Philippe are thirty-eight, so at least twenty years in Montreal?"

"Sounds about right. I was eighteen and they followed me a year after that. We've always been tight. First time a cop's been this interested in my family tree."

Despite what she knew about Benoit Manteau, Kala could see his charm. It would be easy to be lulled into carelessness by his deep, melodic voice. His eyes were velvety black and loaded with sexual innuendo. His stare was laser-like, no blinking, no backing away.

"You've heard about Adele Dufour and the child."

"I got a call from Etienne, so yeah, I know about them."

"It must have been a shock." Kala waited.

"What, that she took my kid or that they were both killed?"

"Both."

Benoit sat back in his chair and looked at her. He spoke with icy precision. "She stole my kid and then she died. I have no problem with retribution, Officer Stonechild, but my daughter being drowned? If I could, I would make the man pay. Unfortunately, I can't do much from my cell. I had nothing to do with any of this."

He pulled something out of his pocket and leaned forward, setting a crumpled photo on the table. Kala saw the guard move closer to have a look, then step back once he saw that it was a photo.

She asked, "May I?"

Benoit nodded and she reached for the picture. A baby in a pink sleeper with black eyes open, skin a coffee brown and a tuft of black hair. The baby looked to be a month old. Kala looked at Benoit. He was staring at her, his unblinking eyes watching for her reaction. Calculating, assessing. She thought he was waiting for her to confirm a suspicion.

"Beautiful baby." She kept her racing heart from affecting the evenness of her voice. She met his eyes and smiled. "Do you have other children?"

"No." He shrugged. "I would have liked a son but my daughter is … was what I was living for. I wanted out of here to find her. Cécile sent this photo to me when I was inside, waiting for the bail hearing." He shook his head. "We know how that turned out." He reached for the picture. He tucked it back inside his pocket without looking at it.

"And your appeal?"

"Next month. My lawyer gives me a decent shot. She's come up with enough for a judge to have another look anyhow. She's been working on it for almost three years. I was set up."

That's what they all say. "Well, good luck with that. I guess this isn't too far for your family to visit you since the move."

He paused then shrugged. "My brother Etienne has been once. Philippe is planning to come when he can swing getting away. Cécile says it's too painful but we talk on the phone. My parents are dead. I have an Uncle Maurice in Smiths Falls, but he's gone into assisted living. We used to spend summers at his cottage on Otter Lake. What I'd give for a week there now."

"Has the cottage sold?"

"No. Still there, waiting for me to get out on appeal." Benoit smiled as if seeing himself lying on the dock with the whole wide world open in front of him.

"I understand that Etienne owns the bar now in Montreal."

"That's right."

"You've been essentially cut out of the business. That doesn't bother you?"

Benoit spread his hands wide, palms up. "I have nowhere to spend money in here."

"What happens when you get out?"

"I'm going to pick up Cécile and head somewhere warm for six months. Then, who knows?"

"I guess you haven't heard that the man who was married to Adele hanged himself yesterday."

The dark circles inside Benoit's eyes expanded, the only sign that the news came as a surprise. "I hadn't heard. I won't pretend to be sorry. He might have thought about sparing my kid before he did himself in."

"All of this has been a terrible waste."

She wanted to ask him if he'd ordered the hit that landed him in prison, but she knew he'd deny it. He was no fool. Whatever he said was being picked up by the microphone and his appeal was imminent. That left her with nothing else of relevance to discuss. She signalled the guard. "I'll be going then. Thanks for seeing me, and again, I'm sorry for your loss."

"Yeah, me too."

On the way out Kala asked at the guard desk if she could check the log of Benoit Manteau's visitors. The two guards talked over her request and one put a call in to the warden. Another twenty minute wait and permission granted, she made note of one visit by Etienne Manteau on a Tuesday some two weeks earlier. He'd had two other visitors since Benoit was moved to Millhaven, but she didn't recognize either name. She wrote them both into her notebook.

Head down, deep in thought, Kala crossed the parking lot to her truck. She unlocked the door and climbed inside, taking a moment to jot down her impressions of the visit and the facts she'd gleaned in her notebook. Once done, she took a last look at the imposing prison wall. Dawn's father was also being housed in Millhaven. She'd never met him and had thought about arranging a visit, but not this time. When she wasn't involved in a case, she'd come back and meet him to satisfy her own curiosity.

She looked at the clock on the dashboard as she started the truck. It was nearly two o'clock and her stomach was growling. She unrolled the window and tilted her head outside to take a deep breath of fresh spring air. A low cloud cover had blotted out the sun and the air smelled of rain. *More rain.* She thought about Benoit Manteau and the crumpled photo he kept on his person. She wanted to talk over what she'd discovered with Rouleau but didn't want to burden him any more than he was. That left confiding in Gundersund or going it alone. Her inclination was to forge ahead on her own, but Rouleau had made her swear not to do anything rash after the last close call. She put the truck into gear. First things first. She'd find a family restaurant and have some lunch.

Then she'd give Gundersund a call.

CHAPTER TWENTY-NINE

Kala had just popped the last of the club sandwich into her mouth when her cellphone rang. She chewed quickly and glanced at the number before pressing receive. "Officer Stonechild here."

"Officer Stonechild, it's Fred Taylor on the desk. A call just came in asking specifically for you. Woman by the name of Catherine Lockhart."

"Did she say what it was about?"

"Not really. Just that she needed to speak with you. Didn't sound urgent."

"Well I was on my way into the station but I can swing by her place first."

"I'll log it."

Kala tucked her phone and notebook into her purse and signalled the waitress for her bill. Twenty minutes later, she reached the outskirts of Kingston and the turnoff to the Delaney and Lockhart houses. She passed the Delaney house first. All appeared quiet, although the yellow crime tape wrapped across the front door signalled that the police would soon be returning. A kilometre farther on the Lockhart house came into view — a smaller home with blue shutters and a garden out front. Pansies crowded around a bird bath in jewel shades of purple, red, and yellow. Both houses were set back from the main road with clumps of pine, birch, and alder lining the long driveways.

Drops of rain began to splat on the windshield as Kala made her slow way up the Lockhart driveway to park behind Catherine's car. Thunder rumbled off to the east where the clouds were at their blackest. Kala zipped up her leather jacket and tucked her chin inside the collar before running the short distance to the front door. Catherine must have been watching for her because she swung the door open before Kala had a chance to ring the bell.

"I was hoping you'd make it before school gets out." Catherine left the door open and Kala followed her into the kitchen. A coffee pot sat on the table beside a green glass vase filled with pansies and Catherine got another mug from the cupboard. A plate of butterscotch squares appeared in front of Kala. She took one even though she wasn't hungry. The chewy sweetness filled her mouth. Kala swallowed before asking, "Have you remembered something that could help us with the Delaneys?"

Catherine waited until she'd crumbled a square in her hands and eaten half. She set the rest on a napkin while she poured two cups of coffee and slid one across the table toward Kala. After pouring milk and sugar into her own, Catherine spoke. Her tone bordered on hostile.

"I almost didn't call you after your blond partner practically accused me of having an affair with Ivo. I have to tell you that I'm still quite put out by that."

"I'm sorry. We have to pursue all lines of questioning during an investigation. We are trying to find the truth, which isn't always pretty."

"Well, that was hurtful." Catherine took another drink of coffee as she collected herself. "Sammy's bus will be dropping him off in a few minutes and I wanted to talk to you before he gets home. I might have mentioned that he's been having nightmares since Violet went missing."

"I seem to recall that, yes."

"He keeps saying that he saw a man. At first, I thought his overactive imagination was dreaming him up, but lately I've been wondering if there's more to it."

Kala felt tingling at the base of her neck that she got when her senses told her something was coming her way. She nodded at Catherine to continue but didn't interrupt. Silence could be a powerful tool to draw out a story.

"I mean, he was bound to be upset that his best friend was missing. He said that the man was looking for her. I really thought he was making up nonsense but since he's been so upset and talking in his sleep. Last night, he woke up screaming. It took me forever to settle him down. You said to call if anything out of the ordinary happened...."

"You've done the right thing." Kala spoke as if calming an upset child. "At the very least, I can try to ease his mind about whatever is troubling him. You're right that he's probably experiencing trauma over Violet's disappearance, but best to be sure that's all it is."

"I had to do something." Catherine reached for the coffee pot and refilled their cups. "Rain's getting worse. I'll bet he thanks me now for insisting he wear his raincoat this morning."

"Does he go to school every day?"

"No. I was taking him to playgroup most mornings, but with Violet gone he gets sad and sits off by himself. I finally called the school on Friday and he started afternoon kindergarten again this week. He was enrolled last fall but hated it, I think because Violet was too young to go too. My son needs to be around other kids, otherwise he'll never learn to cope and get along. He likes the bus ride, anyhow." She looked at the clock on the wall and heavily pushed herself to her feet. "If you'll wait here a minute, I'll just go watch for him at the front door. The driver will be letting Sammy off within the next few minutes and he dawdles if he doesn't see me in the window."

"I'll keep myself occupied with another square. They're delicious."

Kala chewed on a mouthful while she checked her messages. Gundersund had texted asking where she was. She typed a reply and asked if he could come by that evening to catch up on the case. Once she finished interviewing Sammy, she'd have to get home. Dawn would be there ahead of her and they needed to talk. She heard the door open and close and a bag hitting the floor. A moment later Sammy trailed Catherine into the kitchen.

"Sit at the table, Sammy, and I'll get you a glass of milk." Catherine opened the fridge door. "You remember Officer Stonechild, don't you? She's dropped by for a visit."

"Hey, Sammy." The kid reminded Kala of a little bulldog, solid and pug faced.

He climbed onto the chair and grabbed squares with both hands from the plate. He'd stuffed one into his mouth while Catherine had her back to him getting a glass out of the cupboard. Kala smiled at him when he finally made eye contact.

"Your mom has been telling me that you've been having bad dreams about a man. Can you tell me about what's upsetting you, Sammy?"

Catherine returned and set the glass of milk on the table. She shook her head at the sight of his full cheeks before moving her chair up next to him and sitting down. "Swallow what's in your mouth and tell Officer Stonechild about what's worrying you. She can help make it better."

They waited while he chewed and swallowed. He looked at Kala with intense blue eyes, oddly disconcerting. "He asked me where Violet is."

"Who asked you?"

"The man."

Catherine looked at Kala with an expression that said, "See?"

Kala avoided looking at her and focused in on Sammy, who was stuffing the second square into his mouth. She waited for him to swallow. "Where did you see this man?"

"In the trees," his eyes darted over to his mother and back to Kala. "Near the road. I was on my bike."

"What did he look like?"

"Big."

"Was his skin white?"

"White and brown."

Not helpful. "What colour was his hair?"

"I don't remember."

"Come on, Sammy." Catherine poked his arm. "You remember everything. What did he look like?"

Sammy started kicking the table leg with one foot. "He was big and he wore black."

Kala thought for a moment. "When did you see him?"

"After Violet was gone."

"Did he say anything else to you?"

Sammy shook his head. "Can I go play now?"

Kala said, "Why are you dreaming about this man, Sammy? What upset you about him?"

Sammy's eyes widened. She saw confusion in their depths and sat still, waiting for him to find the words.

"He followed us. Violet was talking to him and I called her to come. He asked her my name and she told him. Sammy Lockhart."

Catherine sighed, breaking the moment. She pushed herself to her feet. "I'll just go cut some more squares. You can have one more, Sammy, for helping Officer Stonechild. No matter how little."

She mumbled the last sentence in Kala's ear on the way to the counter.

Kala moved her chair a little closer to Sammy. "If you saw the man after Violet went missing, how could he have been talking to her?"

Sammy closed his eyes tightly and scrunched up his face.

Very softly, "Sammy? How could that be?"

His eyes shot open. Brilliant blue and suddenly remembering. "He was at the flower store when Violet and I were looking at the birds. Then he was in our yard after she went missing." Sammy puffed out his cheeks and jumped off the chair. "I'm going now, Mom." He gave Kala a mischievous grin and scooted out of the kitchen before she could stop him.

Catherine returned and plunked a full plate of sweets onto the table. "He won't give you any more now. I doubt any of it's true anyhow. I guess he's just upset about Violet. Thanks for coming by and talking to him though. I'm hoping your visit will be enough to get the nightmares to end."

Kala wasn't so certain that Sammy's jumbled story didn't hold grains of relevant information. She thought over what he'd told her, cryptic as it might have been. "You said that you went to a plant nursery with Violet and Adele earlier in the week that she went missing, is that right?"

"Yes. It was our last outing. We stopped at Country Kitchen on Highway 2 for lunch first."

"Can you remember if anybody else was in the restaurant?"

"It was busy. We had to wait for a booth."

"Is it possible that a man approached Sammy and Violet while you were at the nursery?"

Catherine pursed her lips and thought it over. "I was going to say no, but I had to ask the clerk if I could use their washroom and I was gone, oh five minutes, maybe ten. Adele said she'd watch them, but when I got back she wanted to leave right away. The kids didn't argue for once and home we came. I managed to buy the pansies out front while Adele got the kids into her car."

"Were there birds?"

"In cages. Little brown songbirds and yellow and green budgies. The kids love going to the nursery to see the birds."

"You don't remember a man alone either in the restaurant or the nursery?"

"Nobody stands out."

"And Adele didn't mention anybody?"

"No." Catherine leaned her dimpled arms onto the table and reached for a square. "But now that you mention it, she kept checking the rear-view mirror when she was driving home. She seemed on edge. Do you think Sammy really could have seen a man?"

"I don't know." Kala didn't want to worry Catherine Lockhart unduly, but Sammy's story raised alarm bells. "Maybe keep a close eye on Sammy while I check out his story. Keep your doors locked too, just to be on the safe side. We'll look into this tomorrow and I'll let you know what I find out."

"As if I'm not already paranoid enough. I tell you, Officer Stonechild, between the deaths and Sammy's nightmares I'm about ready to move back to Toronto. I never thought I'd say this, but my old Regent Park apartment is starting to look like a safe haven."

"Like this, Gundersund?" Dawn slid the spatula under half of the hardening egg and folded it over the bottom half. She looked up at him, her eyes seeking approval.

"Perfect. Two more minutes and we can slide this one into the oven with the other two to keep warm."

"Aunt Kala works late a lot."

"She should have more time soon. The case she's working on is nearly over." He looked at Dawn's bowed head. She was a striking girl and self-contained for a thirteen-year-old. Other kids this age who'd experienced what she'd been through were already broken, but she was still reachable. Her desire to please and the spark to learn weren't far under the surface.

He reached into the oven and pulled out the pan with the other two omelettes and held it steady while she scooped the last one from the frying pan and laid it carefully next to the others. He set the pan on top of the stove and covered it in tin foil before sliding it back into the oven. Taiku got up from his spot next to the table and barked once before going to the back door with Minny at his heels.

"I hear her truck. I'll start the toast." Dawn smiled and jumped across to the toaster.

"And I'll pour the milk."

He always liked the first moment when Stonechild walked into the house. She'd look around for Dawn and her features would soften at the sight of her niece. She might not have acknowledged it to herself, but the connection was there and deepening. Then her eyes would find him and for the briefest of moments, he could tell that he was included in her circle. Slowly but surely, Kala Stonechild was letting them in.

"Something smells good," she said, kicking off her shoes and dropping her bag on the floor. She knelt and gave Taiku and then Minny a good rub down their sides.

"We made cheese and mushroom omelettes." The toast popped and Dawn got busy with the butter.

"You're wonderful. I'll wash up and we can eat."

Dinner was becoming a comfortable routine. He thought that the three of them made for an unlikely family, for that was how he was beginning to feel around them. Dawn felt like a daughter, and Stonechild ... well, she was someone he liked being around. When they finished the omelettes and toast, Stonechild made tea and Dawn left with the dogs to do homework. Before she reached the bottom of the stairs, Stonechild called to her, "We'll take the dogs for a walk after the tea, so don't plan to spend all evening shut up in your room."

Gundersund stood and walked toward the kitchen window. "Has it stopped raining?"

"It was drizzling when I came in. The weather person on my car radio is calling for it to clear by seven. Shall we take the tea into the living room?"

They settled on either end of the couch. He could tell during supper that Stonechild was bursting to tell him something and she wasn't long getting to it.

"I know Heath believes the Delaney case is closed, but Rouleau felt that I should keep the appointment I made with Benoit Manteau in Millhaven this morning."

"I could have gone with you."

"The fewer people involved the better, because there's going to be hell to pay when Heath finds out. I didn't want to get you into trouble."

She still didn't get it. "We're partners, Stonechild. We have each other's back, so if you're in trouble, so am I."

"I had your back. I was protecting you from Heath's wrath."

"You have to let me have yours."

They stared at each other and he saw something in her eyes that looked a lot like regret. He'd take it. "So what did you find out from Monsieur Manteau?"

"He carries around a photo of his baby daughter, the daughter he's never seen. Problem is, the baby in the picture is not Violet."

"How can you tell? All babies look much the same."

"Violet was blond and had blue eyes. The baby in Benoit's picture has black hair and brown skin, matching his own features. Turns out he has a different mother than Etienne. Benoit's mother was Hispanic. Benoit would have been suspicious if his child didn't have his colouring."

"Are we sure that Violet is Cécile's missing child?"

"Prevost said they came up with one hospital photo taken for ID purposes when Cécile's baby was born and the baby was fair and blue-eyed, like Violet."

"Don't mothers usually take a lot of pictures of their newborn?"

"Cécile apparently wasn't interested."

"Why would Cécile bother trying to fool Benoit? He was bound to find out about the kid's heritage if she hadn't been kidnapped."

"Good question. I'm thinking fear. She had to be screwing around on him and he didn't strike me as someone you'd want to do that to. There's a meanness underneath his charm that made my skin crawl. Maybe she came up with the idea of giving him that photo after she was sure her baby wasn't coming back. I think we have to have another chat with her."

Gundersund took a second to consider the implications. "So we have a violent boyfriend of a pregnant violent girlfriend who was sleeping with ..."

"My money is on one of the other upstanding family members. Etienne to be specific."

"Why Etienne?"

"Well I got a call to go see Catherine on my way back to the station. That's why I'm so late. Her son

Sammy is having nightmares about a man who talked to him and Violet at the nursery while Catherine was in the washroom. When I checked the visitor log at Millhaven today, Etienne happened to be visiting Benoit on the same day. It was right after that when Adele acted spooked and wouldn't leave the house all week. She made plans to take Violet to her sister's, something completely out of the ordinary. A week later, she and Violet went missing. Sammy couldn't give a description of the man, but I think he might have visited the Lockhart house. The other option is that the kid is traumatized and seeing the man in his dreams because on some level he knows the man killed his friends." Kala took a sip of tea and waited for Gundersund to absorb the information.

The linkages and possibilities all were coming up disturbing. Adele had stolen a child from the worst possible people and spent the next four years basically hiding out. Benoit Manteau's transfer to Millhaven had led to a chance encounter between Adele and Etienne that had blown her cover. Gundersund knew that Stonechild was onto something and that she wasn't going to let go of until she had the entire truth. "If what you're saying is true, Ivo Delaney is innocent and Heath isn't going to be happy. The Kingston force might have had a hand pushing Delaney over the edge and killing himself."

"Heath and his sins are the least of our worries. So will you come with me to Montreal tomorrow?"

"Yeah, I'm in." He would have liked to replace the tea with a shot of something stronger. Maybe it was just time to head home to bed. "Will you give Prevost a call and let him know we're coming? I'll leave now and pick you up around seven tomorrow morning if that's okay. It could be a long day."

"I'll call Prevost as soon as you leave and I'll be ready in the morning."

"What about Dawn? Tomorrow's Saturday and she'll be alone all day."

"I don't want to bring her with us." Stonechild hesitated. She said as if not convinced, "I guess it's a long time for her to be on her own."

The disturbing thing was that she'd see nothing wrong in leaving the kid for hours on end.

"Let me see what I can do," Gundersund said.

"I'd be in your debt."

They both stood and she walked him to the door, keeping a few steps behind. Her voice was quiet.

"Thanks Gundersund. I know I haven't always been the best partner."

He opened the back door and turned to look at her. Her expression was unsure for one of the few times he'd known her. He smiled and said, "Goodnight, Stonechild. Get some sleep and I'll see you bright and early tomorrow."

CHAPTER THIRTY

Stonechild and Gundersund dropped Dawn off at Vera's condo just after seven o'clock the following morning and left the two of them preparing for a day at the spa. Gundersund hadn't been sure how the idea would go over when Vera proposed it the night before, but Dawn seemed excited after Vera described the rejuvenating power of manicures and pedicures. Kala had looked unconvinced but gamely agreed that Dawn should give the spa a try.

"I really hope leaving Dawn with Vera wasn't a mistake," Kala had said walking back to his car. "I don't know if I could deal with a teenager obsessed with looking like a fashion model."

"You do know that you're an anomaly, right?" Gundersund teased, but he honestly didn't know what to make of her. She was the polar opposite of Fiona, who never left the house without perfect makeup and hair and a designer outfit. His limited experience with women had not included anyone like Kala Stonechild.

The weather had cleared overnight although the air was cool. The highways were dry and they made good time, reaching the outskirts of Montreal at ten o'clock. Stonechild's phone rang a minute later.

"It's Michel Prevost," she said to Gundersund before answering. "Hello?"

Gundersund could hear Prevost's voice from where he sat. Stonechild grabbed her pen and notebook from her bag. She scribbled down an address and directions and said they'd meet him there within the half hour. When she closed her phone, she shot him a smile.

"Prevost managed to get Cécile's address. She's living in a second-floor apartment at the corner of Davidson and Hochelaga near the Olympic Stadium."

"I know the area well," Gundersund said. "I used to be an Expos fan. She's living in an area called Hochelaga-Maisonneuve, or Ho Ma as the locals call it. An old working-class district close to the Saint Lawrence River that's being rejuvenated. It's a ways further east from Chez Louis on Sainte-Catherine. How do you want to play this interview?"

"Bad cop, bad cop. Let's use whatever we have to in order to get her to talk."

"You don't like her much."

"I can't say that she's my favourite person. She seemed ... mean, and I'm not a fan of mean."

"I'm with you, but we can't cross any lines, especially since this isn't our jurisdiction."

"Don't worry. I'll restrain myself."

They cut across the city toward the Big O towering large against the horizon. The grey stone, three-storey apartment building was on the right, a pizza restaurant taking up a chunk of the main floor. The door to Cécile's apartment on Davidson had been spray painted with blue graffiti.

"There's Prevost waiting across the street." Stonechild pointed to the bear of a man with black curly hair.

"Who's that with him?"

"No idea. He must have brought a friend."

Gundersund drove the length of the street until he found a parking spot. He and Stonechild hustled back on foot to where Prevost and his sidekick stood waiting. Montreal was considerably warmer than Kingston had been when they set out that morning. Such were the vagaries of a spring day in Canada.

"*Salut!*" Prevost greeted them and turned to the heavyset man next to him. "This is my colleague, Normand Duguay. He is here in case we need back up."

Duguay nodded. "*C'est vrai.*"

They crossed the road and Duguay remained at street level and the others climbed the stairs to knock at the door to Cécile's apartment. The pizza smell permeated the hall and a layer of shiny grease coated the walls.

"Whew! Imagine living here." Prevost waved a hand under his nose.

The door swung open with some force.

"What do you want this time?" Cécile's pale blue eyes darted from one to the other. "You may as well come in." She turned without waiting for an answer. Following her down the short hallway into the living room, Gundersund saw the green tattoo stencilled across the back of her neck, where her hair was pulled into a ponytail. The pattern was vertical and disappeared past the top of her T-shirt. He wondered how painful it must have been to have the needles inserted in that tender part of the body. It was beyond him why someone would pay to have another person hurt them and scar them permanently with ink.

The apartment was small and he had a view of all the rooms from where he stood. Through the open bedroom door directly ahead, he could see a mattress on the floor, the sheets and blanket a twisted mess, half on the floor and half on the bottom of the bed. The kitchen galley on the left was well stocked with a fancy coffee maker and new toaster. A small table and two chairs fit snugly into a corner. They stepped right and entered the living room; a larger space with parquet floors and a door leading onto a small balcony encased with black wrought-iron railing. Cécile had left the door open and a breeze stirred the blind and kept the air cool and fresh, diluting the smell of pepperoni and tomato sauce from the restaurant below and the stink from the smoked cigarettes in the overflowing ashtray.

"Have a seat." She pointed to a gold couch

against the wall beneath a print of nuns running down a street in old Montreal. The wind had caught under their wimples and they looked to be flying. "I'd offer you a beverage but know you're on the job."

Gundersund sat squished in next to Prevost. Stonechild wisely chose to position herself on one arm of the couch next to him looking down on Cécile, who took the recliner on the other side of the coffee table. Cécile tapped a cigarette out of the pack lying on the table and lit it as she watched them trying to get comfortable. It was the closest Gundersund had seen to a smile on her pinched face. She reached for the half-full beer bottle next to the overflowing ashtray and took a long drink.

"You haven't been truthful with us," Stonechild said in a voice so cold that Gundersund stopped pulling his notebook from his pocket. "And I have half a mind to have Prevost throw you back in jail." He looked up at Stonechild where she perched above him. Her eyes were fixed intently on Cécile, who returned her stare with equal animosity.

"How do you figure that?" Cécile sucked on her cigarette and blew the smoke toward them like a blast from a dragon.

By force of will, Gundersund kept himself from opening his mouth wide and inhaling. He'd given up the habit several months before and missed everything about smoking: the smell, the taste, the feel of one in his hand. Speaking of self-harm.

Cécile crossed one leg over the other and Gundersund saw another tattoo. This one a black dragon on the inside of her calf. She said, "Should I call my lawyer and see what he has to say about your unfounded accusation?"

"If you like." Stonechild shrugged. "Or you could tell us the truth and get it over with. For instance," she paused for a few beats, "why does Benoit Manteau, the man you claim is father to your child, have a photo in his pocket of a kid who has no resemblance to your daughter?"

Cécile blinked. Her eyes narrowed and she took another pull on her cigarette. Her voice was less defiant. "When did you see him?"

"It doesn't matter. How do you think he'd feel knowing that you've pulled a fast one on him for the last four years?"

"You didn't tell him?"

"That the picture of the baby he's been carrying around like a good luck charm isn't his? Not yet."

Cécile's shoulders relaxed perceptively. She watched them through another puff of cigarette smoke. She had the look of a poker player about to cut their losses. "Perhaps it was easier to let him believe the kid was his. He wouldn't have been pleased to find I'd been less than faithful when we were together."

"Who's the father?"

"That's not important."

"Oh, but I think it is."

They sat staring at each other without speaking. When it reached the point when Gundersund thought the impasse wouldn't be broken, Cécile mumbled out a name. "Etienne Manteau."

"Benoit's brother. I could see how he wouldn't take kindly to that." Stonechild's voice was deadpan. Prevost hadn't moved since the exchange began but he shifted his bulk forward at her comment.

Cécile barked out a laugh. "Are you kidding me? We'd both be feeding the fishes at the bottom of the Saint Lawrence. Benoit is in jail because he ordered a hit. He would not have lost sleep over two more bodies."

"Did Etienne tell you that he'd seen your daughter with Adele that day?"

"No. He kept the sighting to himself. I didn't know he'd found Pauline. If I had, I would have gone to Adele and taken my baby back."

"So to recap, Etienne is Violet's father and not Benoit, even though you let Benoit believe that he was the father. You had no idea that Etienne had found Adele and Violet, and you didn't go to Kingston on the day they went missing."

"*C'est vrai*. Etienne and I are not together since he took up with Li Li while I was inside. We speak but I am not his friend."

"Why did Adele really take your baby?"

"How would I know?"

The staring match was on again. Gundersund felt Prevost reposition himself next to him. His legs began to cramp.

Cécile's eyes were like a used car salesman's, assessing what Stonechild knew and how much she could get away with. Finally she sighed and said, "Okay, Etienne arranged it. Adele was to take my baby, Pauline, and keep her until I got out of jail. He had her do it because I was scared that Benoit would get wind that the baby wasn't his and then my life would be worth nothing. Etienne didn't tell me what he was up to until after the baby went missing. The problem was that Adele disappeared. The bitch double crossed him."

"You weren't in on this plan from the start?"

"*Mais non*! Good luck getting Etienne to admit anything, even that my baby was his daughter. Li Li is jealous and her father also knows how to make people pay."

"You could have come forward instead of letting the police search high and low for Pauline."

"It would have been suicide. We thought that Benoit was going to beat the prison rap. One look at the kid and we'd have been done for if she didn't stay hidden. I was frantic that he did not see any photos except the one I gave him. Benoit was already suspicious that Etienne and I were getting it on." Her eyes narrowed. "You can't tell Etienne that any of this information came from me. I will deny everything."

"Benoit's transfer east must have been a worry for you and Etienne. But at least your daughter was already missing."

Prevost spoke for the first time. "Convenient that we got the evidence that put Benoit away from an anonymous source."

Cécile's mouth lifted in a sideways smile. "No comment."

"And now he's mounting an appeal, saying that the evidence against him was rigged."

"No comment."

Prevost shook his head. "I would not like to be in your shoes, madam. If Benoit gets out and discovers the traitors inside his own circle, he will have anger in his heart. Etienne won't be happy either if he knows that you talked."

"But you cannot say anything."

"For now I will not reveal your name as long as you continue to cooperate."

"I don't want to go back to prison. I'll help you if you promise me that I won't go back inside."

"I will do what I can." He paused. "Perhaps it was best for you that the child was not found."

For the tiniest fraction of a second, the truth of his statement flashed across Cécile's face but she immediately dropped her head and moaned. "You have no idea the agony that I've been in, wondering what became of my daughter. I cry myself to sleep many nights. Years ago, when Etienne and I were in love, we wanted to raise her together, and with Benoit locked up for life, we could have. What will you do to me now?"

Prevost pushed himself up from the coach and groaned at the effort. Standing, he looked down at her. "You kept what you knew about your daughter's kidnapping a secret for almost four years. There will be no charges today if you come with me to the station to answer more questions and make a statement. That's all I can promise."

"I'll cooperate fully. I've been devastated by this. If Etienne had a hand in the deaths …" She shrugged. "I won't lift a hand to save him. He's nothing to me now. Our relationship didn't last because I blamed him for the ridiculous scheme that led to our daughter's disappearance."

"One last question." Stonechild had also pushed herself off the arm of the couch. "Do you believe that Etienne could have killed Adele and Violet?"

Cécile raised her head. Her eyes were eerily transparent in the sunlight streaming in from the open patio door. "I want to say no," she said, "but the truth is that I don't know what he might have done when he got his hands on them. He said many times that he could kill Adele for how she'd ruined our lives." Her eyes widened. "I wonder if she killed Violet herself when she knew he'd be coming for her. She was spiteful enough that if she couldn't have her, she would make sure that I couldn't either."

"Nobody has accused Adele of being spiteful except for you."

"She played the role of wife and mother so why not change how people saw her too? I mean, she was a stripper and a party girl when I knew her. She'd spread her legs for anybody if it meant getting paid. If she could shed that skin, how hard was it for her to remake herself as a nice person? But it was an act, Detective. It was all an act. Just look at how she disappeared with my baby and left me heartbroken for all these years if you need proof."

They gathered outside on the sidewalk. Duguay had waited upstairs for Cécile to cancel her work shift before escorting her to their car. "We can bring in Etienne Manteau for a going over but I don't think we have enough to charge him with murder." Prevost looked with questioning eyes at Stonechild before he slipped on his sunglasses.

Kala was quite certain that grilling Etienne would get them exactly nowhere, but she said anyway, "You know him. Do you think he'll reveal anything incriminating under questioning?"

Prevost and Duguay laughed in unison. Prevost said, "Not a chance, but we might shake him up. I'm amazed you got Cécile to admit what she did. Do you have something on her?"

"When I saw the photo Benoit's been carrying around I had a hunch. I never understood why Adele would quit her job and hang around a few months to steal the baby. The whole set up seemed fishy to me."

"Cécile has skeletons. She's as manipulative as they come and a match for the Manteau boys, from what I heard. Benoit was crazy about her."

"Yet, she isn't adverse to throwing him under the bus," said Gundersund. "Seemed to relish it, actually."

"These people would throw their own mother under the bus to save their bacon," said Prevost. "Perhaps Cécile is the vindictive one. Etienne is happy with Li Li who has better family connections than Cécile."

"A jealous ex-lover. They can be nasty."

"The first rule about these people is not to trust anything they say, but we're missing something. Cécile was waiting for me to take the conversation in another direction. Did you see how relieved she was when we got up to leave?" Kala felt like she'd let the fish off the hook. Cécile had been too willing to acknowledge the kidnapping. That could only mean that she was hiding a bigger sin. "What question didn't I ask? What was it she was waiting for me to nail her with?"

"We'll try to think on it when we question Etienne." Prevost sounded reassuring and Kala wanted to believe him.

"If you can handle the interview, we have somewhere to be this afternoon. We can return to Montreal this evening or tomorrow if you need us," Gundersund said.

Prevost looked momentarily surprised but nodded. "We'll make a full report and will let you know late this afternoon if we have anything."

CHAPTER THIRTY-ONE

If nature had been in sync with his feelings, the day would have been grey and overcast, not filled with summery warmth and sunshine that poured in through the stained-glass windows. Rouleau felt outside his own body, sitting in the small funeral home chapel next to his father with Frances's ashes in a blue urn on the altar. The entire week had been surreal. He took a look around.

"A good turn out." His dad commented. He was also craning his neck to have a look around the church. He swivelled his head back to face Rouleau and said, "Frances had a lot of friends."

Rouleau knew some of them on sight but nobody well. Frances had been the sociable one. The one people naturally gravitated toward. His job had kept him from socializing except on the odd occasion, but if he was honest with himself, he'd liked it that way. Frances had attended many functions without him when they were together and she'd carved a new life these last years since she'd left the marriage. Her present husband's family took up four pews alone.

The smells in the chapel caught in the back of Rouleau's throat — roses, incense, and grief from the families who'd sat in these pews before. He knew you couldn't smell grief, but today it filled all of his senses like dense fog. He couldn't pull himself out from under the depression that had settled into his being since Frances drew her last breath. Gordon had been with her when she slipped away. Rouleau had waited in his father's hotel room for the news.

Jim Croce's "Time in a Bottle" played through speakers at the front of the room and the murmur of conversations stilled. Frances had loved this song. She would have chosen the music before she got too sick. Rouleau bowed his head and closed his eyes.

"Well, well," said his father. He touched Rouleau's arm. A flurry of activity at the end of the pew and Kala Stonechild slid past knees until she was in the space next to him. Gundersund caused more disruption as people stood to let him by. He squeezed his bulk into the remaining space next to Stonechild.

"You didn't have to come," Rouleau said.

"Accept that we're here for you." Stonechild turned her head to smile at him.

He returned her smile and felt something of the emptiness lift. He felt her arm rest against his and the warmth penetrated the cloth of his suit jacket. She kept it there until they stood to watch Frances's family walk together up the aisle to the reserved pews at the front of the chapel.

* * * *

Later, after the service and reception of tea, finger sandwiches, and assorted cakes, they found a bar on Elgin Street and settled in with a round of Scotch and Stonechild's usual soda and cranberry. Two refills later and Henri left them to walk back to his hotel, refusing company, saying he could use the time to clear his head. Rouleau knew that his father was giving them room to discuss the case before the third round of Scotch left him and Gundersund the worse for wear.

"I'll be back to the hotel soon, Dad."

"Take as much time as you need, Son. I'm going to go to bed as soon as I get to the room."

Gundersund walked with his father to the entrance before heading for the washroom, leaving Rouleau alone with Stonechild.

"This must have been a hard week. You should have been walking up the aisle with the family." Her eyes were compassionate.

Rouleau couldn't return her stare for long. "No, it was better that I didn't. Gordon is her husband now."

"But you're still her family, even if you weren't together. Anyone can see that."

Rouleau was quiet for a moment. He'd shared some of his story with her at Christmas in Ottawa when they'd been drawn together over a lonely holiday. He thought he might owe her an explanation having let her into his confidence as far as he had. "The rage I felt for Gordon when I found out about their affair should have been directed at me. I was the one who neglected our marriage and let her slip away. Gordon stepped in to give her the attention that I should have given all along. It was only right that he be with her at the end."

"Your call."

He could tell that she wasn't convinced. Part of him liked that she was ready to come to his defence, however misplaced.

Gundersund arrived with two glasses of Scotch. He put one in front of Rouleau before settling into the seat next to him. If he noticed the silence at the table, he gave no sign. "So should we go over the case before the whisky takes hold?"

"I've kept up with the reports," Rouleau said. "Reading them has been a break, believe it or not. What happened in Montreal today?"

Stonechild hunched forward. "Cécile now says that Violet's father is Etienne Manteau and that they purposely led Benoit to believe that he's the father. She was scared about what he'd do to them if he found out his brother was sleeping with his girlfriend. The real kicker is that she said Etienne dreamed up the plot to have Adele kidnap the baby and to keep her hidden until they knew Benoit would be staying in prison. The plan went awry when Adele disappeared with the child."

Rouleau took a second to process the information and its implications. "How trustworthy is Cécile?"

Gundersund said, "All of them are serial liars. They take a grain of truth and embellish to put themselves in the best possible light. Cécile is no different, although she's managed to keep herself out of the kidnapping plot. Her only crime would be not reporting Etienne and Adele when she found out."

"It's difficult to trust what she's saying."

"She's been careful to lay the blame for that on Etienne, who's currently being interviewed by Prevost." Stonechild pulled out her cellphone and checked for messages. "Prevost promised updates on Etienne but we have nothing yet, although he texted an hour ago that they've let Cécile go after a few hours of questioning. They're considering charges."

Gundersund added, "Benoit Manteau's appeal is moving forward, and from what I hear he stands a chance of getting out. The key evidence has been found to have holes. However, nobody doubts that he ordered the hit that landed him there."

"Making Etienne and Cécile very nervous, I would imagine." Rouleau took a drink while he considered the angles. The drink was peaty amber with a satisfying burn that lingered in the throat. "If we go with this theory that Ivo Delany didn't kill Adele and Violet, but their murders were a result of her kidnapping the child, where did the killer hold Adele for the day and night before her body was tossed on the highway?"

They were silent as they each pondered the question.

"They could have gone to Montreal and back in that time." Gundersund spoke hesitantly, as if he didn't believe his own suggestion.

Rouleau nodded. "The question is why would the killer go to all that trouble? Any distance with a body in the vehicle is a bigger chance of getting caught."

Kala said, "Maybe he has a friend who lives in Kingston. These guys are connected to the biker network."

"Might even have been Benoit directing her murder from inside if Etienne had let him know where Adele was living."

"That's unlikely," said Kala. "Etienne would want to keep the child's location a secret from his brother. Remember that Benoit believes the photo he's carrying around of a mixed race child is his daughter, not a blond, blue-eyed girl with his brother's DNA."

"What if Benoit found out another way?" Gundersund asked. "He'd have good reason to kill Adele, and drowning the child would exact a twisted revenge on Etienne and Cécile. It would send a message."

"Who would have told him and what are the odds he'd discover their location the same time as Etienne did? Makes no sense whatsoever." Stonechild moved her chair back. "I'll be right back. I need to use the washroom."

Rouleau watched Gundersund watching Stonechild walk away. "She's not one to mince her words."

Gundersund looked at Rouleau. "I don't think we should rule out Benoit. He's conniving and ruthless. Someone could have tipped him off, especially if he might be getting out soon."

"We still haven't ruled out Ivo killing his family. Some might say that his suicide confirms his guilt."

"Yeah, we haven't managed to narrow this down much." Gundersund's phone vibrated on the table. He took a minute to read the incoming message. "That was Prevost. Etienne denies everything, even being father of the child. Prevost is holding him overnight while they search his apartment and car. He says there's no need to return to Montreal this evening."

"So you'll be heading back to Kingston?"

"Looks that way. And you?"

"I'll drive Dad back in the morning. He's still got to pack and will need some rest after today. I should be in the office early afternoon. Where's Dawn, by the way?"

"She's with Vera. She should be a fashionista by the time we pick her up."

Rouleau raised his glass and smiled. "Stonechild's going to love that."

CHAPTER THIRTY-TWO

"There's a spot over there." Gundersund pointed to a space at the end of the lot. "Next to the white van."

"Are you sure Vera said to meet them at this ball diamond?"

"Positive."

He could hear the cheering as soon as he stepped out of Stonechild's truck. The stands were filled with parents, grandparents, and kids, who sat in the higher rows. The team that was up to bat took up the bottom row of one of the two stands. As Gundersund and Stonechild approached, a boy swung at a ball and it bounced past the pitcher to the shortstop. A great throw to first and the boy was out. The kids sitting in the bleachers grabbed their ball gloves and headed for the field while the team in the field raced toward their bench. Gundersund saw Dawn running in from second base. She was the only girl on either team that he could see.

Vera waved from the top of the farther set of bleachers where Dawn's team was gathering.

"This way," Gundersund said to Stonechild. Dawn was standing near home plate wearing a batting helmet with her back to them, taking practice swings. She'd be first up. "We'll let her know we're here after she has her turn at bat."

They climbed past legs and bodies until they reached the empty space next to Vera. He'd never seen her dressed down, as she was now in faded jeans and a plaid shirt that tied at the waist, although she had on her red high heels. She'd pulled her hair into a ponytail that poked out from the back of her Blue Jays ball cap.

Stonechild sat between them and kept her eyes on Dawn. "What's going on?" she asked Vera.

"Dawn told me she'd been asked to play in this tournament but she didn't think she should because the girls in her class were jealous. I convinced her to give it a try. You can't spend your life giving in to what other people want you to be. This is her fourth game since yesterday and it's the final. She's better than most of the boys out there." Vera stood and yelled, "Hit the cover off that ball! You got this Dawn!" She put her fingers to her mouth and let out a piercing whistle.

Four heads turned to look up at her. They were girls who looked to be from Dawn's class. They nudged each other and one of them said something and they all laughed.

"I think I'm starting to understand," Stonechild said under her breath.

Gundersund leaned forward, elbows on his

knees, to watch Dawn. She stood at the plate holding the bat with easy assurance, elbows bent, feet planted, body turned slightly with her eyes on the pitcher. The pitcher looked around at his players and the outfielders moved in.

"She got to first two innings ago but the batter after her swung out. We're down one."

"What inning?" Stonechild asked.

"Eighth and we have last bat."

"Is she the only girl out there?"

"Some of the other teams had a girl or two but she's the only one on the teams that made the final."

The pitcher threw an overhand fast ball but Dawn didn't swing. It looked low but the umpire called a strike.

"Have an eye, ump!" Now Gundersund was on his feet.

A second pitch, low and away. The umpire signalled ball. Another pitch. Another ball called.

The catcher got up from his crouch and raced out to the pitcher's mound. They talked with hands hidden behind their gloves. Dawn took a few practice cuts across the plate while she waited.

This time the ball came hard and fast, waist level across the middle of the plate. Dawn put her body into her swing and a sharp crack split the silence. All heads moved to follow the arc of the ball as it rose over the head of the left fielder and hit the ground and bounced its way toward the fence. Dawn sprinted, past first, past second, and slid into third before the throw landed in the third baseman's glove with a sharp pop. He swung the ball down to tag her, but Dawn's hand was on the bag, her body stretched out at his feet. A groan and boos came from the bleacher next to them but everyone sitting behind Dawn's team was on their feet clapping and cheering. Even the four girls in front were celebrating with high fives. Dawn stood up and wiped off the dirt from her jeans and got set to run.

The next two batters didn't fare so well. The first popped out to the shortstop and Dawn had no chance to run home. The next batter swung out. A tall boy stepped up to the plate.

"Go, Cody!" Vera yelled.

"How do you know him?" Stonechild asked.

"He's the one who got Dawn out here. Apparently Cody's the class heartthrob. He was emailing, texting, and calling her so many times after you dropped her off that I was concerned because I thought someone was harassing her. She finally told me about the tournament. He seems like a nice kid."

The four girls in front began jumping up and down and calling his name. Cody glanced over before he got into position. The pitcher whipped the ball to third but Dawn made it back to the base before she was tagged out. She took a shorter lead off and the pitcher squared his body to throw. Cody connected with a fast ball down the centre of the plate. This time the ball cleared the fence and he loped around the bases. Dawn waited for him at home plate and they hugged before racing back to the bench.

The girls ran over to jump all over Cody. Dawn

stepped back and turned to look up into the stands. She smiled and waved when she saw Gundersund and Kala sitting with Vera. Some of her teammates stood up to pat her on the back and give high fives.

"One mystery solved," said Stonechild. "Nothing like a pack of jealous adolescent girls to torment a perceived threat. What should I do about it, Gundersund? My inclination is to go down there and punch the crap out them."

"My gut tells me she's handling it okay on her own. I have to say though, she's nobody's doormat." He could have added "like you," but he didn't.

Stonechild was quiet for the next inning while Dawn's team held off a late rally by the opposing team, keeping them from scoring. With a one run lead, they didn't need their final at bat and the celebrations began after the teams shook hands. Gundersund led the way down from the bleachers to congratulate Dawn. He saw Stonechild sizing up the group of girls who'd gathered around Cody and the pitcher. He could tell she wanted to do something to make them regret having gotten Dawn into trouble, and was relieved when she turned her back on them and left that battle for another day.

CHAPTER THIRTY-THREE

Kala arrived at work early after a restless night's sleep. The night before had proved anti-climatic following the excitement of the game. Dawn had been exhausted from her weekend of baseball and headed straight to her room to read before falling asleep. Kala hadn't thought it a good time to get to the bottom of the school drama, but she planned to as soon as a good opening presented itself. The opening might even be later today when she finally sat in on one of Dr. Lyman's sessions.

The thought of someone probing her motivations and psyche made her want to run for the hills, but if this soul-baring would make the difference between keeping or losing Dawn, she'd give it a shot. If Marci Stokes went ahead and published her article, Kala feared that Tamara Jones, in her earnest suit and black-and-white view of the world, would decide that Dawn had to go to a more suitable family. The thought of losing Dawn because of her own past life was a pricking worry at the back of Kala's mind. She knew now that keeping Dawn was the right thing to do. Not just because they needed each other, but also because Dawn deserved a stable home. Kala accepted that she had lots to learn about being a guardian, but she was going to do her best — all made easier because she was more attached to the kid with every passing day.

She'd put on a pot of coffee and was pouring herself a cup when Bennett walked into the office. He grabbed a mug from his desk and reached her as she set the pot back on the hot plate.

"You're the early bird. How'd it go in Montreal?" he asked.

She picked up the pot again and filled his cup as she spoke. "Good. Michel Prevost is holding Etienne Manteau and trying to get him to come clean about visiting his brother in Millhaven and possibly doing something to Adele and Violet. I doubt Prevost is going to make any headway, but you never know. How was your day?"

"Not as productive as yours."

Kala glanced over and could see that Bennett was holding back on something. "What's going on?"

"Nothing."

They headed back to their desks. He flopped down in his chair, looking like he'd lost his best friend.

Kala rolled her chair closer to his desk. "What is it, Bennett?"

He looked at her for a few beats, then shrugged. "I'm just having trouble with the way we handled

Ivo Delaney. I keep thinking we could have done something so he didn't resort to killing himself."

"He had mental issues and he'd just lost his entire family. You have to factor these into his decision."

"I guess."

"He was in incredible pain. Sometimes people can't take carrying on anymore and you have to respect their choice, no matter how abhorrent."

"You sound like you've had experience with this before."

"Yeah. A few times." She turned away and returned to the document on her computer. As in every investigation, she was rereading all of the reports. Making a chart of the facts, the suspects, motives, timeline. Drawing connections in the hopes that something would spark.

For the moment, keeping at bay memories of the friends who'd taken their own lives.

Woodhouse came in just before nine. Kala lifted her head and watched the terse exchange between him and Bennett. Something was going on. Bennett was keeping it bottled but it didn't take a mind reader. She thought about Woodhouse and the way he'd glommed onto Ivo Delaney as being the only suspect in his family's death. She looked at the report open on her computer screen. Woodhouse and Bennett had taken the break-in call the night before Ivo killed himself.

She filed away her unease and clicked on her report from her interview with Benoit Manteau in Millhaven. What had she missed?

Gundersund sauntered into the office a few minutes later with a box of muffins, and broke her concentration. She stood up and refilled her coffee cup and selected a fruit-explosion bran concoction. Woodhouse joined them and reached into the box for a muffin before saying, "Heath just sent a note that the Delaney file is closed. It's going to be ruled a murder-suicide, even though Delaney waited a few days to off himself."

"I didn't get that message." Kala wanted to wipe the smug look off his face.

"Check your inbox," Woodhouse said before he walked back to his desk.

She looked at Gundersund. "This is bullshit."

"I didn't get the email either." He smiled. "So until we hear from Rouleau ..."

"We carry on."

She sat back at her desk with a renewed sense of urgency. Her desk phone rang as she was going over her conversation with Benoit for the second time. She picked up, her mind still back in the prison reliving the expression on Manteau's face as he handed her the photo of his baby daughter. What had she seen in his eyes that had alerted her to keep her face expressionless? Because she'd known instinctively that he was watching for a reaction. *I have no problem with retribution, Officer Stonechild....*

"Hello?"

"Kala Stonechild? This is Marci Stokes from the *Whig*. I'm glad I caught you."

Kala straightened. "How can I help you?"

"I wanted to give you a heads up. We're short of stories for tomorrow's paper and the editor got wind of my article on you. He's running with it. I'm sorry. I don't know how he found out."

"Is there no way to stop it?"

"No, I'm really sorry. If it's any consolation, I went with the admirable way you turned your life around angle. You shouldn't have a backlash."

"You can't know that."

"I'm not pleased how this turned out."

Kala hung up without saying goodbye. *Shit.* What next? This day was getting worse and worse.

Her eyes travelled back to the computer screen. *Said Etienne has been to visit once. Mentioned summers at uncle's cottage outside Smiths Falls, still in family.* She blinked. Why had she put that detail in her report? She looked over at Gundersund then back at her computer screen.

"Find something?" He stood up and came up behind her to look over her shoulder.

"I'm thinking about what Rouleau asked, you know, about where Etienne might have kept Adele from that morning until the next night when he dumped her body. Benoit told me about his uncle's empty cottage outside Smiths Falls."

"Do you know where it is?"

"No, but the uncle's name is Maurice and he's in a home, I'm guessing in Smiths Falls."

"If we're lucky he's related on their father's side and his last name is also Manteau."

"That would be the easiest scenario."

"I'll make some calls."

Vera waylaid Rouleau in the hallway as he entered the station and directed him into Heath's office. She placed a hand on his arm. "My condolences," she said. "How're you holding up?" Her eyes were liquid pools of sympathy.

"I'm okay, but thanks, Vera."

"If there's anything I can do...."

They reached Heath's corner office. He stood and crossed the floor to meet Rouleau just inside the door. He shook Rouleau's hand and said, "So sorry to hear about your ex-wife's death. Never easy to lose someone you care for to cancer."

Vera hovered in the doorway as if unsure about leaving Rouleau alone with Heath. "Close the door on your way out," Heath said to her. "Shall we sit by the window, Jacques?"

Rouleau turned to thank her but the door was already closing and she was gone before he could call her back. He took a leather chair warmed by the morning sunshine while Heath poured coffee from a carafe on the table. He accepted the mug and waited as Heath settled across from him in the other leather chair.

"Well," Heath said. He took a sip of coffee. "I'm glad to put the Delaney case to bed. We can use our resources elsewhere."

Rouleau felt a great weariness come over him all of a sudden. He wished he could make himself still care about this case but Frances's death had drained him. Why not go along with Heath and let the investigation end? Barely anybody was even left to mourn this family, wiped from the face of the earth in cruel swiftness. His mind conjured up Stonechild's face next to him at the funeral. He could picture the betrayed look in her black eyes if he didn't fight for every ounce of truth, turn over every stone to make sure they had justice. The Delaneys might not have family who cared, but they had Stonechild … and they had him. He said, "I understand we still have a lead in Montreal. Etienne Manteau is being held and questioned overnight. I'd like to see it through."

Heath lifted a hand. "But there's no concrete evidence that proves Adele's past life was the cause of her death, what, three years later?" He sat forward as if to convince Rouleau. "What clinched it for me is the fact Delaney was out driving the night his wife's body was found on the highway. He couldn't account for his whereabouts and nobody saw him in the places he claimed to have been. He found out the week before that the child wasn't his wife's as she'd led him to believe, and unfortunately this betrayal played on his fragile psyche. Stacked alongside his dead sister, whom he likely killed as well, and we have a man who couldn't live with what he'd done. His suicide is, in fact, an admission of guilt."

Rouleau sat quietly and drank from his cup. Everything that Heath said made perfect sense. Blaming Ivo Delaney in death tied everything up neat and tidy. The thing Heath was neglecting in this scenario, however, was that they had no concrete proof that Ivo had killed his sister or his family. Rouleau set his cup on the table. "I'd like another few days to see how the Montreal angle plays out. It's already in motion with the Sûreté and we could look foolish if we call it off at our end and they find something we've missed."

Heath set his cup on the table next to Rouleau's. He leaned back and steepled his fingers together under his chin. "You believe there is anything to this Manteau business?"

Rouleau wasn't surprised that Heath was up on the file. He was nobody's fool, no matter his youthful cherub-like appearance and hands-off approach to investigations. The real puzzle was his obsessive need to look good in the press. He guarded a squeaky-clean image at odds with the extra-marital affair he was carrying on with Laney Masterson.

"There could be," Rouleau said finally. "I think we should at least rule them out if we can. The press won't be able to say later that we didn't pursue all the leads … relentlessly." The last word was added to appeal to Heath's vanity.

"I suppose we are quieter than usual at the moment."

Rouleau took that as assent. He changed the subject and didn't push the issue any farther.

Twenty minutes and another cup of coffee later, and he was on his way back to his office. Gundersund and Rouleau must have been watching because they appeared at his door as he was turning on his computer.

"Mind if we go for a drive to Smiths Falls?" Gundersund asked.

"Is this about the Manteau family?" Rouleau asked.

"We're not wanting to put you in an awkward position again," said Stonechild, "but we think we might have stumbled across the location where Adele Delaney was held that day when she went missing. The uncle, Maurice Manteau, owns a cottage at Otter Lake that's been vacant since he went into a nursing home."

"You're working on the theory that she was taken and not killed by her husband."

Stonechild nodded.

"Okay. See about a search warrant and contact the Smiths Falls police to clear it."

"We've already got that started," said Gundersund. "I have a buddy on the force so it shouldn't be a problem. We expect the warrant to be faxed before lunch. Will Heath put up a fuss?"

"I've bought us a few days." Rouleau was rewarded with a smile from Stonechild. "If you see anything suspicious, call me and I'll send a forensics team. Are they still questioning Etienne Manteau?"

"We haven't heard from Prevost this morning."

"All the more reason to follow up on this today then."

CHAPTER THIRTY-FOUR

Leanne Scott cursed the hot flashes that woke her up in the middle of the night in soaking sheets that were hot to the touch. More mornings than not she was exhausted before the day got underway, and this morning was no different. Her new ritual upon waking was to descend to the kitchen, make an extra strong pot of coffee, and down a cup before climbing back upstairs for a cool shower. Today, she sat in a semi-stupor at the kitchen table while she had her first cup. She thought about fetching the paper from the front stoop but that would involve movement. Much better to sit and think about nothing.

She heard Randy's feet hit the floor above her head and she pictured him moving around their bedroom, choosing his clothes for the day. She smiled knowing he'd be humming some country song totally out of key while he got dressed. The man loved to hum. He also slept on his back and snorted like a pony periodically, not quite as endearing, but she'd had a reprieve the last few months. He'd moved into the spare bedroom rather than suffer through her nightly three hours of tossing and turning that began like clockwork at two a.m., and who could really blame him? She would have liked to get away from herself too if she could.

She finally pushed herself to her feet and set her cup next to the coffee pot. Randy passed her on the stairs and gave her a kiss on the cheek as they squeezed past each other. He was wearing his Home Hardware shirt and smelled of Old Spice. "Meeting some of the guys for breakfast before work. I'll give you a call at break."

"Have a good one." She rubbed a hand across his cheek before continuing on upstairs. "You okay with pork chops for supper?" she called down from the landing.

"Sure," he yelled back before she heard the back door slam.

She sighed and considered going back down to lock the door because he never thought of it. She didn't mind being alone in the house with it unlocked, but not while she was in the shower. "This is Gananoque," Randy always said when she asked him to lock the door on his way out. "Last time I checked, nobody's done any raping and pillaging."

"Always a first time," she'd answer, but he never took her seriously.

She entered their bedroom and checked through her closet for something to wear to the clinic. Her navy pants were clean and it had been a while since she'd worn the thin grey pullover. Maybe she wouldn't sweat too much since the weather forecast was calling for a cool, rainy day again. She'd throw on the red silk scarf with the butterfly pattern to give the outfit some interest. She wouldn't even have to do any ironing. Bonus.

She thought about washing her hair but checked in the mirror and decided it could go one more day. She was never going to win any beauty prizes, but she liked to look respectable. Adele had been the one to get the pretty gene. Leanne swallowed hard. "Don't think about her," she said to her reflection.

The water took a while to reach a decent temperature. Leanne put on a shower cap and stood in the centre of the jets while she squirted shower gel labelled orchid bouquet onto a sponge. She'd never known an orchid to have a scent but was willing to accept that this is how they'd smell if given the chance. Randy had installed state-of-the-art shower heads from Germany that blasted water from four directions at the same time. He'd gotten a good employee discount and the project had kept him happy for an entire weekend. She was fine with the old showerhead but had to admit that the multiple jets were relaxing.

She towelled off and went back into the bedroom to get dressed. Then a second trip into the bathroom to brush her teeth, put on some blush and eye shadow, and pee out the first cup of coffee. Ten minutes later, and she was on her way back downstairs. She'd taken longer than she should have in the shower and would have to take the second cup of coffee in a mug on her walk to work. She couldn't remember if she'd brought her travel one home but would use her favourite Starbucks cup if not. It held a good amount.

Just as she was halfway down the hallway into the kitchen, she heard the weight of a floorboard shifting behind her. Having lived thirty years in the house, she'd come to learn its sounds — the furnace cycling on, the wind whistling through the cracks around the windows, the slam of the screen door. She could tell where Randy was in the house by creaks of the floorboards. The creaking behind her only happened when somebody stepped on a spot on the floor just outside the living room. It drove Randy nuts. He kept talking about taking up the floor and fixing it so that this wouldn't happen. She'd agreed, knowing that he never would get around to it. The noises didn't bother her and she didn't want the disruption that would come from ripping up the hallway. Randy always took forever to finish a project because he'd head off fishing or moose hunting when he had some days off.

Her first thought was that Randy had come home for something. Her second thought was that he would have announced his arrival so as not to startle her. Even as she discarded the idea of Randy being home, she knew that nobody had been waiting in the living room when she came downstairs or she would have seen them. These thoughts were followed by a surge of fear and the mother of all hot flashes. She stopped walking and froze in place for all of three seconds before she forced herself to spin around. The sight of a man less than a metre away made her blink and suck in air like a fish. She'd never seen him before, but she had a good idea who he was.

"How did you get in?" she asked, knowing full well he'd walked through the unlocked back door. "I want you to get out of my house right now."

"Not without Violet." He took a step closer.

"Violet? I'm sorry to tell you that she drowned a week ago. Why would you think —"

"Adele would never drown her. We both know that. Where have you hidden her?"

"You're out of your mind." Leanne took two steps back and then turned to run. She screamed as she felt his arm wrap around her neck, pulling her backwards. She flailed against the pressure of his body and twisted to get away but she was no match for his strength. The chop of his hand in the middle of her back made her scream again as pain shot through her shoulders and down her spinal cord. He let her go all of a sudden and she dropped to her knees. She whimpered when he kicked her in the ribs.

"Get up," he said. "We're going for a drive."

"Please," she gasped as she struggled to catch her breath. "I don't know anything."

"And I'm betting my kid's life that you do."

Her body picked that moment for a second hot flash to pulse through her like a blast of heat from a furnace. She could feel sweat bead on her face and roll down her freshly washed back. The feverish heat made her lightheaded. His kick to her ribs made her feel sick to her stomach. She slowly pushed herself from all fours to her feet and swayed while she tried to wrap her brain around the reality of who was in her house.

This nasty man is Violet's father.

Adele had told her that she'd been careful not to let anyone at Chez Louis know she had a sister. She'd lied about her hometown from the start, being fully aware of the kind of people she was living amongst and knowing she'd want out when she'd had enough. She'd liked the adventure at first, the novelty and the danger, but she'd never planned to spend her life in Montreal. *I just want to have a good time for a few years before I become old and staid like you, Leanne.* She'd laughed when she said it. Then her eyes had gotten serious. *I want to experience life and have some excitement before I die. Is that so wrong? Tell me how enjoying myself can be so terrible.*

The last Christmas that Adele had made the trip to Gananoque before she'd shown up with Violet, she hadn't been so bright eyed. She wasn't talking anymore about her exciting life in the big city, and Leanne could see the toll that living the lifestyle had taken. "Why don't you just leave?" Leanne had asked her.

Adele had shrugged and avoided meeting her eyes. "Soon," she'd said. "I just have a few things to wrap up first. I don't want them coming after me."

"Let's go," the man said, giving Leanne a shove toward the kitchen. "Out the back way."

Leanne worked some saliva into her mouth. "Where are we going?"

"Same place I took Adele. And if you still don't feel like telling me where my daughter is, maybe a call to your husband, Randy, will change your mind. I imagine he'll do anything to get you back safe and sound."

"Why? Why would you kill Adele?"

"Why? Because she took my daughter! That's why! She double crossed us. Cécile and I are getting our kid back and we're going to start our lives somewhere new. Your sister had a choice. So do you."

She turned her head and saw his mouth sneer sideways. His eyes were as cold as a January day. Adele had told her that these people were badass and nasty as snakes. This man and Cécile were the reason Adele had taken the baby and fled to a house in the country with dull, safe Ivo Delaney. *I can't give her back, Leanne. They're violent and she's so small and helpless. She won't stand a chance. I'd rather do us both in than let them have her.*

Leanne said, "I can't tell you where Violet is because my sister drowned her. You have to believe me."

The man's mouth lifted in a smile even as he kept his eyes on hers. "The thing is, lady, Adele told me that you *do* know." He gave her another hard shove just below her collarbone that sent her crashing into the wall. As she struggled to keep from sliding to her knees, she heard his words through a pink blur of pain.

"It was the last thing your sister told me before she died, and I'd have been here sooner if she'd stopped begging long enough to give me your real name and address."

CHAPTER THIRTY-FIVE

"Any word yet?" Gundersund asked.

Kala shook her head. "The assistant says Judge Dixon will sign as soon as she gets back from court. She's due in the office around one thirty."

"Well, I guess I can wait that long. The cottage isn't going anywhere."

"Yeah." Kala drummed her fingers on the top of her desk. She wanted to get moving. She pulled up the map of Otter Lake again and had another look at the road to Maurice Manteau's property. It looked to be off from the other cottages on a piece of pie-shaped land, ending in a narrow stretch of beachfront. The acreage spread like a fan back toward the road. She guessed the road would be more of a dirt track by the distance it was from the main road. Her cell rang and she checked the number.

"*Salut*, Prevost. Any news?" She was watching Gundersund as she spoke. He lifted his head and looked across at her. Woodhouse and Bennett were on a call. Prevost's voice was low and heavily accented.

"Etienne Manteau *dit rien d'important*. I had to let him go after breakfast. With sad misgivings."

"I didn't believe he would say anything, but thanks for trying."

"Ah, but I have something else to tell you. Chez Louis did not open today. It is the first time in the history of the bar. Many patrons were left *sans bière*."

"Could it have stayed closed because Etienne Manteau was in custody?"

"I don't think so. The cousin, Philippe Lebeau, runs the bar. He would still open without problem. I have one other odd thing to report."

"What's that?" She saw Gundersund get up from his chair and come toward her.

"Cécile did not go to the appointment with her parole officer yesterday afternoon. She's not in her apartment. I drove over myself to find her. We have put a bulletin out."

"So Chez Louis remained closed and Cécile has disappeared." She repeated for Gundersund's benefit. He was standing uncomfortably close, leaning across the desk to listen in.

"And Etienne is on the loose."

"Could they all be making a run for the border?" She was only half joking. Something was going on and they were a step behind. She hung up after thanking Prevost and looked up at Gundersund. "Our suspects in Montreal are on the move, it appears. What do you think it could mean?"

He stepped back and leaned against her desk, arms folded across his chest. Kala became aware of the smell of Irish Spring soap and freshly washed clothes dried in the outdoors. She took a closer look. His hair had been trimmed since she'd last seen him and he'd shaved the two days growth from his cheeks. If Kala had to guess, she'd say he'd been on a date with Fiona, or she'd moved back in.

"No idea," he said. "Feel like grabbing some lunch while we wait?"

"Why not?"

They got club sandwiches and coffee and found a table in the far corner of the lunchroom. A lot of support staff were on break and the noise level was high. Kala looked for Fiona as she balanced the tray and wove through the rows of chairs but didn't see her. Gundersund was walking ahead with his head lowered and didn't appear to be searching for his wife. Kala decided not to read anything into it.

Gundersund knew Kala well enough to stop talking while they dug into the food, something she appreciated about him. She liked to enjoy what she was eating, even if just a cafeteria sandwich. When she was onto the last wedge, she looked up and saw him staring at her with a smile on his face. She reached for the napkin and wiped her mouth. "What?"

"I don't know. I like watching you eat."

"Great. So I'm a freak show."

"No, that's not it. I like that you get so much enjoyment out of your food. It's refreshing."

"Well, I like to eat."

"That makes two of us." He took a big bite of sandwich as if to prove his point. After chewing and swallowing, he said, "Say, have you seen how Woodhouse is strutting around lately like the cat that ate the canary?"

"That's the way he's always been." She tried to think if Woodhouse had said anything out of the ordinary and couldn't come up with anything. "He's probably showing off for Bennett. You know, doing that dominant male stuff to make certain Bennett knows his place in the pecking order."

"Maybe. How's it going with Dawn since the baseball tournament?"

"I have a meeting with her counsellor Dr. Lyman today. Dawn and me both."

"You seem worried."

"Because I am. I have no faith in the system, in case you haven't noticed."

"They'd be crazy to move Dawn now. She's settling in with you and getting happier. You're doing a great job, Stonechild."

"I'm not so sure, but thanks. Tomorrow I might have a fight on my hands to keep her."

"Why's that?"

"Nothing for you to worry about."

"Well, if I can help ..." His phone buzzed on the table. He grabbed it and checked the message. "Time to roll. The search warrant just came through."

"At last." She slurped the last of her coffee as she stood. "Let's hope I'm not taking us on a wild goose chase."

* * * *

Randy pulled two green plastic lawn chairs off the pile and carried them to the cash for Mrs. Fielding. She tried to slip a five dollar bill into his hand but he gently refused it. "You keep that for your grand-kids," he said and was rewarded with a wide smile. Mrs. Fielding had lost her husband two years before and Randy worried that she was showing signs of dementia. He'd passed the information along to Leanne in the hopes she could warn Mrs. Fielding's doctor at the clinic. He waited around until she'd paid for the chairs and then took them into the parking lot and slid them into her hatchback. The clouds were looking ominous and the wind had come up since he'd driven to work. Another spring storm rolling in. On the way back across the parking lot he spotted Chuck Darenger having a smoke on the far side of the building.

"What's going on?" Randy asked as he approached.

"Nothing. Just finished putting out the fertilizer and compost." Chuck pointed inside. "Did you hear them paging you just now?"

"No, I was helping Mrs. Fielding."

"Well somebody wants you."

"Guess I'll go check."

He headed back to the main doors, figuring Leanne had finally gotten some free time at work to call him back. He'd left a message on her cellphone at his ten o'clock break just before his phone ran out of juice. It was charging in the office so if she'd been trying to reach him unsuccessfully she'd try the store line.

Kelly was behind the customer service desk. She waved him over.

"Hey, Randy. The clinic just called a minute ago and asked that you phone them back."

"Was it Leanne?"

"I don't think so."

"Great, thanks."

An uneasy feeling made him quicken his steps to the back office to get his cellphone. It was three quarters charged and the light was flashing to show he had a message. Looked like Leanne had tried to get ahold of him. He hit her speed dial number and listened to it ring five times before going to her voice mail. Strange but not worrisome. He squinted at the screen and scrolled through the address book until he found the clinic. A few seconds later, the other receptionist, Wendy, picked up.

"I'm looking for Leanne," he said. "Can you pass me over to her?"

"Randy? I just called you because she hasn't come in this morning and she's not answering her phone."

"That can't be right. She was getting ready for work when I left the house this morning around eight."

"It's not like her to miss work without notifying us. I hope everything's okay."

"I'm sure it is. I'll make a run home and will call you after I speak with her."

He disconnected and stood for a moment

looking out the office window. It had gotten darker since he helped Mrs. Fielding with her chairs. He heard a rumble of thunder and looked around for his rain jacket. It was hanging on a hook on the back of the door. He grabbed it on his way out.

"Just heading home for a minute," he said to Kelly on his way by. "Call this my early lunch."

He drove above the speed limit and arrived home ten minutes later at the same time as a lightning flash jagged across the sky off to the east. The clouds had darkened and hung low over the town. The rain would be starting any second. Leanne walked to work so he wasn't alarmed to see her car in the driveway. He parked behind it and skirted around the house into the backyard. One of her flower boxes was tipped over near the walkway and he tried to remember if it had been upright when he left for work that morning. He would have sworn it had been. The wind was strong but not that strong.

What the hell was going on?

He opened the back door and called her name but silence greeted him. He spotted her purse hanging on a hook just inside the door. She never left home without it. His voice rose to a higher pitch as he yelled for her and ran from room to room. Back in the kitchen he tried to get his breathing under control and think this thing through. His phone buzzed in his pocket and he quickly checked the number. Kelly was calling him from the store.

"Yeah, Kelly. I seem to have a problem here at home so I probably won't be in for the rest of the afternoon until I get it sorted." He listened and then said. "Thanks. You too."

He leaned against the counter with the phone in his hand. Her call reminded him that he hadn't checked his voice mail and he logged into the system. The second message was from a number he didn't recognize. He clicked on the right button to listen to it. A stranger's voice filled his ear.

"I have your wife. We're having a friendly chat about where the two of you've hidden Violet. If you want Leanne back in one piece, I'd say you better get my kid to me ASAP. Call me back at this number."

Randy clicked on the next message. This time it was Leanne's voice, shakier than he'd ever heard it.

"Randy, he means what he says but I keep telling him we don't know where ..." A scream, and the line went dead.

Randy clicked back through the messages until the man rhymed off his phone number again. He logged out of the voice mail system and punched in the digits with sweating fingers. The phone rang once before the man picked up.

"I'll bring her." Randy said into the silent phone. "Tell me where to make the trade."

After he tucked his phone back into his pocket, he jotted down the instructions on a notepad in the shape of a cat that Leanne kept by the home phone. Then he took the steps two at a time into the basement. He used a key on his key ring to unlock a cabinet partially hidden behind the couch and pulled out his hunting rifle. From a separate location he took cartridges from a box and loaded the chamber.

The rain soaked him on his way back to his truck but he barely registered the wet or the cold. He unlocked the front door and hid the loaded gun on the back seat under a Hudson's Bay blanket. The fear he'd felt at hearing the man say he had his wife had turned to fury when he heard Leanne scream. If this guy thought he was going to do to her what he'd done to Adele, then he had another thing coming.

He'd blow the bastard away without a second's hesitation.

CHAPTER THIRTY-SIX

They left the cafeteria and stopped by the office before heading to Otter Lake. Gundersund crossed the floor to Rouleau's office to check in while Stonechild went to the washroom. Bennett and Woodhouse were back at their desks, both speaking on their phones. An unnatural darkness had settled outside the windows, making it look as if night had fallen. Wind battered the glass but so far no rain.

"We're on our way to Smiths Falls," Gundersund said, standing in the doorway.

Rouleau looked up from a document he was reading. He'd turned on his desk lamp and the light was a circle of brightness in the dark room. "There you are. I'm sorry to make you put off your trip, but Heath wants you to take a call at the mayor's office. It's a sensitive case of a staff member being stalked and he specifically asked that you take it. I've opened a new file in the system under today's date and sent the case number to you in an email."

"Woodhouse and Bennett should be able to handle the interview."

"Normally I'd agree, but Heath was adamant that it be you and Stonechild."

Gundersund rubbed his jaw and thought about how he'd tell her that their jaunt was on hold. He heard her laugh and looked over his shoulder. Stonechild and Bennett had their heads together at her desk.

He looked back at Rouleau. "What if I go to the mayor's office alone and Stonechild and Bennett have a look at the cottage?"

"You think it's that urgent?"

"To be honest, I have no idea, but this feels like something that has to be done sooner rather than later." He must have caught some of Stonechild's bloodhound instincts because he was as disappointed as he knew she'd be at the thought of waiting another day.

"So, ready to hit the road?" Stonechild had come up behind him. She was holding a black raincoat. "I want to make sure we're back in time for my appointment with Dawn at four-thirty."

"We've got a change of plans," Rouleau looked past Gundersund to where she was standing. "Take Bennett. Call in when you've had a look at the cottage and I'll have a forensics team on standby." She stared uncertainly at Gundersund and he nodded. "I've got another call. I'll see you later."

Her eyes told him that she found this odd but she would roll with the change. She nodded back and went to tell Bennett he'd be her partner for the afternoon.

Gundersund took another look out the window as he walked back to his desk. Was it the impending storm that was making him apprehensive about letting Stonechild go on this trip without him? Driving might get rough when the rain struck, but she was more than competent. He tried to shake off the worried feeling, but it was still with him when he sat at his computer to check the messages. "Take your sidearm," he said as she passed by him on the way to the door.

Stonechild stopped as if considering. "Yeah, okay, although probably not necessary."

"I've got mine," said Bennett, rounding his desk to follow her.

"That'll be enough. We're not going to arrest anybody." Stonechild kept walking and was out the door before Gundersund voiced his unease.

"Don't worry," called Bennett, stopping and turning as he reached the exit. "I'll keep a good eye on her." He grinned and dimples appeared in his cheeks, making him look all of fifteen years old.

Gundersund watched the door close after him before turning back to the task at hand. He rubbed the scar on his cheek and told himself to relax. The feeling in his gut was simple indigestion from having eaten too quickly and drinking one too many cups of coffee. The two of them would be fine. He'd get this call over with and pick up some groceries on his way home. It would be good to finish work early for a change. Maybe he'd even get some laundry done. He was down to his last pair of clean socks.

* * * *

"When will this damn rain stop?" Randy craned his neck and looked up at the sky through the windshield wipers. He was waiting for a chain of cars to pass by on the left so that he could turn onto Otter Lake Road from Highway 15 north. The drive had been slow going with the rain coming down in buckets and a bunch of slow-moving cars in front of him. Normally, he would have passed them in a nanosecond, but vision was limited and he wanted to make sure he wasn't in an accident. That's all he'd need.

A break came in the oncoming traffic and he made the turn. He took a second to pull over and check the map. The cottage was on the left side of Otter Lake, toward the southern tip. It was a fair-sized lake and the cottage lots looked to be big and well treed. Lots of cedar and deciduous trees, not yet in full leaf. Some of the lots had grass to mow once the season got going but others had kept a wilder tangle of bushes and forest. They'd give him some cover. He didn't spot any cars on the properties as he drove slowly past. This weather and the lousy spring would have kept people from opening their cottages for the season. The road was paved but narrow with a yellow line painted down the centre, for which he was thankful with the rain making it difficult to see far ahead.

The man had told him to drive about ten minutes until he saw a red scarf tied to a post on his left. The cottage would be down the incline heading toward the water. He was to pull in and park and wait for the man to come to him. "Yeah, right," Randy said out loud. "Wait in the cab like a sitting duck while you take a shot at me from wherever you've settled yourself."

About five minutes down the road, Randy pulled off and backed his truck through a tangle of weeds to park behind a string of cedar trees. When he was satisfied that the truck couldn't be spotted from the road, he put on his rain poncho and grabbed his rifle from under the blanket. He slid out of the cab and shut the door as quietly as he could, leaving the key in the ignition. With the nose of his truck pointing toward the road, he'd be ready for a quick getaway if it came to that.

The sound of the rain pattering on the cottage roof and trees made Randy feel like he'd stepped into a world cut off from civilization. The rain muffled sounds and gave a dreamy feel to the woods. He figured he had a few kilometres to go before his destination but he'd be careful and stay hidden just off the road, keeping to the trees and bushes. He was going to need the element of surprise to separate this guy from Leanne so he could get off a good shot. Hopefully, there was only one of them; he had no reason to think otherwise. His first choice would be to shoot the guy in the leg to immobilize him, but he'd do what he had to do. Shooting a man would be like shooting a moose. He had to think of it that way. He had to remember what this animal had done to Adele.

CHAPTER THIRTY-SEVEN

"The turnoff is coming up on your left," Bennett said, checking his phone. "Otter Lake Road."

"Glad you can see it on your map because I can't see much through this rain." Kala had made good time considering the steady downpour since they left Kingston. They'd veered north on Highway 15 outside Gananoque.

"Have you figured out how we're going to gain access to the cottage?"

"I can pick the lock."

"Really?"

"It's better than breaking in the door. We have the search warrant so we can get in however we need to."

Bennett looked at her and grinned. "I like how you northern cops operate."

She glanced at him. "How's it going with Woodhouse?"

"I asked Rouleau to partner me with you if that's any indication." He pointed. "There's the turnoff. Hang a left."

She swerved a little too quickly onto the side road and the back tires skidded before she regained control. "That came up fast."

"Sorry. I almost missed the turnoff."

Kala geared down to a crawl. "Sometimes working with a partner takes a while to become an easy relationship."

"I prefer when it's easy from the start." He looked down at the directions in his lap. "We continue on a ways. This road circles the west end of Otter Lake and the Manteau cottage is at the south end. I'll keep an eye for the Coopers' sign because Manteau's is the next lot over."

They were silent for a while, Kala concentrating on the narrow road slick with rain and flooded in spots. Bennett kept his eyes on the side of the road, searching for the Cooper sign, which should be at eye level and nailed onto a post.

"The lots are long and narrow but the cottages aren't that far apart," he said. "The good thing is that they've kept a lot of trees and wild growth so it doesn't feel too civilized."

"A lot of these properties have lawns. Why would you have a lawn that you have to mow all summer? And a cottage the size of a house. I don't get it."

"Where do you go to escape from it all?"

She didn't answer for a while, but then said, "North in the bush with my canoe. I think we're getting close." She thought she saw movement in the trees to her left and slowed even more. She looked back using the side and rear-view mirrors speckled with rain drops. Nothing. Maybe she'd seen a deer. Whatever it was had been a dark, blurry form through the side window. She sped up the truck again as fast as she dared.

A minute later, Bennett pointed toward a track leading onto a property next to a sign that said THE COOPERS. "There's the sign. Manteau's place should be the next one over."

The Manteau property was a thicket of overgrown cedar bushes and long grass, beaten down by the rain. She spotted a small cottage with faded red siding and a black roof with weathered shingles nestled partway down a rutted hill. The lake was grey and choppy farther down the incline. Thick stands of trees surrounded the dwelling.

"I guess I'll turn around and park on the road," Kala said. No point driving down there and getting stuck in the mud."

She drove a bit farther until she saw an opening wide enough to turn the truck. A half minute later and she was back in front of the Manteau cottage and parked just off the road with two tires in the thick grass. She turned off the engine and looked over at Bennett. "Well, shall we go have a look?"

"I'm pumped to see you pick the lock."

"Doesn't take much to amuse you, does it?"

"Not usually." He flashed her a wide grin and opened the door.

They'd put on their rain jackets in the truck and both pulled up their hoods and started walking, Bennett in the lead. Stonechild reached for his arm as she spotted tire tracks off to her right, almost hidden by the swaying grass. Her heart jumped.

"Bennett, somebody's been here recently. I think we should slow down and scout this out."

Bennett turned. He tilted his head and began to say something at the same time as a gunshot blasted through the curtain of rain falling all around them. For Kala, the next surreal seconds happened in slow motion, beginning with the startled expression in Bennett's eyes at the moment of impact. Immediately afterward, his mouth opened into a round circle of surprise and he looked to be trying to say something before his eyes rolled back and he slumped hard against her. Kala reached for him and they both tumbled into the wet grass, her managing to break his fall with her body. She lay winded for several seconds afterward, struggling to catch her breath, frantically trying to make sense of what had just happened. When she finally let go of him and lifted her hands from his back, bright red blood coated her palms and dripped from her fingers.

This can't be happening. "Bennett? Can you hear me?"

Somehow, she rolled him sideways and scrambled out from under him. She crouched as low to the ground as she could and searched for the shooter. The rain was running into her eyes and she blinked to clear her vision. She couldn't see anybody near the cottage or in the trees, but there were lots of places to hide. They could be anywhere. She looked down at Bennett's wound. The bullet had entered near his shoulder and blood was spreading from under his rain jacket. They were sitting ducks where they were. Her police training kicked in.

She got to her feet and grabbed him around the waist, pulling him toward a clump of bushes several feet away. Another gunshot and a bullet whizzed by, ricocheting off a tree behind them as they reached cover. She ducked and rolled Bennett onto his side and felt under his jacket until her hand grabbed the handle of his handgun. She worked it out of the holster and then turned Bennett onto his stomach. She checked to make sure the gun was loaded and set it next to her as she tried to stem the flow of blood from his exit wound. She made a compress from a scarf she had in her pocket. It wasn't great, but was better than nothing. The shot looked to have gone through his shoulder but could have hit his lung. It must have missed his heart because he was still breathing. She lifted one hand and felt for her cellphone. As she pulled it out, she looked up.

"Drop it in the grass," said Philippe Lebeau. He had a handgun pointed at her face. Rain had plastered his long hair to his head and his beard was dripping water. "Then get up real slow and walk ahead of me to the cabin."

She dropped her phone and raised her hands, palms facing him before carefully getting to her feet. "I don't want to leave my partner. He needs medical attention."

Lebeau didn't say anything. He motioned with the gun for her to get moving. Then he crouched down with the gun still pointed at her while he picked up Bennett's service revolver.

Kala took a last look at Bennett and started walking with her hands in the air at chest level. How had this gone sideways so quickly? Was Benoit Manteau directing Lebeau from his prison cell or was Lebeau working on his own? Were Etienne and Cécile in the cottage? She stumbled and slipped on a muddy patch but managed to remain upright. Lebeau was a few feet behind her and she could hear him curse when he slid on the same piece of ground. She thought about turning and lunging at him but he wasn't close enough and she didn't like her odds. They reached the back door and she looked behind her. He was right there, the gun inches from her neck. She stepped sideways and opened the door. As she went to step inside, Lebeau gave her a shove from behind and she stumbled into the kitchen and landed on all fours.

She lifted her head. Through a wide doorway, she saw a small living room with a brown couch under three large picture windows with an external door on their right. The floor was gritty with dirt under her throbbing hands and the room smelled of mildew and something rotting. Lebeau was on her before she could get up. He yanked her arm and pulled her to her feet. "Stand still," he ordered and she felt his left hand patting her down, resting longer than it needed to on her breasts and rear end. She could feel rage growing inside her and it took all of her will power not to lash out. She closed her eyes and counted to five in her head. She'd try talking him down first and hope he lowered the gun. Then she'd strike.

He grabbed her arms from behind and pulled her roughly over to the counter. She heard him rummaging around in a drawer before she felt a rope bite into her wrists as he tied her arms behind her back. When done, he let her go and pushed her into the living room.

She managed to stay standing and turned to face him. "Let's talk about what's going on." She kept her voice neutral, non-accusatory. "Is Etienne with you?"

"Sit on the couch."

She looked toward the two bedrooms as she crossed the distance to the couch. Someone's legs and feet were stretched out on a bed through the closest open door. She reached the couch and sat down awkwardly, her wrists aching from where he'd tied them. "Who's that in the bedroom?" she asked. "Are they okay?"

"All I wanted was to get my kid and get out of here. Why the hell did you show up? Did he call you?"

"Who? Did who call me?"

"Her husband."

Kala tried to think. She had no idea what was going on and felt on slippery, shifting ground. Lebeau's face was red and angry and he was jumping around while he talked, the gun always pointed in her direction. She had to remain calm. She had to get him to calm down too. This could be her only chance.

"I think we need to get some medical help," she said. "You don't want to hurt so many people."

Lebeau rubbed his fist across his jaw. "It didn't have to be this way. She could have just told me where she had my kid. None of this had to happen."

Kala felt the first toehold. "You tried to get Adele to hand over Violet. You're the father, not Etienne or Benoit."

His eyes signalled that she was right. "Cécile and I are going away as soon as he brings our daughter."

She risked another question. Keep him talking. Use his name. "Philippe, how do you know she's your daughter and not Etienne's?"

"Because she wasn't sleeping with him. She was sleeping with *me*."

"Not Etienne?"

Lebeau started pacing, checking out the kitchen window as if waiting for someone. He came back and looked at her. "I was the poor cousin with the crackhead mother. They looked at me like a charity case, always giving me the leftovers, making me feel like dirt. Giving me a fucking bartender job and cutting me out of being an owner. Like I owed them for the air I breathed. Well, I got the last laugh on Benoit and I'm about to have the last laugh on Etienne too when they arrest him for Adele's murder ... and yours." He slowly raised the gun. "Cécile picked me over the two of them. We used to lie in bed and laugh at them. We talked about taking their money and going where they'd never find us. That kid is mine and nobody is going to take her from me. Not Adele. Not her sister. And not you."

Kala heard the click of the gun hammer being pulled back. A deep calm filled her as she considered that these would be her last moments alive. She hoped Dawn would be spared knowing how this ended.

He sounded almost sorry. "Hell of a shame it had to come to this. Would have been better for all of us if you'd pinned Adele's murder on Ivo."

She closed her eyes and prepared herself for the impact. In what she knew was a futile effort to save herself, she twisted her body and rolled sideways at the same time as a gunshot blasted through the closed window. Shards of glass exploded into the room. She fell onto the floor and banged her cheek and forehead hard as she landed. Her ears were ringing and felt stuffed with cotton batting. Through one eye she watched Lebeau's arms fly up over his head and his gun go flying across the room, crashing into the wall. Blood pumped from his chest and he fell backwards onto the floor, his feet landing not far from her own.

"You okay in there?" She heard through the hole where the window had shattered and thought she recognized the voice. She lifted her head as Randy Scott rammed in the door like some avenging angel. He towered over her for a second before kicking Lebeau in the legs to see if he was alive. Satisfied, he grunted and crouched down next to her. He eased her into a sitting position. "Have you seen my wife?"

Kala licked her lips. "I think she's on the bed."

He stood and took a step toward the bedroom. "Leanne!" he called as he started running.

Kala pushed herself to her feet, using the couch as leverage. Philippe Lebeau had believed Leanne and Randy had his daughter. He'd gone completely off the deep end. She was dizzy but stepped around Lebeau's lifeless body and staggered toward the bedroom. She leaned against the door jamb and saw Randy cradling Leanne in his arms. Her face was bruised and her lip was bleeding onto his shirt.

"Is she…?"

"Still breathing strong. My wife is hardy stock."

"Thank God." The second of relief disappeared as quickly as it came. "Can you untie me? I have to get to my partner. He's been shot and is lying outside."

"I saw him and bandaged him up with my shirt. He was coming around. I left him propped against a tree. That's why I took a bit of time getting around back to get a shot off. I called for help on my cell and they should be here soon. I asked for a couple of ambulances. Looks like we're going to need them."

For the first time, Kala noticed Randy's bare chest inside his open raincoat. "Thank you for all you've done. I hate to think how this would have ended without you."

Randy lay Leanne gently back on the bed and took a hunting knife out of a sheath on his belt. He held the rope around her wrists steady with one hand and said as he cut, "You're hurt too. Your face is puffing up on the one side and I think there's glass in your other cheek."

After he said it, she began to feel sharp jabs of pain. The rope fell to the floor and she shook her hands to get the blood circulating. She gingerly touched her forehead with tingling fingers. When she removed her hand, warm blood dripped into her left eye from a piece of embedded glass. There was no time to worry about fixing herself now.

"I'm going to find Bennett and wait with him for the paramedics. Did they say how long?"

"The dispatcher was sending the police and ambulances from Smiths Falls, so not too long. I pressed the urgency."

She turned before leaving. "I'm going to kiss you when this is all over."

He'd already picked up Leanne and was rocking her in his arms. "I might just hold you to that."

Gundersund was in the emergency waiting room watching for Kala when the doctor finished with her physical and released her. He sat in the closest row of chairs facing the corridor and his worried eyes caught sight of her as soon as she entered from the direction of the examination rooms. He was out of his chair and next to her before she'd taken another step. He reached out and took her by the arm.

"I must look a sight," she said by way of greeting, "but I've got the clean bill of health." She tucked a prescription for painkillers into her jacket pocket. "Been here long?" She aimed for lightness, trying to counter the shakiness in her limbs that she was certain he could feel.

"An hour. Dawn is having some girl time with Vera." He moved his hand from her arm and wrapped his arm firmly around her waist. "Do you want to sit for a minute?"

"What I want is to get out of here. Any word on Bennett?"

"Rouleau and Woodhouse are with him. Woodhouse sent a text a few minutes ago. Bennett's being prepped for surgery. His vital signs are strong and the doctor says he expects a full recovery."

"Thank God for that." She let herself lean into him. "I'd like to stay but feel the need to lie down all of a sudden."

"Rouleau will call when he's out of surgery. I'm to take you home."

They made it to Gundersund's car and he helped her into the passenger seat. They'd given her a shot of something and the world felt floaty and pain-free. She pulled down the visor and looked in the mirror for the first time. Her face was a mess of cuts and bruises. She snapped the visor back into place. No wonder Gundersund was treating her as if she was about to keel over.

He got into the driver's side and turned on the engine but he didn't make any move to back out of the parking spot. He looked over at her. His eyes were filled with regret and a smouldering anger.

"I should have been with you, not Bennett. I have more experience and I had this feeling…. I would have been expecting trouble." He hit the steering wheel with the palm of his hand.

She turned her head sideways to face him. "You warned me. *I* should have been more careful. This is on me, Partner. Not you."

He shook his head. "If anything had happened …"

"But we're alive and Lebeau isn't. It all worked out. That is, except for Bennett being in surgery."

Gundersund held her eyes for a few seconds more before he rested an arm across the seat and started backing up. "You're aging me, Stonechild," he said. He glanced over at her and smiled. "My hair has gotten a darker shade of grey since the phone call came in about the shooting." He straightened the wheel and aimed the car toward the exit. "Next time you decide to investigate a crime scene, I won't let us get separated. I promise you that."

She knew that fear and guilt were driving his words but they made her feel warm inside all the same. He was concerned about her, and for this moment she'd pretend that he cared for her more than a little bit. Her eyes began to get heavy. She said, "When Lebeau was aiming that gun at me, my last thought was that you'd take care of Dawn. I could die with no regrets knowing."

Gundersund stopped the car at the entrance to Division Street and reached over to take her hand. She opened her eyes and he was watching her, the fierce look making his blue eyes even bluer. "I'll always have your back," he said. "Just like I know you'll always have mine. We're in this together, Stonechild. Don't ever forget."

"I won't," she said, and for the first time, she believed it to be true.

Chapter Thirty-Eight

Kala agreed to meet Tamara Jones at her office in the Family and Children's Services building on Division Street, not far from the police station. The building was new — three storeys of brown and grey rectangles layered on top of each other. Tamara greeted her at the front door and they took the elevator to a third-floor meeting room. Even though they'd rounded the corner into May and the temperature hovered around twenty degrees Celsius, Tamara was dressed in a winter blue pant-suit and severe white blouse buttoned to the top of her neck. Her eyes weren't as chipper as on their last encounter.

"Can I get you some tea or coffee?" she offered as they sat down.

"I'm good." Kala was eager to get this over with so that she could finish the last of her days off with Dawn, who was reading a book and listening to music with her iPhone in Kala's truck in the parking lot. She hadn't wanted to come in and Kala hadn't pressed her.

"I understand you had quite the horrific experience a few weeks ago. How's your partner doing?"

"Better. He's with his parents in Ottawa recuperating."

"And the aunt?"

"Leanne is coming along too." Kala saw Tamara's eyes linger on the bandage above her eye. The scar on her cheek was healing although still bruised and rough looking. Gundersund said he and she were now a matching set. "I was hit by flying glass but no lasting effects."

"Good. That's good." Tamara crossed her legs and shuffled some papers on the table with her head down. She seemed to find what she was looking for and looked up at Kala. "The thing is, and there's no easy way to say this, after talking over your file with my supervisors, we've decided that Dawn should be placed with a foster family who has some experience with traumatized children or adolescents."

Kala stared at her. "I don't understand. She's doing well with me. I want to keep her, as I promised my cousin."

"But her mother isn't really your blood cousin, is she? Legally you're not family. We have to think what's best for Dawn. I know we can agree on that."

A condescending edge had entered her voice and Kala struggled to keep her own voice level.

"What's best for Dawn is that she lives with me. She's happy, and so am I. You can't do this."

"I'm sorry, but I can and I will." Tamara's mouth tightened. "The newspaper story that came to light about your alcoholism and past living on the street is a factor, I will admit. More importantly, however, you missed all the appointments with Dr. Lyman and your job has you working long hours with danger involved. Dawn needs more stability. A foster family will provide this."

"I missed the last appointment because my partner got shot. Another officer picked Dawn up for me. My past on the street has nothing to do with my situation now."

Tamara pursed her lips and looked back at the papers on the desk. The silence lengthened.

Kala knew by the stubborn look on Tamara's face that she wasn't going to win this round today. Tamara was taking her rebuttal as a personal attack and digging in her heels. Kala gave it one more try. "Have you asked Dawn what she wants? If she isn't happy with me, she'll tell you."

"These decisions are best left to the professionals. She's too young to know what's best for her future."

And you think you're old enough? This conversation was useless. Tamara was not going to budge. Kala asked, "How long before you move her?"

Tamara looked up and past Kala's right shoulder. "I have a placement lined up for Tuesday."

"In Kingston?"

"Yes. You'll still be able to visit her. You can have a big part in her life if you choose. I know we recommend that you do."

Kala wanted to weep. She heard herself begging. "What do I have to do to get her back? I'll do whatever you say."

"I'm sorry, but that won't be possible at this time. The papers have already been drawn up and approved. Perhaps, in time, we can reassess, but for now this is what is best for Dawn."

"Then I guess I won't waste any more of your time."

She took the stairs and exited the building still trying to absorb what had just taken place. She needed time to figure out what to do because she had no intention of letting this happen. Tamara Jones was playing God with their lives, but there had to be a way to stop her.

Kala opened the cab door and climbed into the truck. Dawn had her feet on the dashboard and was leaning against the passenger door. She closed her book and smiled. "Hey, Aunt Kala. How'd it go?"

"Fine, but I think we should enjoy my last day off and go for a drive. We can talk about the meeting later. What do you say?"

Dawn's face brightened. "Yes, please!" She dropped her feet from the dash and tossed her book on the seat before doing up her seatbelt

Kala drove out of the city and took the turn-off to Gananoque. She'd booked tickets for the Thousand Island boat tour and was glad now that she had because the trip would be a distraction. They reached the dock with minutes to spare. Dawn's delight at being on the water and seeing the islands was bittersweet. Kala had no idea how to tell her that she'd be moving away in two days. The boat docked at an island and they disembarked to tour

Boldt Castle. Dawn stayed at Kala's side the entire time, wide-eyed, taking everything in.

"I love it here," she said when they stood in the great hall under the stained-glass ceiling. Her eyes shone with wonder. "Can we come again in the fall, Aunt Kala?"

Kala forced a smile. "I'm sure I can arrange it."

The trip back to the dock went too quickly. Dawn jumped in front of Kala onto dry land raced over to watch a mother duck with her string of ducklings bobbing off shore. She knelt down and reached out a hand, trying to coax them over.

Kala sat on the park bench behind her and laughed along with Dawn as two of the ducklings paddled over to her. Dawn turned to look at Kala. "If only I had something to feed them."

"How about we get some lunch, speaking of food, and then I have one more stop."

"Okay."

They ate at the pub across the street. It was a cozy spot down a few steps with a bar along one wall and booths and tables tucked into every available space. They both ordered hamburgers, fries, and chocolate milkshakes. The food tasted like sawdust in Kala's mouth, and she had to choke it down. Dawn looked at her curiously a few times, but didn't say anything.

At two o'clock, Kala parked across the street from the Scott house. The front yard was fragrant with flowering lilac bushes and Leanne had planted a bed of pansies along the sidewalk. She answered the door before Kala lifted her hand to ring the doorbell. She looked at Kala for a moment before hugging her tightly.

Leanne poured cups of coffee and they sat in Adirondack chairs in the backyard, which was also filled with purple and white lilac bushes and flowering apple trees. Dawn took her book and a glass of lemonade and went to sit by the pond at the far end of the garden.

"You're looking so much better than last time I saw you," Kala said. "How're you feeling?"

"I'm good. Randy hovers like an old mother hen, but he'll get back to normal given a bit of time. We'll be putting the house up for sale next week."

Kala nodded. The news didn't come as a surprise. "Where will you be moving?"

Leanne's face reddened and she fanned herself with one hand. She couldn't seem to fix her eyes on anything. "Well, we always wanted to live in British Columbia. We haven't decided on our exact location but it will be near the sea."

Kala leaned forward until her head was close to Leanne's. She waited until Leanne lowered her coffee cup and looked her in the eyes. "Where's Violet?" she asked. "I know you took her that morning before Philippe Lebeau arrived at Adele's."

Leanne began to deny, but something in Kala's eyes made her stop. Kala waited motionless, keeping her gaze on Leanne's face.

Leanne said softly, "What will you do if I tell you?"

"Nothing. I'm not going to tell anyone where Violet is because then her mother Cécile will get her back. Even if Cécile was to gain custody, I believe that Violet will end up in the child welfare system before long because Cécile will do something illegal and end up serving more time. She managed to keep herself from being implicated in Adele's murder and your kidnapping, but I have no doubt she knew what was going on. She was waiting for Lebeau to join her at a motel in Cornwall when she was located. So, I will do nothing if you tell me the truth. I'm here as a citizen, not a cop."

Leanne listened without saying anything. She was silent for several seconds afterwards, appearing to consider Kala's words and searching her face. Finally, she slapped her hands on her knees and said, "Then let's go for a drive."

Kala called to Dawn and they got into Leanne's car. Kala also thought it might be wise not to have her truck spotted wherever it was they were going. Dawn sat in the back seat and Kala rode up front with Leanne. Dawn put on her headphones to listen to music while she read her book.

Leanne backed out of the driveway and glanced over at Kala.

"You were right. I was there that morning. I got a frantic call the night before from Adele. She told Ivo she was getting milk but went and used a payphone because she knew she'd be disappearing and didn't want the call traced later. She'd seen one of the men from her past in a restaurant the week before on an outing with her neighbour, but thought he hadn't seen her — that is until he followed her car to the plant nursery. She was even too scared to tell me his name."

They were driving east. In the centre of town, Leanne was silent as she put on her turn signal and took the main road north. After a few minutes she resumed talking as if there'd been no break in her monologue.

"Adele called me a few times that week later in the evening, using Ivo's phone when he was in bed sleeping. I have a work phone that she called me on. I never shared it with your officers." Leanne smiled an apology at Kala. "Adele was jumpy as a cat until she came up with this plan, which I thought was sheer lunacy. When she called me that last night, she asked me to get to her place by seven the following morning to take Violet. Once we were gone, she was going to make it look as if Violet had gotten out of the house while she was making breakfast and drowned in the creek. Adele figured that the people she knew from her time in Montreal believed Violet was dead, they might not come after her. She was just buying time until she could disappear again and collect Violet. She was out of her mind with panic."

"Why did she think they were after her?"

"She saw Violet's father in town that morning, asking questions at the corner store. She figured he wouldn't come after her that night with Ivo home."

"We learned that Etienne had booked a visit with his brother Benoit at Millhaven the day Adele went to the plant nursery. He asked Lebeau to call and cancel it, but Lebeau decided to make the trip in his place. He borrowed some ID from Etienne's wallet and convinced Benoit to say that he was Etienne once he arrived so that he wouldn't get into trouble. Seemed like a harmless enough switch to Benoit at the time. Lebeau signed the visitor log as Etienne. It was only later when and we showed up asking questions about Adele's past and murder that Lebeau used the lie to implicate Etienne."

"Such horrible men."

"What about Ivo? Was she going to leave him behind? Was she going to let him believe their child was dead?"

"She never said, but I imagine so. It sounds harsh when you put it like that."

They drove thirty minutes until they reached a town named Cheeseborough. Leanne slowed but kept driving north. "Not much farther," she said.

Kala asked, "So, was Adele planning to confront Lebeau at her home?"

"Oh no. She was going to call the police and tell them Violet had disappeared from the house. Media would pick up the story as they do, and Lebeau and the Manteau brothers would hear about it. After a few weeks, Adele was going to leave for a weekend change of scene, get Violet, and disappear. She hoped the bunch of thugs in Montreal would stop trying to find her if they thought she didn't have their kid. Lebeau must have shown up that morning before she could finish her plan."

"Did Adele know who Violet's father was?"

"She knew because Cécile and Lebeau had her kidnap the baby to keep Benoit from finding out that he wasn't the father. She never told me the name of the father, though. I only figured all this out after Lebeau tried to get Violet from us. The pieces connected from things Adele told me. Anyhow, Cécile and Lebeau hated Benoit and Etienne for reasons that were unknown to me. I found the whole situation a soap opera but Adele was petrified of them. She said they told her that they owned her. I think they had her hooking, if truth be told. She tried to tell me once but I wasn't sympathetic." Leanne sighed. "I told her that she'd made her bed and she should figure a way out. I'm ashamed to say that I was a bit of a judgmental prig at the time. I've been trying to make up for it."

They came upon a few houses tucked in from the road in clear-cut properties surrounded by woods. "This is Maple Grove. My friend lives in the last house before the intersection."

Not even a minute farther on and Leanne turned into a driveway lined in pine, birch, and maple trees. She honked her horn and continued slowly up the drive. By the time they reached the front door, a woman in her fifties was standing on the front steps, wiping her hands in an apron. Her smile turned to a frown when she saw Kala and Dawn get out of the car.

She walked down the steps and over to Leanne. "I wasn't expecting company," she said.

"It's okay, Sharon. Kala knows but she's not interested in telling anybody."

Sharon didn't look convinced but reached out a hand. "Let's shake on that."

Kala extended her hand. "You have my word."

"She's out back playing with Mia and Tom. I was keeping an eye on them from the kitchen. You can just follow the flagstone path around that side of the house."

Leanne said, "I'll take them."

Kala and Dawn followed her to a closed gate and a six-foot-high wooden fence. They stepped inside and Kala stopped by the steps. The yard had several oak and poplar trees but the rest was grass. A boy and girl who looked to be about seven were rolling a beach ball to the blond-haired girl Kala had seen in the photos in Ivo's study. They'd cut Violet's hair into a pixie cut but Kala still recognized her. Violet was giggling and running between the boy and girl, clutching onto the ball. They pretended to try to catch her. All of a sudden, Violet spotted Leanne standing near the fence. She threw the ball onto the grass and ran on chubby legs into Leanne's outspread arms. Leanne picked her up and hugged her hard before turning her to face Kala.

"Violet, meet my friends Kala and Dawn. Can you say hi?"

"Hi." Violet fixed them with her blue eyes. She scrunched her face. "Is Mommy coming soon?"

"No, sweetheart." Leanne gave her a kiss. "We just stopped for a minute. I'm going to come back for supper."

"Later!" Violet squirmed out of her arms and waved at Dawn and Kala before racing back to the join the others.

Leanne looked at Kala. "Randy and I are going to give her a good life. We owe that to Adele. I promised her."

Kala nodded. She reached her arm around Dawn's shoulders and gave her a squeeze. "I know what that feels like," she said. "Thanks for putting my mind at ease. It's time Dawn and I get on our way home."

CHAPTER THIRTY-NINE

Kala didn't know what to do with herself. The house felt empty and confining so she put on her running shoes and sweater and took Taiku down to the beach. She threw a stick into the lake for him to retrieve for half an hour or so before they walked the length of the shoreline and back.

The sun was into its descent and the shadows were lengthening when they made it back to the house. She sat on the steps of the back deck with Taiku resting in the grass. He seemed as lost as she felt. A slight wind had come up off the lake and was keeping the bugs at bay. She'd sit until darkness came before going in for supper. Her appetite had disappeared but she knew she had to eat because she had to work in the morning.

A few moments later she heard a car pull into the driveway. It would be too much to hope for that Tamara Jones had had a change of heart and brought Dawn home, so Kala remained seated. Getting up to greet them would take more energy than she possessed at the moment. She lifted her head to watch whoever it was come around the corner of the house.

Taiku bounded across the lawn to greet their guest. He made his way to her with Taiku loping along beside him. Kala stood at his approach.

"Sir, I hadn't expected to see you here."

"Don't get up." Rouleau looked around the property. "This is my first visit. What a lovely spot near the water and away from town." He sat on the steps and she lowered herself beside him.

"Would you like a beer or tea?"

"No. I'm fine sitting here enjoying the evening. How are you?"

She felt tears fill her eyes and she gritted her teeth. When she was okay to talk without crying, she said, "I'm just fine. Back at work tomorrow. Thanks for approving a couple of more days of leave."

"You more than earned it."

They sat without speaking and the sun sank lower, turning from yellow to orange and red above the trees. Kala wondered how nature could be so perfect when her heart was breaking.

"Gundersund called." Rouleau said after a while. "He said that Dawn was taken to a foster family today."

"Why would he worry you with my problems?"

"Because we care about you. You're important to us. Did that article have anything to do with the decision to remove Dawn?"

"The counsellor said I was an unreliable person in a dangerous job. She wasn't happy that I'd been a homeless alcoholic, so yeah, I guess the article had an impact on her decision."

"Then she's a fool. Your past has made you a good role model and you are one of the most reliable people on my team. I wish they'd come to me. Are you going to fight this?"

Kala looked straight ahead toward the lake. "I would if I thought I could win. Maybe I should let her be with a family that can care for her. I've convinced myself that this might be for the best."

"How does Dawn feel?"

The question that Tamara Jones had said was unimportant. Kala smiled. "Dawn refused to go at first. Tamara almost met her match but Dawn gave in when Tamara told her that I'd signed the forms and agreed she should leave. When Dawn asked me, I didn't deny it." Kala rubbed her eyes. "The look of betrayal. I'll never forget it."

"We can go over the social worker's head. Make a complaint."

Kala knew it would be hard on everyone, especially Dawn. The odds of winning her back didn't make it worth the pain. "No. Dawn will settle into a stable family and I'll do what I always do. Put this away and keep on going. I'm good at shutting off places and people. I've been doing it all my life."

"If there is any way I can help ..."

Kala shook her head and Rouleau wrapped his arm around her shoulders. He didn't say anything but he didn't drop his arm either, even when she kept her back rigid and her eyes on the horizon.

"I'm sad for you," he said. "For all that you've had to endure. I admire your strength but sometimes ...

it helps to be sad for yourself too. To let yourself grieve. We all do it and it helps us get through. You aren't alone, Kala. You will never be alone as long as I am on this planet. You're the daughter I would have liked to have had." He paused, then chuckled. "And Dad is thrilled to finally get a granddaughter."

She began to laugh but the sound turned into a sob. She rolled sideways into his shoulder and cried for the first time in a very long time. Rouleau held her without speaking and she wept for Dawn and Bennett, Adele and Ivo, and the child she'd never been allowed to be. When she finished, Rouleau was still there, strong and comforting, like the father she'd imagined but never had.

"I'm better now," she said, wiping her eyes with the back of one hand. She turned and looked up at the sky. Complete darkness had descended — the kind you only get in the country — but the stars were poking through and the moon was casting silvery light on the lake. Taiku came over and rested his head on her thigh.

"Let me take you for supper," Rouleau said. "I haven't been eating much and could use the company."

Kala turned and tried to make out his face in the dark but couldn't see more than an outline. She pictured the sadness in his eyes at the funeral. The connection she felt with him was unexpected but gave her a reason to stay in Kingston for a while longer.

"Okay," she said as she got to her feet. "I think I could use the company too."

ACKNOWLEDGEMENTS

I once again owe a debt of gratitude to the Dundurn team, with special thanks to my editor Jennifer McKnight, publicists Karen McMullin and James Hatch, and cover designer Laura Boyle. Vice-president Beth Bruder and president Kirk Howard continue to publish quality Canadian books and to support the mystery genre, for which I also give thanks.

Thank you to publicist Maryglenn McCombs, who helped with promotion as I work to bring my books to the American audience. She has become a friend. Also, thank you to my colleague Françoise Trudeau-Reeves for not only buying all of my books but for helping with the French translation in *Tumbled Graves*. *Merci bien*.

I would like to name every friend and family member and reader who has supported me, propped me up, and cheered me on, but I would need pages and space does not allow. I raise my glass to each of you with my deepest appreciation. Love to my hearts: Ted, Julia, Lisa, and Robin.